O9-BTI-927

ALSO BY MIRANDA JULY

No One Belongs Here More Than You: Stories
Learning to Love You More
It Chooses You

THE FIRST BAD MAN

A NOVEL BY MIRANDA JULY

LIVINGSTON PUBLIC LIBRARY
10 Robert H. Harp Drive
Livingston, NJ 07039

SCRIBNER
NEW YORK   LONDON   TORONTO   SYDNEY   NEW DELHI

FIC

JULY

SCRIBNER
A Division of Simon & Schuster, Inc.
1230 Avenue of the Americas
New York, NY 10020

This book is a work of fiction. Any references to historical events, real people, or real places are used fictitiously. Other names, characters, places, and events are products of the author's imagination, and any resemblance to actual events or places or persons, living or dead, is entirely coincidental.

Copyright © 2015 by Miranda July

All rights reserved, including the right to reproduce this book or portions thereof in any form whatsoever. For information, address Scribner Subsidiary Rights Department, 1230 Avenue of the Americas, New York, NY 10020.

First Scribner hardcover edition January 2015

SCRIBNER and design are registered trademarks of The Gale Group, Inc., used under license by Simon & Schuster, Inc., the publisher of this work.

For information about special discounts for bulk purchases, please contact Simon & Schuster Special Sales at 1-866-506-1949 or business@simonandschuster.com.

The Simon & Schuster Speakers Bureau can bring authors to your live event. For more information or to book an event, contact the Simon & Schuster Speakers Bureau at 1-866-248-3049 or visit our website at www.simonspeakers.com.

Interior design by Kyle Kabel
Jacket design by Mike Mills

Manufactured in the United States of America

1 3 5 7 9 10 8 6 4 2

Library of Congress Control Number: 20014008520

ISBN 978-1-4391-7256-8
ISBN 978-1-4391-7260-5 (ebook)

"Kooks." Words and music by David Bowie. © 1971 (Renewed 1999) EMI Music Publishing Ltd., Tintoretto Music, and Chrysalis Songs. All rights for EMI Music Publishing Ltd. controlled and administered by Screen Gems-EMI Music, Inc. All rights for Tintoretto Music administered by RZO Music. All rights for Chrysalis Songs administered by Chrysalis Music Group, Inc., a BMG Chrysalis Company. All rights reserved. International copyright secured. Used by permission. *Reprinted by permission of Hal Leonard Corporation.*

1 · 8 · 15
LA

For Michael Chadbourne Mills

THE FIRST BAD MAN

CHAPTER ONE

I drove to the doctor's office as if I was starring in a movie Phillip was watching—windows down, hair blowing, just one hand on the wheel. When I stopped at red lights, I kept my eyes mysteriously forward. *Who is she?* people might have been wondering. *Who is that middle-aged woman in the blue Honda?* I strolled through the parking garage and into the elevator, pressing 12 with a casual, fun-loving finger. The kind of finger that was up for anything. Once the doors had closed, I checked myself in the mirrored ceiling and practiced how my face would go if Phillip was in the waiting room. Surprised but not overly surprised, and he wouldn't be on the ceiling so my neck wouldn't be craning up like that. All the way down the hall I did the face. Oh! Oh, hi! There was the door.

DR. JENS BROYARD

CHROMOTHERAPY

I swung it open.
No Phillip.
It took a moment to recover. I almost turned around and went home—but then I wouldn't be able to call him to say thanks for the referral. The receptionist gave me a new-patient form on a

clipboard; I sat in an upholstered chair. There was no line that said "referred by," so I just wrote *Phillip Bettelheim sent me* across the top.

"I'm not going to say that he's the best in the whole world," Phillip had said at the Open Palm fundraiser. He was wearing a gray cashmere sweater that matched his beard. "Because there's a color doctor in Zurich who easily rivals him. But Jens is the best in LA, and definitely the best on the west side. He cured my athlete's foot." He lifted his foot and then put it down again before I could smell it. "He's in Amsterdam most of the year so he's very selective about who he sees here. Tell him Phil Bettelheim sent you." He wrote the number on a napkin and began to samba away from me.

"Phil Bettelheim sent me."

"Exactly!" he yelled over his shoulder. He spent the rest of the night on the dance floor.

I stared at the receptionist—she knew Phillip. He might have just left; he might be with the doctor right now. I hadn't thought of that. I tucked my hair behind my ears and watched the door to the exam room. After a minute a willowy woman with a baby boy came out. The baby was swinging a crystal from a string. I checked to see if he and I had a special connection that was greater than his bond with his mother. We didn't.

Dr. Broyard had Scandinavian features and wore tiny, judgmental glasses. While he read my new-patient form I sat on a meaty leather couch across from a Japanese paper screen. There weren't any wands or orbs in sight, but I braced myself for something along those lines. If Phillip believed in chromotherapy that was enough for me. Dr. Broyard lowered his glasses.

"So. Globus hystericus."

I started to explain what it was but he cut me off. "I'm a doctor."

"Sorry." But do real doctors say "I'm a doctor"?

He calmly examined my cheeks while stabbing a piece of paper with a red pen. There was a face on the paper, a generic face labeled CHERYL GLICKMAN.

"Those marks are . . . ?"

"Your rosacea."

The paper's eyes were big and round, whereas mine disappear altogether if I smile, and my nose is more potatoey. That said, the spaces *between* my features are in perfect proportion to each other. So far no one has noticed this. Also my ears: darling little shells. I wear my hair tucked behind them and try to enter crowded rooms ear-first, walking sideways. He drew a circle on the paper's throat and filled it in with careful cross-hatching.

"How long have you had the globus?"

"On and off for about thirty years. Thirty or forty years."

"Have you ever had treatment for it?"

"I tried to get a referral for surgery."

"Surgery."

"To have the ball cut out."

"You know it's not a real ball."

"That's what they say."

"The usual treatment is psychotherapy."

"I know." I didn't explain that I was single. Therapy is for couples. So is Christmas. So is camping. So is beach camping. Dr. Broyard rattled open a drawer full of tiny glass bottles and picked one labeled RED. I squinted at the perfectly clear liquid. It reminded me a lot of water.

"It's the *essence* of red," he said brusquely. He could sense my skepticism. "Red is an energy, which only develops a hue in crude form. Take thirty milliliters now and then thirty milliliters each morning before first urination." I swallowed a dropperful.

"Why before first urination?"

"Before you get up and move around—movement raises your basal body temperature."

I considered this. What if a person were to wake up and immediately have sex, before urination? Surely that would raise your basal body temperature too. If I had been in my early thirties instead of my early forties would he have said before first urination *or sexual intercourse*? That's the problem with men my age, I'm somehow older than them. Phillip is in his sixties, so he probably thinks of me as a younger woman, a girl almost. Not that he thinks of me yet—I'm just someone who works at Open Palm. But that could change in an instant; it could have happened today, in the waiting room. It still might happen, if I called him. Dr. Broyard handed me a form.

"Give this to Ruthie at the front desk. I scheduled a follow-up visit, but if your globus worsens before then you might want to consider some kind of counseling."

"Do I get one of those crystals?" I pointed to the cluster of them hanging in the window.

"A sundrop? Next time."

THE RECEPTIONIST XEROXED MY INSURANCE card while explaining that chromotherapy isn't covered by insurance.

"The next available appointment is June nineteenth. Do you prefer morning or afternoon?" Her waist-length gray hair was off-putting. Mine is gray too but I keep it neat.

"I don't know—morning?" It was only February. By June Phillip and I might be a couple, we might come to Dr. Broyard's together, hand in hand.

"Is there anything sooner?"

"The doctor's in this office only three times a year."

I glanced around the waiting area. "Who will water this plant?" I leaned over and pushed my finger into the fern's soil. It was wet.

"Another doctor works here." She tapped the Lucite display holding two stacks of cards, Dr. Broyard's and those of a Dr. Tibbets, LCSW. I tried to take one of each without using my dirty finger.

"How's nine forty-five?" she asked, holding out a box of Kleenex.

I RACED THROUGH THE PARKING garage, carrying my phone in both hands. Once the doors were locked and the AC was on, I dialed the first nine digits of Phillip's number, then paused. I had never called him before; for the last six years it was always him calling me, and only at Open Palm and only in his capacity as a board member. Maybe this wasn't a good idea. Suzanne would say it was. She made the first move with Carl. Suzanne and Carl were my bosses.

"If you feel a connection, don't be shy about it," she'd once said.

"What's an example of not being shy about it?"

"Show him some heat."

I waited four days, to spread out the questions, and then I asked her for an example of showing heat. She looked at me for a long time and then pulled an old envelope out of the trash and drew a pear on it. "This is how your body is shaped. See? Teeny tiny on top and not so tiny on the bottom." Then she explained the illusion created by wearing dark colors on the bottom and bright colors on top. When I see other women with this color combination I check to see if they're a pear too and they always are—two pears can't fool each other.

Below her drawing she wrote the phone number of someone she thought was more right for me than Phillip—a divorced
alcoholic father named Mark Kwon. He took me out to dinner
at Mandarette on Beverly. When that didn't pan out she asked
me if she was barking up the wrong tree. "Maybe it's not Mark
you don't like? Maybe it's men?" People sometimes think this
because of the way I wear my hair; it happens to be short. I also
wear shoes you can actually walk in, Rockports or clean sneakers
instead of high-heeled foot jewelry. But would a homosexual
woman's heart leap at the sight of a sixty-five-year-old man in a
gray sweater? Mark Kwon remarried a few years ago; Suzanne
made a point of telling me. I pressed the last digit of Phillip's
number.

"Hello?" He sounded asleep.

"Hi, it's Cheryl."

"Oh?"

"From Open Palm."

"Oh, hello, hello! Wonderful fundraiser, I had a blast. How
can I help you, Cheryl?"

"I just wanted to tell you I saw Dr. Broyard." There was a long
pause. "The chromotherapist," I added.

"Jens! He's great, right?"

I said I thought he was phenomenal.

This had been my plan, to use the same word that he had used
to describe my necklace at the fundraiser. He had lifted the heavy
beads off my chest and said, "This is phenomenal, where'd you
get it?" and I said, "From a vendor at the farmer's market," and
then he used the beads to pull me toward him. "Hey," he said,
"I like this, this is handy." An outsider, such as Nakako the grant
writer, might have thought this moment was degrading, but I
knew the degradation was just a joke; he was mocking the kind

of man who would do something like that. He's been doing these things for years; once, during a board meeting, he insisted my blouse wasn't zipped up in back, and then he unzipped it, laughing. I'd laughed too, immediately reaching around to close it back up. The joke was, *Can you believe people? The tacky kinds of things they do?* But it had another layer to it, because imitating crass people was kind of liberating—like pretending to be a child or a crazy person. It was something you could do only with someone you really trusted, someone who knew how capable and good you actually were. After he released his hold on my necklace I had a brief coughing fit, which led to a discussion of my globus and the color doctor.

The word *phenomenal* didn't seem to trigger anything in him; he was saying Dr. Broyard was expensive but worth it and then his voice began rising toward a polite exit. "Well, I guess I'll see you at the board meeting to—" but before he could say *morrow*, I interrupted.

"When in doubt, give a shout!"

"Excuse me?"

"I'm here for you. When in doubt, just give me a shout."

What silence. Giant domed cathedrals never held so much emptiness. He cleared his throat. It echoed, bouncing around the dome, startling pigeons.

"Cheryl?"

"Yes?"

"I think I should go."

I didn't say anything. He would have to step over my dead body to get off the phone.

"Goodbye," he said, and then, after a pause, he hung up.

I put the phone in my purse. If the red was already working then my nose and eyes would now be pierced with that beautiful stinging sensation, a million tiny pins, culminating in a giant salty rush, the shame moving through my tears and out to the gutter. The cry climbed to my throat, swelling it, but instead of surging upward it hunkered down right there, in a belligerent ball. Globus hystericus.

Something hit my car and I jumped. It was the door of the car next to mine; a woman was maneuvering her baby into its car seat. I held my throat and leaned forward to get a look, but her hair blocked its face so there was no way to tell if it was one of the babies I think of as mine. Not mine biologically, just . . . familiar. I call those ones Kubelko Bondy. It only takes a second to check; half the time I don't even know I'm doing it until I'm already done.

The Bondys were briefly friends with my parents in the early seventies. Mr. and Mrs. Bondy and their little boy, Kubelko. Later, when I asked my mom about him, she said she was sure that wasn't his name, but what *was* his name? Kevin? Marco? She couldn't remember. The parents drank wine in the living room and I was instructed to play with Kubelko. Show him your toys. He sat silently by my bedroom door holding a wooden spoon, sometimes hitting it against the floor. Wide black eyes, fat pink jowls. He was a young boy, very young. Barely more than a year old. After a while he threw his spoon and began to wail. I watched him crying and waited for someone to come but no one came so I heaved him onto my small lap and rocked his chubby body. He calmed almost immediately. I kept my arms around him and he looked at me and I looked at him and he looked at me and I knew that he loved me more than his mother and father and that in some very real and permanent way he belonged to me. Because I was only nine it wasn't clear if he belonged to me as a child or as a spouse, but it didn't matter, I felt myself rising up to the challenge of heartache. I pressed my cheek against his cheek and held him for what I hoped would be eternity. He fell asleep and I drifted in and out of consciousness myself, unmoored from time and scale, his warm body huge then tiny—then abruptly seized from my arms by the woman who thought of herself as his mother. As the adults made their way to the door saying tired too-loud thank-yous, Kubelko Bondy looked at me with panicked eyes.

Do something. They're taking me away.

I will, don't worry, I'll do something.

Of course I wouldn't just let him sail out into the night, not my own dear boy. *Halt! Unhand him!*

But my voice was too quiet, it didn't leave my head. Seconds later he sailed out into the night, my own dear boy. Never to be seen again.

Except I did see him again—again and again. Sometimes he's a newborn, sometimes he's already toddling along. As I pulled out of my parking spot I got a better look at the baby in the car next to mine. Just some kid.

CHAPTER TWO

I was woken early by the sound of limbs falling in the backyard. I took thirty milliliters of red and listened to the labored sawing. It was Rick, the homeless gardener who came with the house. I would never hire someone to lurk around on my property and invade my privacy, but I didn't fire him when I moved in, because I didn't want him to think I was less open-minded than the previous owners, the Goldfarbs. They gave him a key; sometimes he uses the bathroom or leaves lemons in the kitchen. I try to find a reason to leave before he arrives, which is not so easy at seven A.M. Sometimes I just drive around for the whole three hours until he's gone. Or I drive a few blocks away, park, and sleep in my car. Once he spotted me, on his way back to his tent or box, and pressed his smiling, stubbly face against the window. It had been hard to think of an explanation while still half-asleep.

Today I just went to Open Palm early and got everything ready for the meeting of the board. My plan was to behave so gracefully that the clumsy woman Phillip had spoken with yesterday would be impossible to recall. I wouldn't use a British accent out loud, but I'd be using one in my head and it would carry over.

Jim and Michelle were already in the office, and so was Sarah the intern. She had her new baby with her; she was trying to keep it under her desk, but obviously we could all hear it. I wiped down the boardroom table and laid out pads of paper and pens. As a manager this is beneath me, but I like to make it nice for Phillip. Jim yelled, "Incoming!" which meant Carl and Suzanne were about to make their entrance. I grabbed a pair of giant vases full of dead flowers and hurried to the staff kitchen.

"I'll do that!" said Michelle. She was a new employee—not my pick.

"Too late now," I said. "I'm already holding them."

She ran alongside me and pried a vase out of my hand, too ignorant to understand the system of counterbalances I was using. One was slipping now, thanks to her help, and I let her catch it, which she did not. Carl and Suzanne walked in the door the moment the vase hit the carpet. Phillip was with them.

"Greetings," said Carl. Phillip was wearing a gorgeous wine-colored sweater. My breath thinned. I always had to resist the urge to go to him like a wife, as if we'd already been a couple for a hundred thousand lifetimes. Caveman and cavewoman. King and queen. Nuns.

"Meet Michelle, our new media coordinator," I said, gesturing downward in a funny way. She was on her hands and knees gathering up slimy brown flowers; now she struggled to stand.

"I'm Phillip." Michelle shook his hand from a confused kneeling position, her face a hot circle of tears. I had accidentally been cruel; this only ever happens at times of great stress and my regret is always tremendous. I would bring her something tomorrow, a gift certificate or a Ninja five-cup smoothie maker. I should have already given her a gift, preemptively; I like to do that with new employees. They come home and say, "This new job is so great, I can't even believe it—look at what my manager gave me!" Then if they ever come home in tears their spouse will say, "But, hon, the smoothie maker? Are you sure?" And the new employee will second-guess or perhaps even blame themselves.

Suzanne and Carl ambled away with Phillip, and Sarah the intern hurried over to help clean up the mess. Her baby's gurgling was insistent and aggressive. Finally I walked over to her desk and peeked under it. He cooed like a mournful dove and smiled up at me with the warmth of total recognition.

I keep getting born to the wrong people, he said.

I nodded regretfully. *I know.*

What could I do? I wanted to lift him out of his carrier and finally encircle him in my arms again, but this wasn't an option. I mimed an apology and he accepted it with a slow, wise-eyed blink that made my chest ache with sorrow and my globus swell. I kept getting older while he stayed young, my tiny husband. Or, more likely at this point: my son. Sarah hurried over and swung his baby carrier to the other side of the desk. His foot went wild with kicking.

Don't give up, don't give up.

I won't, I said. *Never.*

It would be much too painful to see him on a regular basis. I cleared my throat sternly.

"I think you know it isn't appropriate to bring your baby to work."

"Suzanne said it was fine. She said she brought Clee to work all the time when she was little."

It was true. Carl and Suzanne's daughter used to come to

the old studio after school and hang out in the classes, running around screaming and distracting everyone. I told Sarah she could finish the day but that this couldn't become a routine thing. She gave me a betrayed look, because she's a working mom, feminism, etc. I gave her the same look back, because I'm a woman in a senior position, she's taking advantage, feminism, etc. She bowed her head slightly. The interns are always women Carl and Suzanne feel sorry for. I was one, twenty-five years ago. Back then Open Palm was really just a women's self-defense studio; a repurposed tae kwon do dojo.

A man grabs your breast—what do you do? A gang of men surrounds you and knocks you to the ground, then begins unzipping your pants—what do you do? A man you thought you knew presses you against a wall and won't let you go—what do you do? A man yells a crude comment about a part of your body he'd like you to show him—do you show it to him? No. You turn and look straight at him, point your finger right at his nose, and, drawing from your diaphragm, you make a very loud, guttural "Aiaiaiaiaiai!" noise. The students always liked that part, making that noise. The mood shifted when the attackers came out in their giant-headed foam pummel suits and began to simulate rape, gang rape, sexual humiliation, and unwanted caress. The men inside were actually kind and peaceable—almost to a fault—but they became quite vulgar and heated during the role-plays. It brought up emotions for a lot of the women, which was the point—anyone can fight back when they're not terrified or humiliated, when they aren't sobbing and asking for their money back. The feeling of accomplishment in the final class was always very moving. Attackers and students hugged and thanked each other while drinking sparkling cider. All was forgiven.

We still teach a class for teen girls, but that's just to keep our nonprofit status—all our real business is in fitness DVDs now. Selling self-defense as exercise was my idea. Our line is competitive with other top workout videos; most buyers say they don't even think about the combat aspect, they just like the up-tempo music and what it does to their shape. Who wants to watch a woman getting accosted in a park? No one. If it weren't for me, Carl and Suzanne would still be making that type of depressing how-to video. They've more or less retired since they moved to Ojai, but they still meddle in employee affairs and attend the board meetings. I'm practically, though not officially, on the board. I take notes.

Phillip sat as far away from me as possible and seemed to avoid looking at my side of the room for the duration of the meeting. I hoped I was just being paranoid, but later Suzanne asked if there was a problem between us. I confessed I had shown him some heat.

"What does that mean?"

It had been almost five years since she'd suggested it—I guess it wasn't a phrase she used anymore.

"I told him when in doubt . . ." It was hard to say it.

"What?" Suzanne leaned in, her dangly earrings swinging forward.

"When in doubt, give a shout," I whispered.

"You said that to him? That's a very provocative phrase."

"It is?"

"For a woman to say to a man? Sure. You've definitely shown him—how did you put it?"

"Some heat."

Carl walked around the office with a dirty canvas sack that said OJAI NATURAL FOODS and filled it with cookies and green tea and a container of almond milk from the staff kitchen, then he bounced over to the supply closet and helped himself to reams of paper, a handful of pens and highlighters, and a few bottles of Wite-Out. They also unload things they don't know what to do with—an old car that doesn't run, a litter of kittens, a smelly old couch that they don't have room for. This time it was a large amount of meat.

"It's called beefalo—it's the fertile hybrid of cattle and bison," said Carl.

Suzanne opened a Styrofoam cooler. "We ordered too much," she explained, "and it expires tomorrow."

"So rather than let it rot, we thought everyone could enjoy beefalo tonight—on us!" shouted Carl, throwing his hands into the air like Santa.

They began calling out names. Each employee rose and received a little white package labeled with their name. Suzanne called Phillip's name and my name in quick succession. We walked up together and she handed us our meat at the same time. My meat package was bigger. I saw him notice that and then he finally looked at me.

"Trade you," he whispered.

I frowned to keep the joy in. He gave me the meat that said PHILLIP and I gave him the meat that said CHERYL.

As the beefalo was distributed, Suzanne also wondered aloud if anyone could take their daughter in for a few weeks until she found an apartment and a job in LA.

"She's an extremely gifted actress."

No one said anything.

Suzanne swayed a little in her long skirt. Carl rubbed his large stomach and raised his eyebrows, waiting for takers. The last time Clee had been to the office she was fourteen. Her pale hair was pulled back into a very tight ponytail, lots of eyeliner, big hoop earrings, pants falling down. She looked like she was in a gang. That was six years ago, but still no one volunteered. Until someone did: Michelle.

THE BEEFALO HAD A PRIMAL AFTERTASTE. I wiped the pan clean and ripped up the white paper with Phillip's name on it. Before I was even finished, the phone rang. No one knows why ripping up a name makes a person call—science can't explain it. Erasing the name also works.

"I thought I'd give a shout," he said.

I walked to the bedroom and lay down on my bed. Initially it was no different than any other call except for that in six years he had never once called me on my personal cell phone at night. We talked about Open Palm and issues from the meeting as if it wasn't eight o'clock and I wasn't in my nightgown. Then, at the point where the conversation would normally have ended, a long silence arrived. I sat in the dark wondering if he had hung up without bothering to hang up. Finally, in a low whisper, he said, "I think I might be a terrible person."

For a split second I believed him—I thought he was about to confess a crime, maybe a murder. Then I realized that we all think we might be terrible people. But we only reveal this before we ask someone to love us. It is a kind of undressing.

"No," I said in a whisper. "You are so good."

"I'm not, though!" he protested, his voice rising with excitement. "You don't know!"

I responded with equal volume and fervor, "I do know, Phillip!

I know you better than you think!" This quieted him for a moment. I shut my eyes. With all my throw pillows around me, poised at the lip of intimacy—I felt like a king. A king on his throne with a feast laid before him.

"Are you able to talk right now?" he said.

"If you are."

"I mean, are you alone?"

"I live alone."

"I thought so."

"Really? What did you think when you thought about that?"

"Well, I thought: *I think she lives alone.*"

"You were right."

"I have a confession to make."

I shut my eyes again, a king.

"I need to unburden myself," he continued. "You don't have to respond, but if you could just listen."

"Okay."

"Yikes, I'm nervous about this. I'm sweating. Remember, no response necessary. I'll just say it and then we can hang up and you can go to sleep."

"I'm already in bed."

"Perfect. So you can just go right to sleep and call me in the morning."

"That's what I'll do."

"Okay, I'll talk to you tomorrow."

"Wait—you haven't said the confession."

"I know, I got scared and—I don't know. The moment passed. You should just go to sleep."

I sat up.

"Should I still call you in the morning?"

"I'll call you tomorrow night."

"Thank you."

"Good night."

IT WAS HARD TO THINK of a confession that would make a person sweat that wasn't either criminal or romantic. And how often do people, people we know, commit serious crimes? I felt jittery; I didn't sleep. At dawn I experienced an involuntary total voiding of my bowels. I took thirty milliliters of red and squeezed my globus. Still rock hard. Jim called at eleven and said there was a mini-emergency. Jim is the on-site office manager.

"Is it about Phillip?" Maybe we would have to rush over to his house and I could see where he lived.

"Michelle changed her mind about Clee."

"Oh."

"She wants Clee to move out."

"Okay."

"So can you take her?"

When you live alone people are always thinking they can stay with you, when the opposite is true: who they should stay with is a person whose situation is already messed up by other people and so one more won't matter.

"I wish I could, I really wish I could help out," I said.

"This isn't coming from me, it's Carl and Suzanne's idea. I think they kind of wonder why you didn't offer in the first place, since you're practically family."

I pressed my lips together. Once Carl had called me *ginjo*, which I thought meant "sister" until he told me it's Japanese for a man, usually an elderly man, who lives in isolation while he keeps the fire burning for the whole village.

"In the old myths he burns his clothes and then his bones to keep it going," Carl said. I made myself very still so he would continue; I love to be described. "Then he has to find something else to keep the fire going so he has *ubitsu*. There's no easy translation for that, but basically they are dreams so heavy that they have infinite mass and weight. He burns those and the fire never goes out." Then he told me my managerial style was more effective from a distance, so my job was now work-from-home though I was welcome to come in one day a week and for board meetings.

My house isn't very big; I tried to picture another person in here.

"They said I was practically family?"

"It goes without saying—I mean, do you say your mom is practically family?"

"No."

"See?"

"When is this happening?"

"She'll come with her stuff later tonight."

"I have an important private phone call this evening."

"Thanks a bunch, Cheryl."

I CARRIED MY COMPUTER OUT of the ironing room and set up a cot that is more comfortable than it looks. I folded a washcloth on top of a hand towel on top of a bath towel and placed them on a duvet cover that she was welcome to use over her comforter. I put a sugarless mint on top of the washcloth. I Windexed all the bath and sink taps so they looked brand-new, and also the handle on the toilet. I put my fruit in a ceramic bowl so I could gesture to it when I said, "Eat anything. Pretend this is your home." The rest of the house was perfectly in order, as it always is, thanks to my system.

It doesn't have a name—I just call it my system. Let's say a person is down in the dumps, or maybe just lazy, and they stop doing the dishes. Soon the dishes are piled sky-high and it seems impossible to even clean a fork. So the person starts eating with dirty forks out of dirty dishes and this makes the person feel like a homeless person. So they stop bathing. Which makes it hard to leave the house. The person begins to throw trash anywhere and pee in cups because they're closer to the bed. We've all been this person, so there is no place for judgment, but the solution is simple:

Fewer dishes.

They can't pile up if you don't have them. This is the main thing, but also:

Stop moving things around.

How much time do you spend moving objects to and fro? Before you move something far from where it lives, remember you're eventually going to have to carry it back to its place—is it really worth it? Can't you read the book standing right next to the shelf with your finger holding the spot you'll put it back into? Or better yet: don't read it. And if you *are* carrying an object, make sure to pick up anything that might need to go in the same direction. This is called carpooling. Putting new soap in the bathroom? Maybe wait until the towels in the dryer are done and carry the towels and soap together. Maybe put the soap on the dryer until then. And maybe don't fold the towels until the next time you have to use the restroom. When the time comes, see if you can put away the soap and fold towels while you're on the toilet, since your hands are free. Before you wipe, use the toilet paper to blot excess oil from your face. Dinnertime: skip the plate. Just put the pan on a hot pad on the table. Plates are an extra step you can do for guests to make them feel like they're at a restaurant. Does the pan need to be washed? Not if you only eat savory things out of it.

We all do most of these things some of the time; with my system you do all of them all of the time. Never don't do them. Before you know it, it's second nature, and the next time you're down in the dumps it operates on its own. Like a rich person, I live with a full-time servant who keeps everything in order—and because the servant is me, there's no invasion of privacy. At its best, my system gives me a smoother living experience. My days become dreamlike, no edges anywhere, none of the snags and snafus that life is so famous for. After days and days alone it gets silky to the point where I can't even feel myself anymore, it's as if I don't exist.

The doorbell rang at quarter to nine and I still hadn't heard from Phillip. If he called while I was with her I would just have to excuse myself. What if she still looked like a gang person? Or she might feel terrible about the imposition and start apologizing the moment she saw me. As I walked to the door the map of the world detached from the wall and slid noisily to the floor. Not necessarily an indicator of anything.

She was much older than she'd been when she was fourteen. She was a woman. So much a woman that for a moment I wasn't sure what I was. An enormous purple duffel bag was slung over her shoulder.

"Clee! Welcome!" She stepped back quickly as if I intended to embrace her. "It's a shoeless household, so you can put your shoes right there." I pointed and smiled and waited and pointed again. She looked at the row of my shoes, different brown shapes, and then down at her own shoes, which seemed to be made out of pink gum.

"I don't think so," she said in a surprisingly low, husky voice.

We stood there for a moment. I told her to hold on, and went and got a plastic produce bag. She looked at me with an aggressively blank expression while she kicked off her shoes and put them in the bag.

"When you leave make sure to lock both dead bolts, but when you're in the house it's fine to just lock one. If the doorbell rings, you can open this"—I opened the tiny door within the front door and peeked through it—"to see who it is." When I pulled my face out of the peephole she was in the kitchen.

"Eat anything," I said, jogging to catch up. "Pretend this is your home." She took two apples and started to put them in her purse, but then saw one had a bruise and switched it out for another. I showed her the ironing room. She popped the mint into her mouth and left the wrapper on the washcloth.

"There's no TV in here?"

"The TV is in the common area. The living room."

We walked out to the living room and she stared at the TV. It wasn't the flat kind, but it was big, built into the bookshelves. It had a little Tibetan cloth hanging over it.

"You have cable?"

"No. I have a good antenna, though, so all the local stations come in very clearly." Before I was done talking she took out her phone and started typing on it. I stood there for a moment, waiting, until she glanced up at me as if to say *Why are you still here?*

I went into the kitchen and put the kettle on. Using my peripheral vision, I could still see her and it was hard not to wonder if Carl's mother had been very busty. Suzanne, though tall and attractive, would not be described as a "bombshell," whereas this person leaning against the couch did bring that word to mind. It was more than just her chest dimensions—she had a blond, tan largeness of scale. She was maybe even slightly overweight. Or maybe not, it could just have been the way she wore her clothes, tight magenta sweatpants low on her hips and several tank tops, or maybe a purple bra and two tank tops—there was an accumulation of straps on her shoulders. Her face was pretty but it wasn't equal to her body. There was too much room between her eyes and her little nose. Also some excess face under her mouth. Big chin. Obviously her features were better than mine, but if you just looked at the spaces between the features, I won. She might have thanked me; a small welcome gift wouldn't have been unheard-of. The kettle whistled. She looked up from her phone and widened her eyes mockingly, meaning that's what I looked like.

At dinnertime I asked Clee if she wanted to join me for chicken and kale on toast. If she was surprised by toast for dinner, I was going to explain how it's easier to make than rice or pasta but still counts as a grain. I wouldn't lay out my whole system at once, just a little tip here, a little tip there. She said she had some food she'd brought with her.

"Do you need a plate?"

"I can eat it out of the thing."

"A fork?"

"Okay."

I gave her the fork and turned up the ringer on my phone. "I'm waiting for an important phone call," I explained. She glanced behind herself, as if looking for the person who might be interested to know this.

"When you're done, just wash your fork and put it right here with your other things." I pointed to the small bin on the shelf where her cup, bowl, plate, knife and spoon were. "My dishes go here, but of course they're in use now." I tapped the empty bin beside hers.

She stared at the two bins, then her fork, then the bins again.
"I know it seems like it might be confusing, because our dishes look the same, but as long as everything is either in use, being washed, or in its bin, there won't be a problem."

"Where are all the other dishes?"

"I've been doing it this way for years, because nothing's worse than a sink full of dirty dishes."

"But where are they?"

"Well, I do have more. If, for example, you want to invite a friend over for dinner . . ." The more I tried not to look at the box on the top shelf the more I looked at it. She followed my eyes up and smiled.

BY THE NEXT EVENING, THERE was a full sink of dirty dishes and Phillip hadn't called. Since the ironing room didn't have a TV, Clee nested in the living room with her clothes and food and liters of Diet Pepsi all within arm's distance of the couch, which she'd outfitted with her own giant flowery pillow and purple sleeping bag. She talked on the phone there, texted there, and more than anything watched TV there. I moved my computer back to the ironing room, folded up the cot, and pushed it up into the attic. While my head was on the other side of the ceiling, she explained that someone had come to the door with a free-trial cable offer.

"When you were at work. You can cancel it at the end of the month, after I go. So there's no cost."

I didn't fight her on it because it seemed like a kind of insurance that she would leave. The TV was on all the time, day and night, whether or not she was awake or watching it. I had heard of people like this, or seen them, on TV actually. When it had been three days I wrote Phillip's name on a piece of paper and ripped it up but the trick didn't work—it never does when you lean too heavily on it. I also tried dialing his number backward, which isn't anything, and then no area code, and then all ten but in a random order.

A smell began to coagulate around Clee, a brothy, intimate musk that she seemed unaware of, or unconcerned by. I had presumed she would shower every morning, using noxious blue cleansing gels and plasticky sweet lotions. But, in fact, she didn't wash. Not the day after she arrived or the day after that. The body odor was on top of her pungent foot fungus, which hit two seconds after she passed by—it had sneaky delay. At the end of the week she finally bathed, using what smelled like my shampoo.

"You're welcome to use my shampoo," I said when she came out of the bathroom. Her hair was combed back and a towel hung around her neck.

"I did."

I laughed and she laughed back—not a real laugh but a sarcastic, snorting guffaw that continued for quite a while, getting uglier and uglier until it halted coldly. I blinked, for once grateful that I couldn't cry, and she pushed past, knocking me a little with her shoulder. My face had an expression of *Hey, watch it! It is not okay to ridicule me in my own house, which I have generously opened to you. I'll let it go this time, but in the future I expect a one-hundred-and-eighty-degree turnaround in your behavior, young lady.* But she was dialing her phone so she missed the look. I took out my phone and dialed too. All ten numbers, in the correct order.

"Hi!" I yelled. She whipped her head around. She probably thought I didn't know anyone.

"Hi," he said, "Cheryl?"

"Yep, it's the Cher Bear," I barked, walking casually to my room. I quickly shut the door.

"That wasn't my real voice," I whispered, crouching behind

my bed, "and actually we don't have to talk, I just needed to make a demonstration phone call and you were the number I happened to dial." This felt more plausible at the start of the sentence than the finish.

"I'm sorry," said Phillip. "I didn't call when I said I would."

"Well, we're even now, because I used you for the demonstration call."

"I guess I was just scared."

"Of me?"

"Yes, and also society. Can you hear me? I'm driving."

"Where are you going?"

"The grocery store. Ralphs. Let me ask you a question: Does age difference matter to you? Would you ever consider a lover who was much older or much younger than you?"

My teeth started clacking together, too much energy coming up at once. Phillip was twenty-two years older than me.

"Is this the confession?"

"It's related to it."

"Okay, my answer is yes, I would." I held my jaw to quiet my teeth. "Would you?"

"You really want to know what I think, Cheryl?"

Yes!

"Yes."

"I think everyone who is alive on earth at the same time is fair game. The vast majority of people will be so young or so old that their lifetime won't even overlap with one's own—and those people are out of bounds."

"On so many levels."

"Right. So if a person happens to be born in the tiny speck of your lifetime, why quibble over mere years? It's almost blasphemous."

"Although there are some people who *barely* overlap," I suggested. "Maybe those people are out of bounds."

"You're talking about . . . ?"

"Babies?"

"Well, I don't know," he said pensively. "It has to be mutual. And physically comfortable for both parties. I think in the case of a baby, if it can somehow be determined that the baby feels the same way, then the relationship could only be sensual or maybe just energetic. But no less romantic and significant." He paused. "I know this is controversial, but I think you get what I'm saying."

"I really do." He was nervous—men are always sure they'll be accused of some horrific crime after they talk about feelings. To reassure him I described Kubelko Bondy, our thirty years of missed connections.

"So he's not one baby—he's many?" Was there an odd pitch to his voice? Did I hear jealousy?

"No, he's one baby. But he's played by many babies. Or hosted, maybe that's a better word for it."

"Got it. Kubelko—is that Czechoslovakian?"

"That's just what I call him. I might have made it up."

It sounded like he had pulled over. I wondered if we were about to have phone sex. I'd never done that before, but I thought I would be especially good at it. Some people think it's really important to be in the moment with sex, to be present with the other person; for me it's important to block out the person and replace them, entirely if possible, with my thing. This would be much easier to do on the phone. My thing is just a specific private fantasy I like to think about. I asked him what he was wearing.

"Pants and a shirt. Socks. Shoes."

"That sounds nice. Do you want to tell me anything?"

"I don't think so."

"No confessions?"

He laughed nervously. "Cheryl? I've arrived."

For a moment I thought he meant here at my house, right outside. But he meant Ralphs. Was this a subtle invitation?

Assuming he was on the east side, there were two Ralphs he could be going to. I put on a pin-striped men's dress shirt that I'd been saving. Seeing me in this would unconsciously make him feel like we'd just woken up together and I'd thrown on his shirt. A relaxing feeling, I would think. The reusable grocery bags were in the kitchen; I tried to get in and out without Clee's seeing.

"You're going to the store? I need some stuff."

There was no easy way to explain that this wasn't a real shopping trip. She put her feet on the dashboard, dirty tan toes in light blue flip-flops. The odor was unreal.

After changing my mind a few times, I chose the more upscale Ralphs. We promenaded up and down the aisles of processed food, Clee pushing a cart a few feet ahead of me, her chest ballooning ridiculously. Women looked her up and down and then looked away. Men did not look away—they kept looking after they passed her, to get the rear view. I turned and made stern faces at them, but they didn't care. Some men even said hi, as if they knew her, or as if knowing her was about to begin right now. Several Ralphs employees asked if she needed help finding anything. I was ready to bump into Phillip at every turn and for him to be delighted and for us to shop together like the old married couple we had been for a hundred thousand lifetimes before this one. Either I had just missed him or he was at the other Ralphs. The man ahead of us in the checkout line spontaneously began telling Clee how much he loved his son, who was sitting fatly in the grocery cart. He had known love before he had a kid, he said, but in reality no love could compare to his love for his child. I made eye contact with the baby but there was no resonance between us. His mouth hung open dumbly. A red-haired bagger boy hastily abandoned his lane to bag Clee's groceries.

She bought fourteen frozen meals, a case of Cup-o-Noodles, a loaf of white bread, and three liters of Diet Pepsi. The one roll of toilet paper I purchased fit in my backpack. On the drive home I said a few words about the Los Feliz neighborhood, its diversity, before trailing off. I felt silly in the men's shirt; disappointment filled the car. She was scanning her calves for ingrown hairs and picking them out with her nails.

"So what exactly do you aspire to, acting-wise?" I said.

"What do you mean?"

"Like do you hope to be in movies? Or theater?"

"Oh. Is that what my mom said?" She snorted. "I'm not interested in acting."

This wasn't good news. I'd been imagining the big break, the meeting or audition that would remove her from my house.

Kale and eggs, eaten from the pan, I didn't offer her any. Early to bed. I listened to each thing she did from the dark of my room. TV on, then padding to the bathroom, flush, no hand washing, a trip to get something from her car, car door slam, front door slam. The refrigerator opened, the freezer opened, then an unfamiliar beeping. I jumped out of bed.

"That doesn't work," I said, rubbing my eyes. Clee was poking the buttons of the microwave. "It came with the house but it's a million years old. It's not safe, and it doesn't work."

"Well, I'll just try it," she said, pressing start. The microwave whirred, the dinner turned slowly. She peered through the glass. "Seems fine."

"I would step away from it. Radiation. Bad for your reproductive organs." She was staring at my bare legs. I don't usually expose them, which is why they're unshaven. It's not for political reasons, it's just a time-saver. I went back to bed. Microwave dinged, door opened, slammed shut.

ON THURSDAY I SLIPPED OUT before seven o'clock to avoid Rick. Just as I stepped into the office, he called.

"I am very sorry to bother you, miss, but there's a woman here and she just asked me to leave."

I was surprised he even had my number, or a phone.

"Excuse me, she would like to talk to you."

There was a bang, the phone was dropped, Clee came on.

"He just walked onto your property, no car or anything." She turned away from the phone. "Can I see some ID? Or a business card?" I cringed at her rudeness. But also maybe I wouldn't have to deal with him anymore.

"Hello, Clee. I'm sorry I forgot to mention Rick; he gardens." Maybe she would forbid him to return and there would be nothing I could do about it.

"How much do you pay him?"

"I—sometimes I give him a twenty." Nothing; I'd never given him anything. I suddenly felt very judged, very accused. "He's practically family," I explained. This wasn't true in any sense—I didn't even know his last name. "Can you please put him back on?"

She did something that sounded like tossing the phone on the ground.

Rick was back. "Perhaps it is not a good time?"

"I'm so, so sorry. She's not well-mannered."

"I had an arrangement with the Goldfarbs . . . they appreciated . . . but perhaps you—"

"I appreciate it even more than the Goldfarbs did. *Mi casa es tu casa.*"

"What?"

I had always thought he was Latino, but I guess not. In any case, it probably wasn't a smart thing to say.

"Please keep up the good work, it was a misunderstanding."

"The third week of next month I will have to come on a Tuesday."

"Not a problem, Rick."

"Thank you. And how long will your visitor be staying?" he asked politely.

"Not long, she'll be gone in a few days and everything will be back to normal."

CHAPTER THREE

The ironing room and bedroom were my domain, the living room and the kitchen were hers. The front door and the bathroom were neutral zones. When I got my food from the kitchen I scurried, hunched over, as if I was stealing it. I ate looking out the too-high ironing-room window, listening to her TV shows. The characters were always shouting, so it wasn't hard to follow the plots without the picture. During our Friday video conference call Jim asked what all the commotion was.

"That's Clee," I said. "Remember? She's staying with me until she finds a job?"

Rather than take this opportunity to jump in with accolades and sympathy, my coworkers fell into a guilty silence. Especially Michelle. Someone in a burgundy sweater sauntered across the office, behind Jim's head. I craned my head.

"Is that—who was that?"

"Phillip," piped Michelle. "He just donated an espresso machine to the staff kitchen."

He walked past again, holding a tiny cup.

"Phillip!" I yelled. The figure paused, looking confused.

"It's Cheryl," said Jim, pointing to the screen.

Phillip walked toward the computer and ducked into view.

When he saw me he brought his giant fingertip right up to the camera—I quickly pointed at my own camera. We "touched." He smiled and moseyed away, offscreen.

"What was that?" said Jim.

AFTER THE CALL I THREW on my robe and strolled into the kitchen. I was tired of hiding. If she was rude, I would just roll with it. She was wearing a big T-shirt that said BUMP, SET, SPIKE IT . . . THAT'S THE WAY WE LIKE IT! and either no bottoms or shorts completely covered by the shirt. She seemed to be waiting for the kettle. This was hopeful; maybe she'd reconsidered the microwave.

"Enough hot water for two?"

She shrugged. I guessed we would find out when it came time to pour. I got my mug out of my bin: even though the sink was full of dishes, I had continued using only my set. I leaned on the wall and kneaded my shoulders against it, smiling lazily into the air. Roll, roll, roll with it. We waited for the kettle. She poked a fork at the layers of calcified food on my savory pan as if it were alive.

"It's building flavor," I said protectively, forgetting to roll for a moment.

She laughed, heh, heh, heh, and instead of growing defensive, I joined her, and laughing somehow made it funny, truly funny— the pan and even myself. My chest felt light and open, I marveled at the universe and its trickster ways.

"Why are you laughing?" Her face was suddenly made of stone.

"Just because—" I gestured toward the pan.

"You thought I was laughing about the pan? Like ha ha you're so kooky with your dirty pan and your funny way of doing things?"

"No."

"Yes. That's what you thought." She took a step toward me, talking right into my face. "I was laughing because"—I felt her eyes move over my gray hair, and my face, its big pores—"you're so sad. Soooo. Saaaad." With the word *sad* she pressed her palm into my chest bone, flattening me against the wall. I made an involuntary *huh* sound and my heart began to thud heavily. She could feel this, with her palm. She got a revved-up look and pressed a little harder, then a little harder, pausing each time as if to give me a chance to respond. I was getting ready to say *Hey, you're about to cross a line* or *You're crossing the line* or *Okay, that's it, you've crossed the line*, but suddenly I felt that my bones were really being harmed, not just my chest but my shoulder blades, which were grinding into the wall, and I wanted to live and be whole, be uninjured. So I said, "Okay, I'm sad." The kettle began to whistle.

"What?"

"I'm sad."

"Why would I care if you're sad?"

I quickly gave a nod of agreement to show how completely I was on her side, against myself. The kettle was screaming. She pulled her hand away and poured the water into a Styrofoam cup of noodles—not appeased, just revolted by our affiliation. I walked away, a free woman on rubbery legs.

I curled up on my bed and held my globus. What was the name of the situation I was in? What category was this? I had been mugged once, in Seattle in my twenties, and that had had a similar feeling afterward. But in that case I had gone to the police and in this scenario I couldn't do that.

I called my bosses in Ojai. Carl answered immediately.

"Business or pleasure?" he said.

"It's about Clee," I whispered. "It's been lovely having her, but I think—"

"Hold on. Suz—pick up! Clee's making trouble! Not that phone—the hall one!"

"Hello?" Suzanne's voice was almost inaudible through the crackling connection.

"You're on the crappy phone!" Carl shouted.

"I'm not!" Suzanne yelled. "I'm on the hall one! Why do we both need to be on at the same time?" She hung up the hall phone but could still be heard distantly through Carl's phone. "You get off the phone, I'll talk to Cheryl alone!"

"You've been snapping at me all day, Suz."

Suzanne picked up the phone but paused before putting it to her mouth. "Can you go away? I don't need you monitoring my every move."

"Are you going to offer her money?" Carl said in a whisper that seemed louder than his regular voice.

"Of course not. You think I'm just handing out—" Suzanne put her hand over the phone. I waited, wondering what there was to argue about since they both agreed I should not be offered money.

"Cheryl!" She was back.

"Hi."

"Sorry about that, I'm not having fun in this marriage right now."

"Oh no," I said, although this was the only way they ever were, like this or loudly entranced by each other.

"He makes me feel like shit," she said, and then to Carl, "Well, then go away—I'm having a private conversation here and I can say what I like." And then to me: "How are you?"

"Good."

"We never thanked you for taking Clee, but it means so much"—her voice became thick and halting, I could see her mascara starting to run—"just to know she's getting exposed to good values. You have to remember she grew up in *Ojai*."

Carl picked up.

"Please excuse the theatrics, Cheryl, you don't have to listen to this. Feel free to hang up."

"Fuck you, Carl, I'm trying to make a point. Everyone thinks it's such a terrific idea to move out of the city to raise your kids. Well, don't be surprised when that kid is pro-life and anti–gun control. You should see her friends. Is she going on auditions?"

"I'm not sure."

"Can you put her on?"

I wondered if I was still allowed to hang up if I wanted to.

"She might need to call you back."

"Cheryl, hon, just put her on." She could tell I was scared of her daughter.

I opened my door. Clee was eating ramen on the couch.

"It's your mom." I held out the phone.

Clee took it with a swipe and strode out to the backyard, the door slamming shut behind her. I watched her pacing past the window, her mouth a little spitting knot. The whole family exerted tremendously toward each other; they were in the throes of passion all the time. I held my elbows and looked at the floor. There was a bright orange Cheeto on the rug. Next to the Cheeto was an empty Diet Pepsi can and next to the can was a pair of green-lace thong underwear with white stuff on the crotch. And this was just the area right around my feet. I touched my throat, hard as a rock. But not yet to the point where I had to spit instead of swallow.

Clee stormed in.

"Someone named"—she looked at the screen—"Phillip Bettelheim called you three times."

I CALLED HIM BACK FROM my car. When he asked me how I was, I did my equivalent of bursting into tears—my throat seized, my face crumpled, and I made a noise so high in pitch that it was silent. Then I heard a sob. Phillip was crying—out loud.

"Oh no, what is it?" He had seemed fine when we touched fingers through the computer.

"Nothing new, I'm okay, it's just the thing I was talking about before," he sniffed soggily.

"The confession."

"Yep. It's driving me nuts."

He laughed and this made room for a larger cry. Gasping, he said, "Is—this okay? Can I just—cry—for a while?"

I said of course. I could tell him about Clee another time.

At first the permission seemed to stifle him, but after a minute he broke through to a new kind of crying that I could tell he liked—it was the crying of a child, a little boy who can't catch his breath and is out of control and won't be consoled. But I did console him, I said, "Sh-sh-shhh," and "That's it, let it out," and each of these seemed to be exactly right, they allowed him to cry harder. I really felt a part of it, like I was helping him get somewhere he'd always wanted to go and he was crying with gratitude and astonishment. It *was* pretty incredible, when you thought about it, which, as the minutes wore on, I had time to do. I looked at the curtains of my own house and hoped Clee wasn't breaking things in there. I doubted if any man had ever cried this much, or even any adult woman. We would probably switch roles at some point, down the road, and he would guide me through my big cry. I could see him gently coaxing me into wet tears; the relief would be overwhelming. "You look beautiful," he'd say, touching my tearstained cheek and bringing my hand to the front of his pants. With a little fiddling the car seat went almost flat; as his wail renewed itself I quietly unclasped my pants and slid my hand down. We'd blow our noses and take off our clothes, but only the clothes we needed to. For example, I would leave my blouse and socks and maybe even shoes on and Phillip would do the same. We'd take our pants and underpants off completely but wouldn't fold them up because we'd just have to unfold them to put them back on. We'd lay them out on the floor in a way that would make them easy to put on again later. We'd get side by side in the bed and hug and kiss a lot, Phillip would get on top of me and insert his penis between my legs and then, in a low, commanding voice, he would whisper, "Think about your thing." I'd smile, grateful for the permission to go within, and shut my eyes—transporting myself to a very similar room where our pants were laid out on the floor and Phillip was on top of and inside me. In a low, commanding voice he said, "Think about your thing," and I was flooded with gratitude and relief, even more than last time. I shut my eyes and was again transported to a similar room, a fantasy within a fantasy within a fantasy, and it continued like this, building in intensity until I was so far inside myself that I could go no further. That's it. That's my thing, the thing I like to think about during intercourse or masturbation. It ends with a sudden knotting in my groin followed by a very relaxing fatigue.

As I reclasped my pants he began to slow down, to try to catch his breath. He blew his nose a few times. I said, "That's it, there you go," which made him cry a little more, perhaps just politely to acknowledge my words. Finally it was all quiet.

"That felt really, really good."

"Yes," I agreed. "It was incredible."

"I'm surprised. I usually don't cry well in front of other people. It's different with you."

"Does it feel like we've known each other for longer than we really have?"

"Kind of."

I could tell him or I could not tell him. I decided to tell him.

"Maybe there's a reason for that," I ventured.

"Okay." He blew his nose again.

"Do you know what it is?"

"Give me a hint."

"A hint. Let's see . . . actually, I can't. There are no little parts to it, it's all big."

I took a deep breath and shut my eyes.

"I see a rocky tundra and a crouched figure with apelike features who resembles me. She's fashioned a pouch out of animal gut and now she's giving it to her mate, a strong, hairy pre-man who looks a lot like you. He moves his thick finger around in the pouch and fishes out a colorful rock. Her gift to him. Do you see where I'm going?"

"Kind of? In that I see you're talking about cavemen who look like us."

"Who *are* us."

"Right, I wasn't sure—okay. Reincarnation?"

"I don't relate to that word."

"No, right, me either."

"But sure. I see us in medieval times, huddling together in long coats. I see us both with crowns on. I see us in the forties."

"The 1940s?"

"Yes."

"I was born in '48."

"That makes sense because I was seeing us as a very old couple in the forties. That was probably the lifetime right before this one." I paused. I had said a lot. Too much? That depended on what he said next. He cleared his throat, then was silent. Maybe he wouldn't say anything, which is the worst thing men do.

"What keeps us coming back?" he said quietly.

I smiled into the phone. What an amazing thing to be asked. Right now, tucked into the warmth of my car with this unanswerable question before me—this might have been my favorite moment of all the lifetimes.

"I don't know," I whispered. I quietly leaned my head against the steering wheel and we swam in time, silent and together.

"What are you doing for dinner on Friday, Cheryl? I'm ready to confess."

THE REST OF THE WEEK glided by. Everything was fantastic and I forgave everyone, even Clee, not to her face. She was young! Over a standing-up lunch in the staff kitchen Jim assured me that young people these days were a lot more physically demonstrative than we had been; his niece, for example: very physical girl.

"They're rough," I said.

"They aren't afraid to show their feelings," he said.

"Which is maybe not such a good thing?" I suggested.

"Which is very healthy," he said.

"In the long run, yes," I said. "Perhaps."

"They hug more," he said. "More than we did."

"Hug," I said.

"Boys and girls hug, unromantically."

The conclusion I came to—and it was important to come to a conclusion because you didn't want these kinds of thoughts to just go on and on with no category and no conclusion—was that girls these days, when they weren't hugging boys unromantically, were busy being generally aggressive. Whereas girls in my youth felt angry but directed it inward and cut themselves and became depressed, girls nowadays just went *arrrrgh* and pushed someone into a wall. Who could say which way was better? In the past the girl herself got hurt; now another unsuspecting, innocent person was hurt and the girl herself seemed to feel just fine. In terms of fairness maybe the past was a better time.

On Friday night I put on the pin-striped dress shirt again and a very small amount of taupe eye shadow. My hair looked great—a little Julie Andrews, a little Geraldine Ferraro. When Phillip honked I scooted through the living room, hoping to bypass Clee.

"C'mere," she said. She was standing in the kitchen doorway, eating a piece of white toast.

I pointed at the door.

"Come here."

I went to her.

"What's that noise?"

"My bracelets?" I said, shaking my wrist. I had put on a pair of clangy bracelets in case the men's shirt made me look unfeminine. Her big hand closed around my arm and she slowly began squeezing it.

"You're dressed up," she said. "You wanted to look good and this"—she squeezed harder—"is what you came up with."

He honked again, twice.

She took another bite of toast. "Who is it?"

"His name's Phillip."

"Is it a date?"

"No."

I focused on the ceiling. Maybe she did this all the time and so she knew something about skin, like that it could withstand a certain amount of pressure before breaking. Hopefully she would keep that amount in mind and not go over it. Phillip knocked on the front door. She finished her toast and used her free hand to gently lower my chin so that my eyes were forced to meet hers.

"I'd appreciate it if you told *me* when you have a problem with me, not my parents."

"I don't have a problem with you," I said quickly.

"That's what I told them." And we stayed like that. And Phillip knocked again. And we stayed like that. And Phillip knocked again. And we stayed like that. And then she let me go.

I opened the door just wide enough to slip out.

When we were safely out of the neighborhood I asked him to pull over and we looked at my wrist; there was nothing there. He turned on the interior lights; nothing. I described how big she was and the way she had grabbed me and he said he could imagine she might squeeze a person thinking it was a normal amount of squeezing, but to someone delicate like me, it might hurt.

"I'm not really delicate."

"Well, compared to her you are."

"Have you seen her recently?"

"Not for a few years."

"She's big-boned," I said. "A lot of men think that's attractive."

"Sure, a woman with that kind of body has a fat store that

allows her to make milk for her young even if her husband isn't able to bring meat home. I feel confident about my ability to bring meat home."

The words *milk* and *fat store* and *meat* had fogged up the windows faster than leaner words would have. We were in a sort of creamy cloud.

"What if, instead of going to a restaurant," Phillip said, "what if we ate dinner at my house?"

He drove like he lived, with entitlement, not using the blinker, just gliding very quickly between lanes in his Land Rover. At first I kept looking over my shoulder to check if the lane was actually clear or if we were going to die, but after a while I threw caution to the wind and sank back into the heated leather seat. Fear was for poor people. Maybe this was the happiest I'd ever been.

Everything in his penthouse was white or gray or black. The floor was one vast smooth white surface. There were no personal items—no books or stacks of bills, no stupid windup toy that a friend had given him as a gift. The dish soap was in a black stone dispenser; someone had transferred it from its plastic container to this serious one. Phillip put his keys down and touched my arm. "Want to know something crazy?"

"Yes."

"Our shirts."

I made a shocked face that was too extreme and quickly ratcheted it down to baffled surprise.

"You're the female me."

My heart started swooping around, like it was hanging on a long rope. He said he hoped I liked sushi. I asked if he could point me toward the restroom.

Everything in the bathroom was white. I sat on the toilet and

looked at my thighs nostalgically. Soon they would be perpetually entwined in his thighs, never alone, not even when they
wanted to be. But it couldn't be helped. We had a good run, me
and me. I imagined shooting an old dog, an old faithful dog,
because that's what I was to myself. Go on, boy, get. I watched
myself dutifully trot ahead. Then I lowered my rifle and what
actually happened was I began to have a bowel movement. It was
unplanned, but once begun it was best to finish. I flushed and
washed my hands and only by luck did I happen to glance back
at the toilet. It was still there. One had to suppose it was the dog,
shot, but refusing to die. This could get out of hand, I could flush
and flush and Phillip would wonder what was going on and I'd
have to say *The dog won't die gracefully.*

Is the dog yourself, as you've known yourself until now?

Yes.

No need to kill it, my sweet girl, he'd say, reaching into the toilet
bowl with a slotted spoon. *We need a dog.*

But it's old and has strange, unchangeable habits.

So do I, my dear. So do we all.

I flushed again and it went down. I could tell him about it
later.

We ate without talking and then I saw his hand shaking a little
and I knew it was time. He was about to confess. I must have sat
across from him at a hundred meetings of the board, but I had
never let myself really study his face. It was like knowing what
the moon looks like without ever stopping to find the man in it.
He had wrinkles that carved down from his eyes into his cheeks.
His hair was dense and curly on the sides, thinner on the top.
Full beard, messy eyebrows. We smiled at each other like the old
friends we on some level were. He exhaled a long breath and we
both laughed a little.

"There's something I've been wanting to talk with you about," he began.

"Yes."

He laughed again. "Yes, you have probably gathered that by now. I've made a big deal out of something that is probably not such a big deal."

"It is and it isn't," I said.

"That's exactly right, it is and it isn't. It is for other people, but it isn't for me. I mean, not that it isn't a big deal—it's huge, just not—" He stopped himself and exhaled with a long *schooooo* sound. Then he lowered his head and became very still. "I . . . have fallen in love . . . with a woman who is my equal in every way, who challenges me, who makes me feel, who humbles me. She is sixteen. Her name is Kirsten."

My first thought was of Clee, as if she were in the room, watching my face collapse. Her head thrown back, a husky heh, heh, heh. I pressed my fingernail into a paper-thin slice of ginger.

"How did you"—I tried to swallow but my throat was completely locked—"meet Kristen?"

"*Kir*—like *ear*"—he touched his ear, a pendulous lobe with a tuft of gray hair sprouting from the hole—"*sten*. Kirsten. We met in my craniosacral certification class."

Heh, heh, heh.

I nodded.

"Amazing, right? At sixteen? She's so ahead of the game. She's this very wise, very advanced being—and she comes from the most unlikely background, her mom is totally out to lunch and involved in drugs. But Kirsten just"—he gasped with pained eyes—"transcends."

I pretended to take a sip of wine but actually deposited the spit that was collecting in my mouth.

"Does she feel the same way?"

He nodded. "She's actually the one pushing for consummation."

"Oh, so you haven't . . . ?"

"No. Until recently she was seeing someone. Our teacher, actually. He's a young man, much closer to her age. A really neat guy—in some ways I think she should have stayed with him."

"Maybe he'll take her back," I offered.

"Cheryl." He suddenly put his hand on my hand. "We want your blessing."

His hand had a heat and weight that only real hands do. A hundred imaginary hands would never be this warm. I kept my eyes on his blocky, primitive fingernails.

"I don't know what you mean."

"Well, I want to, and she wants to—but the attraction is so powerful that we almost don't trust it. Is it real or is it just the power of the taboo? I've told her all about you and our relationship. I explained how strong you are, how you're a feminist and you live alone, and she agreed we should wait until we got your take on it."

I spit into the wine again. "When you were explaining our relationship, what did you say?"

"I said you were . . ."—he looked down at my red knuckles—"someone I had a lot to learn from." With a firm push he pressed his fingers between my fingers. "And I told her how perfectly balanced you are in terms of your masculine and feminine energies." We began making a small undulating wave, threading and rethreading our hands. "So you can see things from a man's point of view, but without being clouded by yang."

Now we were doing it with both hands and looking each other square in the eyes. Our history was bearing down on us, a hundred thousand lifetimes of making love. We rose and stood with just a hot inch between us, our palms pressed together.

"Cheryl," he whispered.

"Phillip."

"I can't sleep, I can't think. I'm going crazy."

The inch was half an inch now. I was throbbing.

"We have no elders," he moaned. "No one to guide us. Will you guide us?"

"But I'm younger than you."

"Perhaps."

"No, I am. I'm twenty-two years younger than you."

"I'm forty-nine years older than her," he breathed. "Just tell me if it's okay. I don't want someone like you to think I'm—I can't even say it. It has nothing to do with her age—you can see that, right?"

Each time I inhaled, the soft dome of my stomach pressed against his groin, and each time I exhaled it gently pulled away. In, out, in, out. My breathing grew sharper and faster, a thrusting kind of breath, and Phillip was gripping my hands. In another second I would use my innocent, fingerless paunch to grope and explore him, shimmying up and down. I stepped away.

"It's a tough decision." I picked my dinner napkin off the floor and placed it carefully over the row of uneaten pink fish meats. "And one I take seriously."

"Okay," said Phillip, straightening up and blinking as if I had suddenly turned the lights on. He followed me to the closet, where I found my purse and jacket. "And?"

"And I'll let you know when I know. Please take me home now."

CLEE WAS HALF-ASLEEP WATCHING TV. When I came in she looked up, surprised, as if it wasn't my house. Just the sight of her pretty face and big chin made me furious. I threw my purse down on the coffee table, which was where I used to put it before she moved in.

"You need to get your act together and start looking for a job," I said, straightening the chair. "Or maybe I should call your parents and tell them what's been going on here."

She smiled slowly at me, her eyes narrowing.

"What's been going on here?" she said.

I opened my mouth. The simple facts of her violence slid out of reach. Suddenly I felt uncertain, as if she knew something about me, as if, in a court of law, I would be the one to blame.

"And anyways," she said, picking up the remote, "I *have* a job."

This seemed unlikely.

"Great. Where?"

"The supermarket, the one we went to."

"You went to Ralphs and filled out an application and had an interview?"

"No, they just asked me—last time I was there. I start tomorrow."

I could see a man's trembling hands pinning a name tag to her bosom and I remembered what Phillip said about her fat store. Just a couple of hours ago we were sitting in his car and I was thinking, *Let's not waste our time talking about her when we have so much else to say to each other.* I lifted the end of her sleeping bag and yanked out one of the couch cushions.

"This couch isn't meant to be used as a bed. You need to flip the cushions so they don't get permanently misshapen." I flipped it over and started pulling at the other one—the one she was sitting on. My muscles were tensed; I knew this was a bad idea but I kept tugging at the cushion. Tug. Tug.

I didn't even see her get up. The crook of her arm caught my neck and jerked me backward. I slammed into the couch—the wind knocked out of me. Before I could get my balance she shoved my hip down with her knee. I grabbed at the air stupidly. She pinned my shoulders down, intently watching what the panic was doing to my face. Then she suddenly let go and walked away. I lay there shaking uncontrollably. She locked the bathroom door with a click.

PHILLIP CALLED FIRST THING IN the morning.

"Kirsten and I were wondering if you'd had you a chance to think it over."

"Can I ask one question?" I said, pressing a bruise on the back of my upper calf.

"Anything," said Phillip.

"Is she gorgeous?"

"Will that impact your decision?"

"No."

"Stunning."

"What color hair?"

"Blond."

I spit into a hanky. My globus had swollen in the night—I couldn't swallow at all anymore.

"No, I haven't decided."

For the next three hours I lay in bed, my head where my feet should be. He was in love with a sixteen-year-old. I had spent years training myself to be my own servant so that when a situation involving extreme wretchedness arose, I would be taken care of. But the house didn't function as it once had; Clee had undone years of careful maintenance. All the dishes were out and the general disarray was beyond carpooling—there was nothing between me and filthy animal living. So I peed in cups and knocked over one of the cups and didn't clean it up. I chewed bread into a puree, moistening it with sips of water until I could slurp it down as a horse would. Only liquids could slip past the globus, and only with a swallowing scenario. The Black Stallion for bready water. For plain water I was Heidi, dipping a metal ladle into a well. It's from the end, when she's living in the Alps. For orange juice I was Sarge from the *Beetle Bailey* comic, where Sarge and Beetle Bailey go to Florida and drink all-you-can-drink orange juice. Glug, glug, glug. It worked because it wasn't me, it was the character swallowing, offhandedly—just a brief moment in a larger story. There's a scenario for every beverage except beer and wine because I was too young for alcohol when I invented this technique. I let my mouth hang open so the spit could roll out easily. Not just a sixteen-year-old, a stunning blond sixteen-year-old. She was driving him crazy. Someone came in the back door. Rick. The TV blasted on. Not Rick.

She was home from Ralphs: it was later than I thought. I pulled myself upright and listened to her flipping channels arrhythmically. My back was sore where she threw me down, but this was almost a welcome distraction from the globus. My neck felt like an object unrelated to me, a businessman's misplaced briefcase. When I tapped my throat it made a bony sound, and then suddenly the muscle began to tighten, and tighten, like a pulled knot—I panicked, shaking my hands in the air—no, no, no—

And then it locked.

I'd read about this online but it had never happened to me. The sternothyroid muscle becomes so rigid that it seizes up. Sometimes permanently.

"Test," I whispered, to see if I could still talk. "Test, test." Very carefully, without moving my neck, I reached for the glass bottle on my bedside table. Using the Heidi scenario I drank all the red. Nothing happened. I gingerly carried my neck to the phone and called Dr. Broyard, but he was in Amsterdam; the message invited me to call 911 or leave my name and number for Dr. Ruth-Anne Tibbets. I remembered the two stacks of business cards in their Lucite holders—this was the other doctor. The one in charge of watering the fern in the waiting room. I hung up, then called back and left my name and number. The message felt too short for a therapist.

"I'm forty-three," I added, still whispering. "Regular height. Brown hair that is now gray. No children. Thanks, please call back. Thank you."

DR. TIBBETS SAW PATIENTS ON Tuesdays through Thursdays. When I suggested today, a Thursday, she countersuggested next Tuesday. Six days of liquids; I might starve. Sensing my anguish, she asked if I was in danger. I might be, I said, by next Tuesday. If I could come right away, she said, we could meet during her lunch hour.

I drove to the same building and took the same elevator to the same floor. Dr. Broyard's name on the door had been replaced by DR. RUTH-ANNE TIBBETS, LCSW—a plastic placard that slid into an aluminum strip. I looked down the hall and wondered how many other offices were shared. Most patients would never know; it had to be unusual for a person to need the services of two different unaffiliated specialists. The receptionist's area was empty. I read a magazine about golf for fifteen seconds until the door swung open.

Dr. Tibbets was tall with flat gray hair and an androgynous horsey face; she reminded me of someone but I wasn't sure who.

This was probably the sign of a good therapist, seeming familiar to everyone. She asked if the room was warm enough—there was a small space heater she could turn on. I said I was fine.

"What brought you in today?"

A bento box sat on top of her day planner. Had she stuffed herself as quickly as possible after the previous patient? Or was she waiting, faint with hunger? "You can eat your lunch if you want, I don't mind." She smiled patiently. "Begin when you feel ready." I turned sideways on the leather couch but quickly discovered there wasn't enough length for my legs, so I swung myself upright again; she wasn't that kind of therapist.

I told her about my globus hystericus and how my sternothyroid had locked. She asked me if I could recall any triggering incidents. I didn't feel ready to tell her about Phillip so I described my houseguest, the way she moved around the living room, swinging her giant, heavy-lidded head like a cow, a dense, stenchy bull.

"Bulls are male," said Dr. Tibbets.

But that was just it. A woman talks, too much—and worries, too much—and gives and gives in. A woman bathes.

"She doesn't bathe?"

"Almost never."

I described her total disregard for my home and acted out the different things she had done to me, pressing on my own chest and squeezing my own wrist. It was hard to yank my own head back.

"This might not look painful because I'm doing it to myself."

"I don't doubt that it's painful," she said. "What have you done to resist?"

I released my arm and sat back down.

"What do you mean?"

"Do you fight back?"

"You mean self-defense?"

"Sure."

"Oh, that's not what this is. It's really more a case of very bad manners." I smiled to myself because it sounded like I was in denial. "Have you heard of Open Palm? Self-defense that helps you burn fat and build muscle? I pretty much invented that."

"Have you yelled?"

"No."

"Or said no to her?"

"No."

Dr. Tibbets was quiet now, like a lawyer who had no further questions. My face crumpled, and my globus swelled painfully; she held out a box of Kleenex.

I suddenly realized why she looked so familiar.

She was Dr. Broyard's receptionist. It was outrageous. Was she even Ruth-Anne Tibbets or was she Ruth-Anne Tibbets's receptionist too? What had she done with Dr. Tibbets? This needed to be reported. Who could I call? Not Dr. Broyard or Dr. Tibbets, since this usurping, masquerading woman would undoubtedly answer the phone. I slowly gathered my purse and sweater. It was best not to agitate her or let on.

"This has been a great help, thank you."

"You have thirty more minutes."

"I don't feel that I need it. It was a twenty-minute problem and you addressed it."

She hesitated, looking up at me.

"I'm going to have to charge you for the whole session."

I had already prewritten the check. I took it out of my purse.

"If possible, please donate the thirty minutes to someone who can't afford therapy."

"I can't do that."

"Thank you."

CLEE WAS AT RALPHS, SO I stayed home and applied hot compresses, working to gradually relax my throat. Occasionally I pressed a warm metal spoon against it; some people say that helps. Just when I thought I might be making progress, Phillip called.

"I'm seeing Kirsten tonight. I'm picking her up at eight."

I said nothing.

"So should I expect to hear from you before eight, or . . . ?"

"No."

"Not at all tonight? Or just not by eight?"

I hung up. A shaking fury quietly rose through my chest into my throat. The lump began to seize up again, tightening like an angry man's fist. Or my fist. I looked at my veiny hands, slowly curling them into balls. Is this what she meant by fight back? The thought of the receptionist's smug, horsey face made my globus even harder. I jumped up and scanned the spines of my DVD collection. I probably didn't even have one. I did: *Survival of the Fittest*. It wasn't our most recent release; Carl and Suzanne had given it to me for Christmas about four years ago. Of course I had many opportunities to learn self-defense in the old studio, just never the desire to embarrass myself in front of my coworkers. The great thing about our DVDs (and streaming video), besides burning fat and building muscle, is you can do them alone without anyone watching. I pressed play.

"Hi! Let's get started!" It was Shamira Tye, the bodybuilder. She doesn't compete anymore but she was still very expensive and hard to get. "I recommend working out in front of a mirror so you can watch your tush shrink." I stood in the living room in my pajamas. Kicks were called kicks but punches were called "pops." "Pop, pop, pop, pop!" Shamira said. "I pop in my sleep! And soon you will too!" A knee-slam-to-groin movement was presented as the can-can—"Yes you can-can!" If someone was strangling you, "the butterfly" would break their hold while toning your upper arms. "It's a catch-twenty-two," Shamira mused at the end. "With your new ripped bod, you may actually get attacked more often!" I fell to my knees. Sweat ran down the sides of my torso and into my elastic waistband.

Clee came home at nine o'clock with a box of trash bags. I hoped this was an olive branch, since we were out of trash bags and I didn't really have any intention of fighting her. But she used all of the bags to gather up the clothes and mildewed beach towels and food items and electronics that apparently had been in her car this whole time. I watched her park the four bags against the wall in the corner of the living room. Each swallow took concentration but I kept at it. Some people with globus only spit; they have to bring a spittoon with them everywhere they go.

At eleven fifteen Phillip texted. *SHE WANTS ME TO TELL YOU I RUBBED HER THROUGH HER JEANS. WE DON'T THINK THAT COUNTS. NO ORGASM.* All caps, as if he was yelling out of his penthouse window. Once read, the image was impossible to keep at bay—the tight jean crotch, his stubby, furry hands rubbing wildly. In the living room I could hear Clee crunching ice like cud. The chewing was so loud I began to wonder if she wasn't doing it sarcastically, to aggravate me. I pressed my ear against the door. Now she was imitating the imitation—it was a chomping sound with a double set of quotation marks around it. Too late I realized there would be no end to this line of thought—her self-impersonation quadrupled, and then sixteeni-fied, her eyeballs popping out of her head, ferociously rubbed jeans, teeth like fangs, tongue whipping around the room, ice flying everywhere. I spit on my sleeve, yanked open the door, and marched over to the couch. She looked up at me from her sleeping bag and quietly regurgitated a single ice cube.

"Could you please not make that sound please?" I shouldn't have said *please* twice, but my voice was low and my eye contact was direct. I held my hands in front of me in a position of readiness. My heart was hitting the inside of my body so hard it made a knocking sound. What if she did a move that wasn't on the DVD? I glanced down to be sure my stance was grounded.

She squinted at me, taking in my hovering hands and planted feet, then tilted her head back and filled her mouth with ice. I grabbed the cup out of her hand. She blinked at her empty palm, slowly chewed the ice, swallowed it and looked past me at the TV. It wasn't going to happen; we weren't going to fight. But she could see I wanted to. She could see I'd gotten all geared up—a forty-three-year-old woman in a blouse, ready to brawl. And she was laughing about it, right now, inside. Heh, heh, heh.

CHAPTER FOUR

It took a day to become calm and gather up my pride. *Delicate* was the word Phillip had used to describe me. A delicate woman would not throw punches in her own home. What a barbaric mentality! As if there weren't a million other ways to deal with conflict. I drafted a letter to Clee. It was clear-cut and unequivocal. Reading it aloud was quite moving, actually; by inviting her to engage in a civilized manner I was probably showing her a respect that few people ever had. Dignity was on its way. I spit into an empty almond butter jar; there's something kind of quaint about a spittoon. She didn't need to thank me for my honest forthrightness, but if she insisted I would be forced to accept. I accepted a few times for practice. I put the letter in an envelope labeled CLEE, taped it to the bathroom mirror, and went out so I wouldn't be home when she read it.

At the Ethiopian restaurant I requested a fork. They explained that I had to use my hands, so I asked for it to go, got a fork at Starbucks, and sat in my car. But my throat wouldn't accept even this very soft meal. I put it on the curb for a homeless person. An Ethiopian homeless person would be especially delighted. What a heartbreaking thought, encountering your native food in this way.

When I got back she was eating Thanksgiving dinner, her favorite kind of microwave meal. I was a little nervous about the letter, but she seemed to be in good spirits—texting and reading a magazine with the TV on. She was taking it well. I put on my nightgown and carried my toiletries bag to the bathroom. The envelope labeled CLEE was still taped to the mirror. She either had seen it and not read it, or had not gone to the bathroom yet. I went to bed and checked my phone. Nothing. Phillip had been rubbing Kirsten through her jeans this whole time, still no climax. The jeans would be in tatters now, his fingers blistered, waiting for my green light. The toilet flushed in the bathroom.

A minute later my bedroom door flew open.

"Who's the guest?" she said. The room was dark but I could see the letter in her hand.

"Who?"

"The one coming Friday that I have to move out for."

"Oh, it's an old friend."

"An old friend?"

"Yes."

"What's the name of the old friend?"

"His name is Kubelko Bondy."

"That's a made-up-sounding name." She was moving toward the bed.

"Well, I'll tell him you think so."

I slid out of bed and backed slowly away from her. If I ran it would be a chase situation and that would be too terrifying, so I forced myself to walk casually toward the door. She slammed it shut before I got there. Galloping heart and micro-shakes. Shamira Tye calls it "your adrenaline event"; once it begins, it has to play forward—it can't be stopped or reversed. The darkness was disorienting, I couldn't figure out where she was until she pushed my head down, dunking me as if we were in a pool.

"Trying to get rid of me?" she panted. "Is that it?"

"No!" The right word but the wrong time. I tried to rise, she plunged me down again. I heard myself gasping, drowning. What move were we on? I needed the DVD. My nose was too near her yeasty feet. I was queasy, green. A scream came out as raspy whispers, stuck to my throat. My peak was nearing; if you don't fight back by the time you hit peak fear then you won't ever fight back. You'll die—maybe not physically, but you'll die.

It came from my bellows, the loudest noise I'd ever made. Not *no*, but the old Open Palm battle cry: *Aiaiaiaiai!* My thighs catapulted upward; I almost leapt into the air. Clee was still for a moment, and then she barreled into me, pulling me down and trying to pin me. It was too much weight. I can-canned with full force, kicking everything in sight, and popped with my hard fist when I could. She repeatedly tried to bring me to the floor until I tried the butterfly. It worked—I broke free. She stood up and walked out of the room. The bathroom door locked with a click. The sink taps blasted on.

I lay next to my bed, sucking down big pulls of air. Long loose thrums of pain were gently vibrating through my limbs. It was gone. Not just the globus but the whole structure around it, the tightness in my chest, my locked jaw. I rolled my head from side to side. Exquisite. A million tiny, delicate sensations. The skin was burning from something she had done but otherwise loose as a goose. I laughed and sent a ripple up one arm, across my shoulders to the other one. What was that called again? The electric slide? Who was this big goof? Señorita Sillypants. I saw myself flamenco dancing, something with castanets. The water was still running in the bathroom, a pathetic attempt at passive aggression. Waste all the water you want! If she moved out tomorrow I could have the house in order by the weekend. My new muscles shook wildly as I reached for my phone. I left my name and number and requested the same time next Tuesday. Dr. Tibbets's receptionist was a fraud and a thief and a pretty good therapist.

CLEE DIDN'T LEAVE THE NEXT DAY. Or the day after that. She was still there on Tuesday but I went to therapy anyway. The receptionist smiled warmly as I placed myself on Ruth-Anne Tibbets's couch.

"How are—"

I interrupted her. "Before I answer that, can I ask you something?"

"Of course."

"Are you licensed?"

"I am, I have a degree in clinical psychology and social work from UC Davis." She pointed to a framed piece of paper on the wall, Ruth-Anne Tibbets's diploma. I was about to ask to see her driver's license, but she continued. "I don't want to violate your patient confidentiality with Dr. Broyard, but I remember scheduling your appointment with him. I am his receptionist, three times a year, when he uses this office. That might have caused some confusion."

Of course. Why hadn't I thought of this obvious and simple explanation? I apologized and she said there was no need and I apologized again. Her shoes. They were a fancy European kind. Did she really need the extra income?

"How much are you paid as a receptionist?"

"About a hundred dollars for the day."

"That's less than what I pay you for an hour."

She nodded. "I don't do it for the money. I enjoy it. Answering the phone and setting up appointments for Dr. Broyard is a wonderful respite from the responsibility of this job."

Everything she said made perfect sense but only for a few seconds, then it expired. A wonderful respite? It didn't sound very wonderful. She leaned back a little, waiting for me to launch into my private life. I waited too, for a feeling of trust to arise. The room was very quiet.

"I need to use the restroom," I said finally, just to break the silence.

"Oh dear. You really have to go?"

I nodded.

"Okay. You have two options. There's a key in the waiting room with a plastic duck on it. You can take that key and go to the bathroom on the ninth floor, which unfortunately you can only get to by taking the elevator down to the lobby and asking the doorman to use his key to unlock the service elevator. This option usually takes about fifteen minutes in total. Alternately, if you look behind that paper screen you'll see a stack of Chinese takeout containers. You can go in one of these, behind the screen, and take it with you when you leave. There are thirty minutes left in your session."

The pee made an embarrassingly loud sound shooting into the container but I reminded myself that she had been to UC Davis and so forth. Overflow was a concern but it didn't. I held the hot container in my hands and peeked at Dr. Tibbets through a tiny tear in the screen. She was looking at the ceiling.

"Is Dr. Broyard married?"

She became very still. "He is married. He has a wife and family in Amsterdam."

"But your relationship with him is . . . ?"

"Three days a year I take on a submissive role. It's a game we like to play, an immensely satisfying adult game." She kept her eyes on the ceiling, waiting for my next question.

"How did you meet?"

"He was my patient. And then, many years later, long after he had stopped analysis with me, we met again in a rebirthing class and he told me he was looking for an office, so I suggested this arrangement. That was about eight years ago."

"You suggested just the part about the office or the whole thing?"

"I'm a mature woman, Cheryl—I ask for what I want, and if the desire isn't mutual, well, at least I haven't wasted any time thinking about it."

I came out from behind the screen and sat down again, carefully placing the takeout container next to my purse.

"Is it sexual?"

"Making love is something he can do with his wife. Our relationship is much more powerful and moving to me if we don't compact our energy into our genitals."

Her genitals, compacted. The image triggered a wave of nausea. I pressed my fingertips against my mouth and leaned forward slightly.

"Are you ill? There's a trash can right there if you need to throw up," she said flatly.

"Oh, that's not why I—" I touched my lips several times to show how it was just a thing I did. "Are you in love with him?"

"In love? No. I don't connect with him intellectually or emotionally. We agreed not to fall in love; it's a clause in our contract."

I smiled. Then unsmiled—she was serious.

"I'm sure the prevailing logic is that it's more romantic to guess at each party's intention." She fluttered her big hands in the air and I saw chickens with ruffled feathers, stupid and clucking.

"Is the contract written or verbal?" My legs were twisted together and my arms held each other.

"How are you feeling about all this new information?" she asked soberly.

"Did a lawyer make it?"

"I downloaded a form from the Internet. It's just a list of what is allowed and not allowed in the relationship. I don't have it here."

"That's okay," I whispered. "Let's talk about something else now."

"What would you like to talk about?"

I told her about fighting back. The story was less triumphant than I thought it would be, especially since Clee was still in my house.

"And how did you feel after she left the room?"

"I felt good, I guess."

"And how about right now? How's your globus?"

The flamenco feeling had not been long lasting. In the morning Clee didn't seem particularly cowed by me—if anything she was more relaxed since the fight, more at home.

"Not great," I admitted, squeezing my throat a little with my hand. Ruth-Anne asked if she could feel it; I leaned forward and she gently pressed my Adam's apple with four fingertips. Her hand smelled clean, at least.

"It is quite tight. How uncomfortable."

Her sympathy set off a crying response. The ball rose and tightened; I winced, holding my neck. It was hard to believe it had been so loose so recently.

"Perhaps you'll get relief tonight."

"Tonight?"

"If you and Clee have another"—she made her hands into boxer's fists—"encounter."

"Oh no. No, no—she needs to go. I've already put up with this much longer than I should have." I thought of Michelle, how quickly she'd booted her. It was Jim's turn now, or Nakako's.

"But if the globus—"

I shook my head. "There's other ways—surgery—well, no, not surgery, but counseling."

"This is counseling."

My eyes fell on Ruth-Anne's mauve fingernails. Polished, but chipped. A receptionist needed nails like those, but a therapist didn't. In three months she'd get another manicure.

I DROVE STRAIGHT TO OPEN PALM: it was my in-office day. All the employees looked strange and shifty to me, as if they weren't wearing any pants under their desks, genitals uncompacted. Was Ruth-Anne pantless behind the receptionist desk when I first met her? It was an icky and unsanitary thought; I swept it away and got to work. Jim and I had a brainstorming session with the web designer on KickIt.com, our youth initiative. Michelle was called over to coordinate the media. Before she sat down she cleared her throat and said, "Jim and Cheryl can take notes alone; they are the best at taking notes—"

Jim cut her off. "Have a seat, Michelle. That's just for group work."

She blushed. The pseudo-Japanese customs were always tricky for new employees. In 1998 Carl went to Japan for a martial arts conference and was blown away by the culture there. "They give gifts every time they meet someone new, and they're all perfectly wrapped."

He'd handed me something wrapped in a cloth napkin. I was still an intern at the time.

"Is this a napkin?"

"They use fabric for wrapping paper there. But I couldn't find any."

I unrolled the napkin and my own wallet fell out.

"This is my wallet."

"I wasn't really giving you a present—I was just trying to show the culture. The gift would be a set of little sake cups or something. That's what the head of the conference gave me."

"You went into my purse and got this? When did you do that?"

"When you were in the bathroom, just a few minutes ago."

He wrote up a list of guidelines for the office, to make the atmosphere more Japanese. It was hard to know how authentic the list was, since none of the rest of us had been to Japan. Almost two decades later, I am the only one who knows the origin of the office rules, but I never go into it since there are now actual Japanese-American people on the staff (Nakako, and Aya in education and outreach) and I don't want to offend them.

If a task requires a group effort—for example, moving a heavy table—it should be begun by one person, and then after a respectful pause a second person can join, with a bowed head, saying, "Jim can move the table alone, he is the best at moving the table, I am joining him even though I'm not much help, because I'm not good at moving the table." Then, after a moment, a third person can join, first bowing his head and stating, "Jim and Cheryl can move the table alone," etc. And so on, until there are enough people assembled for the task. It's one of those things that seems like a drag at first and then becomes second nature, until not doing it feels rude, almost aggressive.

When the meeting was over I asked Michelle to stay for a moment.

"I wanted to discuss something."

"I'm sorry."

"About what?"

"I don't know."

"I wanted to ask you about Clee."

Her face grayed. "Are Carl and Suzanne mad at me?"

"Was she mean to you?"

She looked at her hands.

"She was. Was she violent? Did she hurt you?" I said, continuing. She looked surprised, almost aghast.

"No, of course not. She just . . ." She was choosing her words carefully. "Her manners were different than I'm used to."

"That's all? That's why you kicked her out?"

"Oh, I didn't kick her out," she said. "She just left. She said she wanted to live with you."

I ENTERED THE HOUSE SILENTLY, even though she was at Ralphs. I had never snooped through her stuff or wanted to, but it was no crime to sit on my own couch. Her nylon sleeping bag released a puff of body odor when I sat down. I was careful not to move the old food wrappers or the hairbrush clotted with blond hair or the bulging pink vinyl bag with colorful thong-style underwear spilling out of it. I lowered my head onto her pillow. The scalp smell was so intense I held my breath for a moment, not knowing if I could handle it. I handled it. I inhaled and exhaled. My body was rigid, almost floating, to keep the purple sleeping bag from touching my skin. I counted to three, drew up my knees and slid into it, burrowing down. It was so dirty it was almost moist. Was that the door? I jumped up, caught, speechless—no, just the rain; it roared against the roof. I pulled the nylon maw up under my chin. Her nest without her was utterly vulnerable, each of her junky things exposed in the bleak afternoon light. I swallowed with emotion, smiling a little as my globus tightened. We were in this together. I had a partner, a teammate.

Tonight I'd pop. Butterfly. Bite. Kick.

She chose me.

THE ONLY WAY I COULD get to Ralphs quickly enough was to run. The urgency predated cars—it had to be me alone thrusting through space, chest out, hair blown back. Each driver who saw me thought, *She is running for her life, she will die if she doesn't get there*, and they were right. Except it was quite a bit farther on foot than I had anticipated, and the rain had thickened. My clothes became heavy with water, my face was washed again and again. Each driver who passed me thought, *She is a giant rat or some other wet, craven animal whose hunger strips her of her dignity.* And they were right.

I scared people as I walked through the grocery store, a monster whose grotesqueness is how wet she is. Cashiers' jaws fell and the man behind the deli counter dropped a fish. I squished along the row of aisles, looking, looking. The skinny redheaded bagger boy smiled knowingly and pointed toward aisle 15.

Her back was to me.

She was unloading condiments from a pallet onto a shelf. Yellow mustards in their pointy hats, four at a time. She turned tiredly; *What man is staring at me now?* she was thinking. But it wasn't a man.

Her head reared back in an automatic flinch. Like seeing your mother at school.

"What are you doing here?"

I ran my fingers through my dripping hair and steadied myself. I had no plan for this moment; she was just supposed to see that I knew now—I was in on it. We were playing a game, an adult game. I smiled and raised my eyebrows a couple of times. Her mouth curdled; she wasn't getting it.

"I know," I said. "What's going on." And in case there was any confusion I pointed back and forth between us a couple times.

She blushed angrily and quickly looked behind herself and all around, then turned back to her mustards and began slamming them onto the shelves. She got it.

The rain had stopped. I dried and grew taller as I walked home. Each driver who passed me thought, *Now there is a person who either just graduated or just got promoted or just won an award.* And they were right.

I WAS DOING THE DISHES when she came home. I kept the water very low so I could hear her. Turning on the TV. Doing each thing in the usual way. She walked into the kitchen, got her meal, stood behind me as she watched it spin, and then ate it on the couch. Suddenly it occurred to me that nothing might be happening. I'd done that before. I had added meaningful layers to things that were meaningless many, many times before. It was silly to think Phillip was still rubbing Kirsten's jeans. He'd slid them off by now and done just fine without my blessing. I let the water run over my hands. Clee was twenty; nothing she did meant anything.

I put on my nightgown and went to bed early, lying with my hands folded over my chest. The faucet was dripping in the kitchen. I heaved the covers off and stood up.

When I opened the door she was right there, about to come in.

I was so startled that for a moment I forgot it was a game. I walked past her to the kitchen, dripping faucet, must turn off.

She was right behind me. The moment I was through the door she pressed me against the kitchen wall, same as the first time. The pressure began, my bones panicked, and then a kind of rhythm began to hum in my veins, something like a waltz—so I waltzed. I butterflied her elbows and they bent reflexively. I slid along the wall, using it for balance as I tried to bang her head against it. When I started to can-can she threw me down to the ground face-first, pinning me easily with her knee. Last time she'd been holding back—that was obvious now. Something huge was grinding into my spine and I couldn't keep from screaming, an ugly little noise that stayed in the air. I tried to get my arms under me and push up but she bore down with her upper body, her hard skull against mine.

"You're not allowed in the store," she hissed, her lips against my ear. "I'm there so I don't have to look at you."

I gathered all my strength and tried to roll her off with a guttural bellow. She watched me, unmoving. I gave up. And just when my back began to spark into flames, the endorphins arrived, just like last time but stronger. My throat was a warm easy puddle; my face against the floor felt cold and wonderful. An immensely satisfying adult game, just as Ruth-Anne had said. Looking sideways I could just see the tips of her lowered eyelashes and the top of her upper lip, dotted with sweat and panting. She probably thought I couldn't see her. It was almost poignant to me, this moment we were in, although there was something excruciating about it—or maybe the pain radiating out of my back was excruciating, or maybe that was what I meant by poignant: painful. She slowly rolled off me, I quietly whimpered with relief. Instead of rushing to the bathroom she just lay there, catching her breath, our shoulders lightly touching. The floor spun lazily, my arms and legs trilled and quivered. Was she feeling this too? Minutes passed kaleidoscopically, then, very gradually, the kitchen reconstituted itself, the counters, the sink, up there. As Clee shifted and began moving to her feet, a ridiculous wave of abandonment washed over me. Her blank, dumb face headed to the door. And then, at the last possible moment, her eyes flicked back and met mine. I quickly rose to my elbows, readying myself for a question, but she was already gone.

I WAS SO EXCITED TO see Ruth-Anne that I arrived fifteen minutes early. I cleaned out my car then I browsed the gift shop in the lobby of her building. It smelled like vitamins and was overly warm. A very pregnant Indian woman was inspecting elfin figurines. I turned a spinning rack of reading glasses until I was certain, then I stood discreetly beside her, picking up a skiing elf. The woman's stomach protruded so far that its belly button was closer to me than it was to her.

Kubelko?

Yes. Am I in you?

No. You're in someone else.

A sad and awkward silence followed. I cast about for some way to express the bereavement I felt every time we came across each other. A text vibrated in my pocket.

Excuse me.

SHE STRIPPED FOR ME: SAW HER PUSS AND JUGS. UHHHH. KEPT MY HANDS TO MYSELF. My blessing still reigned. Of course it did. I had to have faith in him. We'd been prehistoric together, medieval, king and queen—now we were this. It was all part of the answer to his question *What keeps us coming back?* He wasn't done with me, and I wasn't done with him. And the details—the text messages—were just riddles from the universe. Clues. When I turned back to Kubelko the pregnant woman was gone.

RUTH-ANNE'S COUCH WAS WARM from her previous patient and she looked flushed and radiant.

"Good session?" I asked.

"Excuse me?"

"You look happy."

"Oh," she said, dimming a little. "I just had my lunch hour—I took a catnap. How are you?"

So the heat of the couch was hers. I pressed the leather with my fingers and tried to think of how to begin.

"The thing you do with Dr. Broyard, that—what did you call it?"

"Roles? An adult game?"

"Right. Would you say that's unusual?"

"Define *unusual*."

"Well, how common would you say it is?"

"I'd say it's more common than you would think."

I told her what had happened—starting with what Michelle said and ending on the kitchen floor.

"And my globus is gone, still! I don't know if you can tell"—I leaned forward and gulped—"but it's much easier to swallow. I owe it all to you, Ruth-Anne." I reached into my purse and pulled out a box.

Sometimes people say thank you before even opening the gift—thank you for thinking of me. Ruth-Anne didn't do that; she glanced at her watch while brusquely pulling off the wrapping paper. It was a soy candle. Not the little kind, but a column in a glass jar with a wooden lid.

"It's pomegranate currant," I said.

She handed the candle back to me without smelling it.

"I don't think this is for me."

"It is! I just bought it." I pointed down, indicating the shop on the ground floor.

She nodded, waiting.

"Who do you think it's for?" I said, finally.

"Who do *you* think it's for?"

"Besides you?"

She nodded by slowly shutting her eyes and opening them again. I held the candle nervously, like a hot potato.

"My parents?"

"Why your parents?"

"I don't know. I just thought because this was therapy that might be the right answer."

"Who might you want to give a candle to? Candle, flame, light . . . illumination . . ."

". . . wick . . . wax . . . soy . . ."

"Who? Think."

"Clee?"

"*That's* interesting. Why Clee?"

"That was right? Clee?"

THE WRAPPING PAPER WAS STILL good so I just retaped it. When Clee was in the bathroom I put it on her pillow but it rolled off with a bang; she came in just as I was reaching under the coffee table. I hadn't wanted to hand it to her in person.

"Here." I put the heavy cylinder in her hand. The fragrance was abundant and nothing like pomegranates or currants, neither of which is famous for its smell. It was so obviously a candle, the very dumbest present you could give a person. Clee undid the tape and she smelled it cautiously. She read the label. Finally she said, "Thank you." I said, "You're welcome." It was horrible and there was no way to undo it.

I locked myself in the ironing room and wrote a long-overdue e-mail to the entire staff about recycling, overpopulation, and oil, then I toned it down a little, then I deleted it. The shower turned on. She was taking a shower. I called Jim and we talked about the warehouse staff.

"Kristof is lobbying for a basketball hoop," he said.

"We tried that once and no one got any work done." I hoped he'd keep pushing for the hoop so I could be really emphatic, but he dropped it. His wife was waiting for him; he had to go.

"How *is* Gina?"

But he really had to go.

It was dusk when I came out of the ironing room. She was sitting on the edge of the couch, knees wide apart. Her wet hair was combed back, a towel hung around her neck; a boxer is what she looked like. Her hands were interlaced in front of her and she was staring past them with a furrowed brow. The TV was off. She was waiting for me.

I'd never really sat in my armchair before. It wasn't comfortable.

She ducked her head, acknowledging my arrival to the meeting, and made a sound in her throat as if she was pulling up phlegm.

"I may have given off the wrong . . ."—she searched for the word—"impression."

She glanced at me, to make sure I was familiar with the word. I nodded.

"I appreciate the gift but I'm not . . . you know. I'm into dick." She coughed huskily and spit into one of the empty Pepsi bottles on the coffee table.

"We're in the same boat, as far as that goes," I said. I saw us in a little dinghy together, liking dick on the big dark sea.

"For me it's a little more intense." She was bouncing her knee unconsciously. "I guess I'm 'misogynist' or whatever."

I'd never heard the word used like this, like an orientation.

"I'll stop if you want," she said, looking abstractly into the distance. At first I thought she meant talking, stop talking. She didn't mean that.

"Do you want to?" I asked.

"What?"

"Stop."

She shrugged, utterly indifferent. It was probably the meanest thing she'd done yet. Then she shrugged again, exactly the same, but added "No" afterward, like that's what she'd been saying the first time. No, she didn't want to stop attacking me.

I felt a little winded, a little light-headed. We were making an agreement; this was real. I gave her a shy glance and realized she was fixated on a repulsive cluster of purple spider veins on my exposed calf. A shiver shuddered through me—she was attached to the super-special angry feeling I gave her.

"Do you want to make a contract?" I murmured, completely inaudibly.

"Make what?"

"A contract that says what we want to do and don't want to do. We can download one from the Internet." I said this too loudly, as if she was deaf.

She blinked a few times. "I don't really know what you're talking about, but I'm not interested in that kind of thing." She pressed her knuckles to her forehead and then dropped her hand suddenly, with a surprising exasperation. "Have you done this before? With the contracts and all that?"

"No," I said quickly. "A friend told me about it."

"You're talking about this with people?" Her knee was bouncing frantically.

"Not a friend. A therapist. It's completely confidential."

Her anguish seemed to level out. She was gazing at the remote control from afar. I handed it to her and she brushed her fingers over the rubber buttons a couple times.

"Is there anything else we need to . . . ?"

"I think we pretty much covered everything," I said, trying to remember what had been established. She nodded gruffly and turned on the TV.

CHAPTER FIVE

It wasn't obvious how or why to fight, now that we had formally agreed to. A few times she seemed to be about to start something and then she'd change her mind. And obviously I couldn't initiate—that would be perverse. The whole thing, if it was a thing, made less and less sense as the days went by, and became more and more embarrassing. I began going to the office as much as possible, yelling, "Informal visit!" as I entered so I wouldn't violate my work-at-home status. Carl gave me some Thai hot sauce to give to Clee. "Have you eaten spicy food with her yet? You have? Isn't she something else?" I nodded mutely and left the bottle in the trunk of my car.

The next morning Clee was in the kitchen when I needed to be in the kitchen and thus we were both in the kitchen at the same time. The air was taut. She dropped a lid and stiffly picked it up again. I coughed and said, "Excuse me." This was ridiculous; it was time to annul the agreement and move on.

"Listen," I said, "neither of us—"

"Go like this," she interrupted, holding her hand over the right side of her face. I mirrored her, squinting in case there was a slap or a punch coming.

"That's what I thought," she said. "One half of your face is way older and uglier than the other half. The pores are all big and it's like your eyelid is starting to fall into your eye. I'm not saying the other side looks good, but if both sides were like your left side people would think you were seventy."

I put my hand down. No one had ever talked to me like this before, so cruelly. And yet so attentively. My eyelid *was* starting to fall into my eye. My left side had always been uglier. Some real thought had gone into this little speech—it wasn't just careless hostility. I looked up at her overly plucked eyebrows and wondered if I could throw some words together about the crass ignorance of her own face and then I saw her hands; they were rubbing the fuzzy legs of her pants with great agitation and her mouth was hanging open. This humiliating little ode had gotten her revved up, she was yearning to strike, and as she registered the fear in my face her body seemed to load itself, to wind up. My forearm deflected her hand with a loud smack.

I ENTERED OPEN PALM WITH big bouncing moon steps, saying, "Hello hello hello!" Our first tussle under the new agreement had been long and dirty and had taken us into all the rooms of the house. I can-canned and popped, not just to defend myself but out of real anger, first at her and then at people *like* her, dumb people. I popped her for being young without humility, when I had had so much humility at her age—too much. I bit and almost broke the skin on her forearm. When she shoved me against my own desk I head-butted her and everyone else who wasn't capable of understanding how nuanced I was. She assaulted me as only a person born to a lifetime of martial arts training can. Succinctly. There was not even a second when I thought I was gaining on her. After about thirty-five minutes we took a moment to recover; I drank a glass of water. When we started up again my skin was tender, bruises were already forming, and every muscle was shaking. It was nice, deeper and more focused. I felt my face contorting with a wrath I didn't recognize; it seemed out of scale for my species. This was the opposite of getting mugged. I'd been mugged every single day of my life and this was the first day I wasn't mugged. At the end she quickly squeezed my hand twice: good game.

I swished through meetings with a secret, raw, achy feeling that made me lighthearted and hilarious; everyone thought so. Organizing the annual fundraiser for Kick It was usually so stressful that I just clawed through, hurting feelings right and left. But everything was different now—when Jim stupidly suggested a live musical act instead of a DJ, I said, "That's interesting!" and let it sit. Then later I circled back and asked a few gentle questions that inspired him to change his mind. Then I said, "Are you sure? It sounded like such a fun idea," and I pretended to play invisible maracas, which was actually taking my new way a tad too far. But this, something in the ballpark of this, was who I really was. When I laughed it was the low chuckle of a wise person, no hysteria, no panic.

But how long would it last? By lunch my limbs had stopped pulsing; she was too skilled to ever really hurt me. At the end of the day I sat in the bathroom stall and swallowed experimentally—my globus wasn't back yet, but the levity, was it still there? I tightened my shoulders and bowed my head, coaxing anxieties to the surface. The chaotic mess of the house . . . really not that big a deal! Phillip? He wanted my blessing—mine! Kubelko Bondy? My eyes fell on the gray linoleum floor and I wondered how many other women had sat on this toilet and stared at this floor. Each of them the center of their own world, all of them yearning for someone to put their love into so they could see their love, see that they had it. *Oh, Kubelko, my boy, it's been so long since I held you.* I lowered my elbows to my knees and dropped my heavy head into my palms.

So it was nice to be apart, to quiver in the afterglow, but after the afterglow it was time to fight again. Now that the globus had softened, I had a new awareness of my whole body. It was rigid and jumpy and not that fun to be in; I'd never noticed because I'd never had anything to compare it to. That week we did it every morning before she went to work. On Saturday we did it and then I went right out; once I felt loose and tingly, I didn't really want to be around her anymore—we had nothing to say to each other. I bought a persimmon-colored blouse that I could picture Phillip loving and wore it right out of the store. I got my hair trimmed. I flitted around the city either turning heads or else walking by heads just as they were turning. I ate a pastry made out of white flour and refined sugar and watched the couple next to me feed each other bites of omelet. It was hard to believe they played adult games but most likely they did, probably with their coworkers or relatives. What were other people's like? Perhaps some mothers and fathers pretended to be their children's children and made messes. Or a widow might sometimes become her own deceased husband and demand retribution from everyone. It was all very personal; nobody's game made any sense to anyone else. I watched seemingly dull men and women zooming past in cars. I doubted they all had written contracts like Ruth-Anne, but some did. Some probably had multiple contracts. Some contracts had been voided or transferred. People were having a good time out here, me included. I waved down the waiter and ordered an expensive juice drink even though there was free water with free refills. Did I still feel loose? Yes. Was it fading? Only a little. I had hours to go.

It was dark when I pulled into the driveway. She was standing on the porch; I didn't even have a chance to put my purse down. She slammed the door behind me and pressed down on my shoulders with a leveling force. I buckled, collapsed to my hands and knees, keys clattering to the floor.

But most nights we didn't do anything. I cooked, took a bath, read in bed; she talked on the phone, watched TV, heated her frozen meals. We ignored each other with a feeling of fullness and ferment. Phillip texted (*KIRSTEN WANTS YOUR PERMISSION TO DO ORAL. ???! NO PRESSURE. STANDING BY UNTIL YOUR GO-AHEAD*) and I felt no animosity. Oh, Kirsten. Maybe she was our cat for the past one hundred thousand lifetimes, always on the bed, pawing around in the covers, watching us. Congratulations, kitty, you're the girlfriend this time—but I'm still in charge. I felt limber and generous. Phillip was working through something—that's how I might put it to a close friend, in confidence. I'd permitted him to have an affair with a younger woman.

You're so brave, you have such faith.

This is nothing. We've seen fire and we've seen rain, I'd reply, quoting the song.

Of course, it was more of a preaffair, since we weren't together yet, at least not in the traditional sense, not in this lifetime. And the fire and rain, that was still to come. Also: no close friends to speak in confidence to. But I held my head up when I saw the postman and I waved at my neighbor—I initiated the wave. I even struck up a conversation with Rick, who was walking around in special shoes that punctured the grass.

"I'd like to pay you," I announced, "for all your hard work." It was lavish, but why not.

"No, no. Your garden is my payment. I need a place for my

green thumb." He held up his thumb and looked at it fondly, then his expression clouded, as if he'd remembered something awful. He took a deep breath. "I brought your trash cans out last week."

"Thank you," I laughed. "That's a big help." It *was* a big help, I wasn't even lying. "If you don't mind, you could do that every week."

"I would," he said quietly, "but I don't usually work on Tuesdays." He looked at me with nervous eyes. "Wednesday is trash day. I usually come on Thursdays. If you are in danger, please tell me. I will protect you."

Something bad was happening, or had already happened. I picked a blade of grass.

"Why were you here on a Tuesday?"

"I asked you if it was okay, if instead of the third Thursday of this month I came on a Tuesday. Do you remember?" He was looking down now, with a red face.

"Yes."

"I had to use the bathroom. I did knock on the back door before I came in but no one heard me. Never mind, it's your private business."

Tuesday. What did we do on Tuesday? Maybe nothing. Maybe he didn't see anything.

"Snails," Rick said.

Tuesday was the morning she cornered me on the floor. I resisted in a defensive huddle position, my wide butt high in the air.

"I need snails." He was trying to switch topics. "For the garden. The African kind—they aerate."

If we hadn't heard him, it could have only been because Clee was yelling verbal harassments.

"I'm in no danger, Rick. It's the opposite of what you're thinking," I said.

"Yes, I see that now. She's your . . . it's your private business."

"No, it's not private, no, no—"

He began to trip away, stabbing the grass with his special shoes.

"It's a game!" I pleaded, following. "I do it for my health! I see a counselor." He was scanning the yard, pretending not to hear me.

"Four or five will be plenty," he called back.

"I'll get seven. Or a dozen. A baker's dozen—how's that?" He was shuffling along the side of the house to the sidewalk. "One hundred snails!" I called out. But he was gone.

SUDDENLY I WAS CLUMSY. WHEN Clee covered my mouth and grabbed my neck in the hallway, I couldn't fight back because I didn't want to touch her. Before every raw impulse there was a pause—I saw us through the homeless gardener's eyes and felt obscene. Being outside society, he didn't know about adult games; he was like me before I met Ruth-Anne, thinking everything that happened in life was real. The next morning I left the house early, but avoiding her caused other problems. A migraine-level headache blossomed; my throat pulsed threateningly. By noon I was frantically trying to concoct a more clinical way to fight, something organized and respectable, less feverish. Boxing gloves? No, but that gave me another idea.

I staggered down the block to the warehouse; Kristof helped me dig through our old stock.

"Do you want VHS?"

"When did we stop doing scenarios? Was that 2000?"

"Scenarios?"

"Like a woman sitting on a park bench and all that. Before self-defense as fitness."

"Those are all pre-2002. Are you putting something together for the twentieth anniversary?"

"Yes?"

"Here's a bunch from '96, '97—is that good?"

COMBAT WITH NO BAT (1996) started with an attack simulation called "A Day at the Park." A woman in espadrilles sits down on a park bench, rubs suntan lotion on her arms, takes a pair of sunglasses out of her purse, and unfolds a newspaper.

I pushed aside Clee's purple sleeping bag and perched on the couch, my purse beside me. I pulled out my suntan lotion. Clee watched from the kitchen.

"What are you doing?"

I slowly finished rubbing in the lotion and pulled out my sunglasses.

"You attack right after I take the newspaper out," I whispered. I opened the newspaper and yawned the way the woman had yawned on the tape, a little theatrically. Her name was Dana something, she used to teach on weekends. She didn't have the abs or the charisma of her successor, Shamira Tye; I doubt we even paid her. Clee hesitated, then sat down beside me. She put her arm around my shoulder sooner than the attacker on the DVD had, but like him she breast-grabbed, so like Dana I elbow-jabbed, yelling, "No!"

She tried to pull me to the floor, which wasn't in this simulation but it was in the next one, so I skipped ahead.

"No! No! No!" I screamed, pretending to knee her in the groin. I jumped to my feet and ran away. Because there wasn't far to run I ran in place for a few seconds, facing the wall. And then jogged a little longer to avoid turning around. The whole performance was quite ridiculous. I pulled off the sunglasses and peeked back at her. She handed me the newspaper.

"Again."

We did that one two more times and then I tried to walk us through "Lesson 2: Domestic Traps," which takes place in a kitchen. I felt silly throwing fake punches but Clee didn't seem to care that we weren't really fighting; she sneered and harassed me with a new thuggy swagger. On the DVD Dana's attacker wore a backward baseball cap and said things like *Hey, baby doll*, or *C'mere, sweetcakes.* In "Lesson 3: A Funny Thing Happened on the Way to the Front Door," he purred, *Yum, yum, yum* from the shadows. Of course Clee didn't say any of these things but I could sort of guide her toward his basic blocking with Dana's flinches and looks of horror, and on a cellular level Clee knew exactly what to do—she'd seen hundreds of demonstrations like this before the age of five.

After an hour we were exhausted but unbruised. She squeeze-squeezed my hand and gave me a long, strange look before we went our separate ways. I shut the bedroom door and rolled my head. The migraine was gone; my throat was soft. I didn't feel euphoric, but I knew this could work. If only Rick had seen "Domestic Traps" instead of whatever it was we were doing before. This wasn't anything, just a re-creation of a simulation of the kind of thing that might happen to a woman if she didn't keep her wits about her.

While Clee was at work I learned the rest of *Combat with No Bat.* "Lesson 4: Fighting from Inside Cars" utilized a couch and set of car keys. "Gang Defense" was too complicated—I skipped it. "Woman Asking Directions" was a quickie; my only line was "Do you know where the nearest drugstore is?" For the wrap-up Dana asked me to call my own answering machine, perform ten maximum-loud nos, and listen back to it: NO NO NO NO NO NO NO NO NO NO.

"Yikes!" she said. "Who's that terrifying woman screaming on your message machine?! That's *you*." I rehearsed not only the kicks and grabs but all the dialogue and staging. Dana really threw herself into the skits; shock, fear, anger—she demonstrated not just what to do but how to feel. My favorite moments were right before the assault—lounging on the park bench, walking casually to the front door. My hair felt long and heavy on my back; I swung my hips a little, knowing I was being watched, hunted even. It was interesting to be this kind of person, so unself-conscious and exposed, so feminine. Dana could have had a career making videos like this for all occasions—waking up, answering the phone, leaving the house; a woman could follow along and learn what to do when she's *not* being attacked, how to feel the rest of the time.

The last three lessons were slightly disturbing; it was obvious why Open Palm never made a dime from this series. Dana asks the viewer to gather up some household items—a soccer ball, a pillowcase, bungee cord—and fabricate a makeshift head. "When you're kicking a real head, it won't bounce as much, but there will be some give and you want to be ready for that. Skulls are softer than you think." By "Lesson 10: Mercy and Advanced Mercy," I wondered if any of us had ever watched this video all the way through; Dana seemed to be doing her own thing. With her high heel pressed against the soccer ball she listed the reasons why a person might be allowed to live. "They have little children. They have pets that are unlikely to be adopted—for example, a smelly old dog with no teeth. Are you killing a dog by killing her owner? Maybe ask if they have pets and then ask to see a picture or for a description of the pet's health level. Lastly: religious reasons. These are personal and fall outside of the scope of this video, but in some people's religions killing isn't allowed, even in self-defense. If you're not sure, you might want to check with a local parish, synagogue, or mosque."

The next morning I took a deep breath and approached Clee on the couch. I had a question for her.

"Do you, um, know where the nearest drugstore is?"

She blinked, a confused half second. Then her left nostril curled and her eyes hardened.

"Yes, I do," she said, slowly rising to stand. Which wasn't the right line, but close enough.

I REHEARSED NEW SCENARIOS EVERY afternoon while she was at work and introduced them each morning before she left. For a few days it was exciting to reveal each one as if I'd just dreamed it up with my own very creative mind. But soon it was frustrating when Clee did and said things that were completely inconsistent with Dana's attacker. It would have been a lot easier if she just watched the DVD and learned her part. On her day off I put *Combat with No Bat* on the coffee table while she was sleeping. I did it without thinking too hard, got in my car and headed to work. At a red light I drew in all my breath and froze. What had I done? The moment she put the disc in she would know I had practiced moves in front of the TV and memorized lines, as if I really cared about this. My cheeks flamed with embarrassment—now she would see me, see who I really was. A woman whose femininity was just copied from another woman.

"Feel my forehead," I said to Jim. "Is it a million degrees?"

"It's not hot but it's clammy. And you look pale."

I could see her sitting on the couch and pressing play on the remote. Every gesture, every scream, every glare and growl I'd made for the last week was Dana's. *Who are you?* she would rightly ask. *Are you Dana? Do you even know who you are? No,* I would sob, *No, I don't.* Jim brought me the thermometer.

"It's the kind you stick in your ear. Or do you want to just go home?"

"No, no. Can't go home." I lay on the floor. At noon Phillip texted a single question mark and a tiny cartoon emoticon of a clock. He'd been waiting for almost two months now. Just two months ago my life had been ordered and peaceful. I rolled onto my stomach and prayed for him to deliver me from this situation I'd gotten myself into. What would be the emoticon for *Carry me to your penthouse and tend to me as a husband?* Jim laid a wet paper towel on my forehead.

At seven P.M. Nakako asked me to turn on the alarm when I left. "You do know the code, right?" I pulled myself up off the floor, stumbled out with her, and drove home shivering. I parked in the driveway and forced myself out of the car, braced for ridicule.

But a funny thing happened on the way to the front door.

"Yum, yum, yum," said a voice from the shadows. She swaggered out and put her hand on the small of my back. She was wearing a backward baseball cap.

"Step away!" I barked, and she hung back for exactly one, two, three seconds before lunging. The next five minutes proved that my neighbors didn't care if I lived or died.

When I finally made it to the front door I shut it behind me and smiled, touching my cheeks. Of course there weren't any actual tears, but I was that moved. She must have practiced all day, rehearsing in front of the TV. Any two foes can fight in anger, but this was something rare. I was reminded of the Christmas

Day soccer game between enemies in World War I or II. She still repulsed me, I'd still shoot her in battle the next day, but until dawn we'd play this game.

The next evening we did the entire DVD, in order. "Gang Defense" was the most confusing because there were two bad men and another man in all denim who didn't want trouble. "Hey," he said to the others. "This isn't cool. Let's scram." Clee switched roles between the three men with no warning; I was constantly stopping to reorient myself.

"What are you doing?" she hissed. "I'm over here."

"Which one are you?"

She hesitated. Until now there had been no overt acknowledgment of the video or that we were anyone but our own angry selves.

"I'm the first man," she said.

"The one in denim?"

"The first bad man."

It was the way she was standing when she said it—her feet planted wide, her big hands waiting in the air. Just like a bad man, the kind that comes to a sleepy town and makes all kinds of trouble before galloping off again. She wasn't the first bad man ever but the first I'd ever met who had long blond hair and pink velour pants. She snapped her gum impatiently.

We sailed through the rest of the scene and then repeated it two more times. It was like square dancing or tennis, I told Ruth-Anne the following week. "Once you get the moves down, it's second nature—a real vacation for the brain."

"So you would describe your pleasure as . . . ?"

"A little theatrical but mostly athletic. And I'm the most surprised of anyone because I've never been good at sports."

"And for Clee? Do you think her enjoyment is also athletic?"

"No." I lowered my eyes. It wasn't really my business to say. "You think it's something else?"

"For her it might not be a game, it might be real. She's a 'misogynist' or something. That's her thing." I described the wolfish intensity that came over her when she simulated. "Of course this is your department, not mine. Do you think it might be psychological?"

"Well, that's a broad term."

"But accurate, right?"

"Sure, okay," she said begrudgingly. She thought I was trying to get two diagnoses for the price of one.

"Say no more," I demurred, holding up the palms of my hands. To change the subject I pointed to the heavy-looking Chinese food cartons lined up on her desk. "Is that all from you?"

"I drink a lot of water," she said, and patted her water bottle. "At the end of the day I gather them up and empty them all in the bathroom at once."

"The bathroom here or the bathroom at home?"

"The bathroom here!" she laughed. "Can you imagine? Me driving home a zillion containers of urine and feces? What a mess!"

She mimed driving a car and we laughed about that. It really was a very funny image. Laughing like friends always emphasized that we weren't. This wasn't real like the laughing she did at home.

She kept driving, and I ponied up another chuckle. Why didn't she stop?

"So what if it's real for her?" she said, suddenly dropping her hands. "Real comes and goes and isn't very interesting."

CHAPTER SIX

The Open Palm fundraiser is a big hassle every year and not
even very lucrative but I'm always giddy as I get dressed for it,
knowing Phillip's getting dressed too. If this were a movie they
would cut back and forth between me pulling up my nylons,
Phillip polishing his shoes, me brushing my hair, and so forth. It
used to be this was the only time I saw him outside the office—
now I could say *He texts me all the time* and it wouldn't be a lie.
When he saw me in the new persimmon blouse he might feel
embarrassed or ashamed about the texts. "Hey," I would say.
"Look right here." I'd point to my eyes. "There's no room for
shame in this relationship, okay?" Would he then pull me toward
him with the farmer's market necklace, which I decided to wear
again? And then what would happen? Someone else might have
to give Clee a ride home, I might not be available. I'd tell her this
when she was done showering. Why was she even coming? She
hadn't been to an Open Palm fundraiser since she was a little girl
charging around the dance floor.

I changed my mind when she clomped out of the bathroom;
she needed a chaperone. Her top forced a person to look at it
even if they didn't want to. It was just two pieces of black mate-
rial attached to a giant gold ring—not a street-safe outfit. I could
drop her off on my way to Phillip's if need be.

"Will there be beverages?" she said on the drive to the Presbyterian Fellowship Hall. Her pungent feet stabbed the dashboard; she'd dug up some very high heels with many crisscrossing straps and buckles.

"Not alcoholic ones. You won't think it's fun." She'd traded her sweatpants for very, very tight jeans. Jeans reminded me of Kirsten. He wouldn't dare bring her.

"That's okay. Jim's got something for me."

"Jim from Open Palm? He's bringing you alcohol?"

"No, something else. You'll see."

We were quiet for the rest of the drive.

Suzanne and Carl hugged their daughter and Clee surprised me by complying. I stood next to the long three-way hug like a guard or a docent.

"Cheryl!" Suzanne squawked as they pulled apart. "What happened to your legs?"

We all looked down at my calves. They were striped with bruises from the old way.

Phillip wasn't here yet. The girls from Kick It did a self-defense demonstration to rap music and then the DJ took over. I asked him if he thought the volume might be a little on the loud side.

"I think it's too quiet," he yelled, one hand holding an earphone up to his ear.

"Well, don't turn it up."

"What?"

"It's perfect the way it is!" I made an A-OK sign.

While the caterer explained a problem they were having with the coffeemaker, I watched Clee talking to the Kick It girls. They were all dressed just like her and she seemed to know some of them—probably the daughters of her parents' friends. I tried to imagine doing scenarios with one of the other girls,

THE FIRST BAD MAN

a girl with brown bangs who was showing Clee something on her phone.

"So we should serve less coffee? Or water it down?"

"Serve less."

It was unthinkable—the girl with brown bangs was just a little girl. Clee glanced at me from time to time; I looked away. Seeing her in public, with her parents, was unsettling. The DJ put on a song that was everyone's favorite, and the girls rushed to the dance floor with their hands in the air. They danced in a hip-hop style and Carl wiggled among them in a purposefully goofy way that made the Kick It girls laugh. He caught sight of me and beckoned. I held my neck to explain I was up to my neck in managerial duties. An invisible lasso began spinning over his head; he roped me. Everyone was watching so I allowed myself to be pulled onto the floor. Clee took one look at my hips swaying in my crinkly ethnic skirt and turned her back, horrified. I snapped a little to show I was having a terrific time and watched the girls do movements that looked more appropriate for a strip club than a fundraiser for self-defense. They were all in high heels—not one of them could run from an attacker, not to mention the amount of self-inflicted foot pain they must have been suffering. "Holla," they kept yelling, "holla!" Was that even a word? Or was it *holler?* People were giving me funny looks; I probably wasn't "on the beat" or whatever. Where was Phillip? Someone bumped into me and I turned to glare. It was Clee. She did it again—as if we could fight right here, wrestle down to the floor. Or else this was just her way of dancing. She bumped again and this time put her hand lightly on my stomach while standing behind me, containing me in a way that forced our rhythms together. I looked around and realized this was an actual dance, a lot of people were doing it. I couldn't see her face but I could tell she thought this was funny, she was trying to make the other girls laugh. And hey, I could take a joke, for a minute, but the song went on and on and it felt, quite frankly, inappropriate. From Suzanne's expression I could tell she agreed with me. I broke away with a little shimmy. My phone vibrated in my pocket.

Phillip. This text didn't mention Kirsten. It pertained only to me and unequivocally revealed his true feelings about us.

SENT A DONATION—PLS SEND RECEIPT WHEN YOU GET A SEC.

A dull and respectable text for a dull and respectable woman. We had never been a couple, not on any level or in any lifetime. But wait—my phone shook again. Maybe he was kidding and this text would say *I was kidding.*

HOPE TONIGHT WAS A BIG SUCCESS!

Polite—the only thing worse than dull. I had waited too long to reply about my decision and this was my punishment. It was hard to type with the music pounding. I used all caps like him, yelling through the night.

I'M CLOSE TO A DECISION!

I stared at the phone, waiting. No reply.

I added: :)

No reply.

I waited twenty more minutes. No reply. I stared grimly at the sea of dancing people. It was time to go home. Jim could manage the rest. I told Clee I was going and she surprised me by immediately walking off the dance floor.

"Let me find Jim."

Jim carried something out to my trunk. He asked Clee what she wanted it for and she shrugged. It was wrapped in a flowery sheet. In the rearview mirror it seemed to be moving.

"What is it?"

96

"You'll see," said Clee.

She carried it into the bathroom with her. A few minutes later I felt a tap on my shoulder. She was in a full pummel suit. I hadn't seen one like this since the late nineties—the giant head and gloves, the shoulder pads and groin guard. She immediately began grabbing me, no script. It was like being hit by a monster, something from a nightmare. I forgot the simulations and fought to kill. No mercy, no advanced mercy, just blood. I punched Phillip in his balding head and Kirsten in her flat stomach, I punched them both at the same time, pounding on them like a door.

"Whoa, whoa, whoa," she said, holding my arms, "slow it down."

I slowed it down.

Clee was almost motionless, not assaulting me so much as moving her padded body into mine. My slow punches felt like tai chi. After a while the giant-headed alien just pinned me. Or held me. A strange minute passed. I counted to seventy and then coughed. She stumbled backward and pulled the foam head off. Her hair was messed up, her face sweaty and red.

"This was a dumb idea," she said. No squeeze squeeze.

THE NEXT DAY CLEE ANNOUNCED she'd been moved to the night shift for two weeks. I crept around her in the mornings, going to the office so she could sleep. Did she miss simulating? She didn't seem to. I was having trouble working or sleeping. My phone was very still. Ever since my reply, Phillip and I were at an impasse. I regretted the smiley face. Sometimes I went to the bathroom at five A.M., when she got home, just to show her I was awake and available, but she ignored me, watching TV with a T-shirt oddly wrapped around her head like a person lost in the desert. Often her pillow was over her face, so I couldn't be sure if she was cocooned in her sleeping bag or still at work. Once I patted it, to check, and she reared up like a mummy awakened, her hair matted, eyes frantic.

"Sorry," I whispered. "I wasn't sure if you were in there."

She stared at me, waiting, as if another explanation was coming.

"The way your sleeping bag puffs up," I reiterated, "sometimes it's hard to tell . . . so I was just . . ." She pulled her head back under the pillow.

AT THE END OF THE two weeks she slept for a full day, then took a shower that seemed to never end. While she was in there Phillip texted: *BATH. MUTUAL SOAPING BUT NOTHING MORE.* And then: *DECISION STILL CLOSE?* He was still waiting for me, of course he was. But instead of relief I felt more agitated. I paced around the kitchen. Clee's shower pounded on and on. It wouldn't be hard to determine the shower's gallons per minute, using a bucket. When the water finally shut off I checked the clock—forty-five minutes. We had never discussed splitting the utilities but maybe it was time. Two checks or I pay and she pays me back half? What was that sound? Blow-dryer. She was blow-drying her hair. She came out of the bathroom dressed in slacks and a satiny blouse, her hair a warm, shiny line. Her feet were coated with some kind of mentholated fungal cream. If she was going out, "A Day at the Park" would be a great option and didn't take too long. Then I could have the house to myself. I put my purse on my shoulder, strolled around the living room and then sat on the "park bench." She looked at my purse.

"You going out?"

"No . . ." I said suggestively.

"Me either."

It was a long night. She tidied the living room, she did her dishes. At one point I found her standing in front of the bookshelf with her head cocked to the side.

"Do you have a favorite one?" she asked.

"Nope." Whatever she was doing was making me extremely tense. With the TV off there was no separation or sense of privacy.

"But you've read them all?"

"Yes."

"Hmmm." She ran her finger along the spines, waiting for a book recommendation. She had a decorative bobby pin in her straight hair. I had been looking at it without understanding what it was.

"Is that . . . ?" I pointed to the pin. "Does that have a rhinestone on it?" It was not at all her style—the way it was placed looked accidental, like a piece of twig.

"What's the big deal?"

"Nothing. I just wasn't sure if you knew it was there."

"How would I not know? Obviously I put it there." She adjusted the bobby pin and pulled a book called *Mipam* off the shelf.

"That's a Tibetan novel," I warned her. "It was written in the eighteen hundreds."

"Sounds interesting."

She sat carefully on the couch as if it had only ever been a couch, never her bed, never a park bench or a car. The book was open in her lap and she read or pretended to read. After a while I gave up and went to bed.

The next morning she was dressed in her usual sweatpants and tank top.

"My friend Kate is coming to visit," she said coolly. "She'll sleep in the ironing room."

"Great." But it was not great. How could we do anything with her friend Kate here? It had been more than two weeks since we'd done a scenario. My globus wasn't back but I felt tight everywhere, wound up and ready to snap. If we could just do it once, then I wouldn't care who visited.

"She's on her way," said Clee. "She left Ojai an hour ago."

I set up the cot in the ironing room. I laid out the towels with the sugarless mint.

"She should be here any second," she said.

I dumped some baking soda down the garbage disposal.

"I see her parking," said Clee. She stood behind me. I turned around. We faced each other. She laughed a little, shaking her head with disbelief. What? What was I supposed to do to make it happen? This felt like the fundraiser all over again, like there was some hip-hop thing that everyone else knew about.

"Holla?" I said.

Her brow furrowed with incomprehension. The doorbell rang.

KATE WAS A BIG ASIAN girl with a loud laugh and a tiny gold crucifix hanging between her breasts. Her truck had a strange vehicle hitched to it. As she came through the door, she said, "Give me some booty," and slapped Clee's butt. Then she stuck out her own butt and Clee slapped it back.

"That's our version of a high five," Kate said, coming toward me with a wide smile. I held my hand up in the air to show I preferred the regular version. She handed me a Tupperware container full of plain cooked spaghetti.

"Don't feel like you have to feed me, I'll just eat that."

I hid in my bedroom until they went outside to look at the thing on the back of Kate's truck. I set up the card table again, plugged in my computer, and began to work. A horrendous noise erupted in the driveway. I ran out to the porch expecting to see smoke but Clee and Kate were just chatting loudly next to the deafening vehicle as it idled.

"It's just like a regular ATV but it's legal anywhere," screamed Kate. She was smoking.

"It doesn't have the horsepower of a regular ATV," yelled Clee.

"For its size it has the same amount—actually more. If you blew it up to regular size it would have more horsepower."

"If you blew up just its back half it would look like you."

They both laughed. Kate dropped her cigarette butt in my driveway.

"My ass is so huge."

"It's really huge."

"Sean likes it. He says he likes to get lost in it."

"I thought you weren't hanging out anymore."

"We're not. He just comes over and gets in my ass for a while and then goes." I looked to the left and right wondering how the neighbors were enjoying this conversation. "Honestly it's so big I can't even feel him. So my dad was right?"

"Yeah, she's a full Beebe. Not as bad as Mrs. Beebe, but bad."

"She sure looks like one."

She meaning me? One what?

I ran down the steps, waving hello, and they fell silent. Clee kicked the vehicle's large tire and then suddenly jumped into its saddle and took off with an earsplitting rumble. We watched her stop at the end of the block; she let out a whoop and yelled something we couldn't hear.

"Who's Mrs. Beebe?"

Kate laughed into the back of her hand in an oddly dainty way. She probably had a tiny dainty mother.

"You heard that? Oh shit, we were just kidding around!" She checked my face to see if I was mad. "Clee's all right. She likes to act all tough, but she's a total softy when you get to know her. I call her Princess Buttercup." She laughed nervously and turned the ring on her pinky. "I think you know my dad. His name is Mark Kwon?"

Mark Kwon, the divorced alcoholic Suzanne had set me up with years ago. That was her dad. Kate Kwon.

Princess Buttercup came roaring back down the street. "That's got some crazy go!" She did a few circles and then jumped off. Kate patted the seat. "Your turn, Cheryl."

"That's okay. I don't think I have the right license for operating—"

Clee walked me over to the grotesque bug. "Ever ridden a motorcycle?"

"No."

"It's easier than that. Get on."

I got on.

"That's your gas, that's your brake. Have fun."

I pushed down on the gas the littlest possible amount. Kate and Clee watched as I very, very slowly pulled away from the curb, and then, like a woman astride a giant tortoise, gradually rolled up the street. It was interesting to be up so high and not enclosed. I'd never moved in such a leisurely way on my own block. My neighbors' houses looked unfamiliar, almost bleached. The putt-putt of the motor overwhelmed all the usual sounds; I was enclosed in a bubble of noise. A dog barked silently; a young mom in a sun hat put sunblock on the silently wailing faces of two toddlers. They grew still as I slowly rolled by. Twins. I'd never seen them before. Except I had.

Where are you going? they asked in unison.

Up the block, I guess.

But you'll be back for us?

I'll be back, but not today.

They were crestfallen, both of them. Somehow both Kubelko

Bondy. Why had this soul been circling me for so long? Did it stay young or was it getting older too? And would it eventually give up on me? This was the wrong question—obviously it was I who would eventually give up. It was just a habit, like memorizing license plates. A silly little tic, that's all. I stomped down on the gas pedal and the mini ATV jumped forward, roaring up the next block. The noise shook everything out of my head. What a magical way to get around. I'd always thought of these types of machines as toys for uneducated people who didn't care about the environment, but maybe they weren't. Maybe this was a kind of meditation. I felt connected to everything and the motor volume held me at a level of alertness I wasn't used to. I kept waking up and then waking up from that, and then waking up even more. Was everything redneck actually mystical? What about guns? I turned around. Clee and Kate were very tiny but I could see them, wildly gesticulating for me to come back. I tried pushing down all the way on the gas. In an instant I was zooming toward them and they were running out of the way, screaming.

THEY WANTED TO HAVE A PARTY.

"It's not a party. It's just some of me and Clee's friends from high school who live here now," Kate said. "Some of our old classmates. Right?" Clee nodded. She was slowly turning the pages of a magazine, recommitted to ignoring me.

"I can't allow anything that will depreciate the value of the house," I said. "I draw the line there."

"The value will for sure not depreciate," Kate said.

"Will there be loud music?"

"No way," she said. "I don't even listen to music."

"What about drinking?"

"No. None."

"You would have to clean up afterward."

"I love to clean; it's, like, my thing."

"Well, I guess there's no harm in a small gathering of classmates."

"I'm thinking about it more now? And actually a few people might be drinking. But I can tell them to keep the bottles in paper bags if you want."

First a big group of loud girls came. Then a group of boys came and Kate plugged her phone into my stereo using a cord that one of the boys had brought. They moved my Mexican artifacts off the top of the speakers, which I appreciated. My phone buzzed. *SHE JUST HELD MY STIFF MEMBER FOR ONE OR TWO MINUTES, BUT NO MOVEMENT.*

Then the boy turned the stereo up to its absolute maximum, which made it so everyone had to scream when they talked.

Then a steady stream of girls and boys came.

Then I went into the ironing room and typed up a note to the neighbors about the noise and printed out six copies. Once I was outside I realized the whole block could hear the music and six was not enough. When I went back to print out more copies the boys and girls were playing a game involving spraying alcohol on each other.

I'LL ADMIT IT, I WANT TO CREAM IN HER MOUTH.

And immediately after that: *I REGRET THAT LAST TEXT, IT WAS TASTELESS AND SHOWED A LACK OF RESPECT FOR KIRSTEN. I HOPE YOU CAN OVERLOOK THAT LAST ONE. WE LOOK FORWARD TO YOUR DECISION. TAKE YOUR TIME!*

Some men came. They didn't even look young; one of them might have been my age. He grinned at me. It seemed as though the men had brought drugs. Definitely hashish or ganja, maybe something else too. It was impossible to use the bathroom—I was waiting in line for more than twenty minutes before Kate bounced over and yelled, "People, people, people! This is the woman who owns this house! Her name is Mrs. Beebe! Let her cut to the front of the line!" She was very drunk. I told her thank you and instead of saying *You're welcome* she yelled, "People like me, they just do!" and handed me her drink.

"Is this alcoholic?" I yelled.

"It's punch!" she screamed in my ear.

I drank it while peeing to save time even though I didn't really need more time right now. It tasted alcoholic. All the towels were on the floor, which was wet. *DO YOU WANT TO SEE A PICTURE OF HER?* he texted. I deleted it.

I leaned against the living room wall and watched Clee. She jumped on a boy's back and yelled, "Foul on the play! Foul on the play!" with one hand up in the air. She knew I was watching her. Now she was saying, "Dang, girl, you need to shave!" and Kate was saying, "No I don't, I'm Asian!" I watched them hold their legs in the air for different boys to compare. Poor Kate, who had to look so ordinary and be best friends with someone who looked like Clee. Someone whose eyes, though a tad far from her nose, were an exotic feline shape, someone whose hair was so sleepy and golden it seemed to be endlessly shifting like water, even in the picture I found online of her making pretend gang signs in a food court. Someone whose mouth was really too tender to be in public. I watched the sweaty, eager faces of the two boys Kate had enlisted in the leg test. She was screaming, "Shut your eyes so you don't know whose leg it is!" The two boys were rubbing their hands up and down Clee's leg and smelly foot and she was looking right at me. I looked back at her. It had been almost three weeks since we'd done a simulation. Why was she even here? My phone vibrated.

I squinted at the photograph on the screen. Kirsten was short with broad shoulders and chin-length dirty-blond hair that was either damp with massage oil or just naturally very stringy. She wore glasses with circular John Lennon–style frames and karate pants with a big white T-shirt that had a picture of a dancing alligator on it. The alligator had green, black, and red dreadlocks and was saying MSC ROCKS, MON. Her smile was enormous and hopeful, full of spitty gums. Her small eyes strained open and her arms were extended like an uncertain opera singer. Or a teenager. She was even less attractive than I had been at the same age.

When I looked up Clee was gone. I went outside, and she wasn't there either. She was probably in some car doing something with someone. I rubbed the side of my head; a pinging. Maybe I was dying or drunk. I walked into the middle of the street and then down the block. On foot it was hard to remember which house it was until I saw the toddlers in the window. Just their silhouettes through a yellow curtain. Because they were twins everything they did was mirrored like inkblots, a symmetrical butterfly, spilled milk, a cow's skull. I could still hear the low part of the beat but otherwise it was quiet when I dialed.

Phillip answered immediately.

"Cheryl?"

"I've decided," I said, my eyes on the yellow curtain.

He exhaled a tight little laugh. "I'm afraid I've been harassing you."

"Yes, definitely, but I've come to my conclusion."

"Some of those texts were pretty inappropriate."

"All of them were."

"I wasn't sure if you got them all."

"I did."

"Because you didn't always write back. I kept telling Kirsten how busy you are."

"I'm not that busy."

"Well, sure, you don't fill your life up with meaningless activity like the rest of us."

"I just didn't have an answer yet."

"Which is what I told Kirsten. Did you get the one I just sent? The picture?"

"I got it."

He was quiet. The light in their bedroom snapped off; the yellow curtain went dark.

"Should I say my decision now?"

"Yes, of course."

"Do it."

When I got back Clee and four other people were standing on the couch singing a song that didn't seem to be in English. The part everyone liked the best went *jiddy jiddy jiddy rah rah*. Phillip was already having intercourse with Kirsten, I could feel it—from his point of view. I was in him, in her. Each time Clee sang *jiddy jiddy jiddy rah rah* she pumped her pelvis forward to the beat and her bosom bounced. Dear God, look at those jugs, Phillip panted. I whispered the word.

"Jugs."

He wanted to rub her through her jeans. *Jiddy jiddy jiddy rah rah*. And cream in her mouth. Mutual soaping. *Jiddy jiddy jiddy rah rah*. My member was stiff. The song was nearing its peak, she and the other girls, the ugly girls, were jumping faster and faster, and the men were screaming at the top of their lungs, not even to the song anymore, just releasing howls because it felt good.

I went into my room, locked the door, took off her purple bra with its shiny, shiny straps, and pressed my balding head into her jugs. My big, hairy hand worked itself down the front of her jeans and my fingers, with their thick blocky fingernails, slid into her puss. She was wet and whimpering. "Phillip," she moaned. "Put it in." So I quietly, forcefully, made love to her mouth. This was the kind of young woman he deserved—a bombshell, not a rat-faced little girl.

After such a long buildup the release was immediate and incredible. When I creamed it was a huge mess, semen everywhere. Not just on her hair and jugs and face but all over my duvet cover and the throw rug. A rope of semen even hit the top of the dresser, splattering across my hairbrush, my earring box, and the picture of my mother as a young woman.

THEY DIDN'T HELP CLEAN UP. They pretended to—at around noon Kate picked up some beer bottles and asked where the trash was, but when I said, "Those are recyclables," she looked overwhelmed and sat down. Clee wandered around groggily in boxer shorts and a tank top, her hair matted in the back. They were both very hungover.

At first I thought it might have been a onetime thing that had a lot to do with the punch. But as I vacuumed and mopped and sponged and wiped down the walls, I had to glance down repeatedly to be sure I wasn't visibly pulsing or swelling, because there was so much energy vibrating in my groin. It was a new experience for me. When Clee parted her legs so I could wipe off the coffee table between them I had to put the sponge down and walk myself to my bedroom. I kept my hand over Clee's moaning mouth so Kate wouldn't hear. Not *my* hand—Phillip's. He thrust so hard his tufty ears shook.

At dusk Kate ordered a pizza.

"It's a thank-you pizza," she said. "Thank you."

Clee dug in and I nibbled at a narrow slice.

"My dad is remarried now, by the way," Kate said, chewing behind her polite hand.

I smiled and nodded. I could barely recall what he looked like but it would be rude to say that. "We had a good time, but it was just one date."

"Do you remember what you wore?" Kate asked.

Clee gave her a sharp look.

"No," I laughed. "It was a long time ago."

Kate took a sip of soda and cleared her throat.

"My dad said—ow!" She paused to inspect the spot where Clee had just kicked her. "My dad said you were dressed like a lesbian."

I smiled. Mark Kwon making a big show out of my failure to attract him was not hard to picture; that's just what he was like. Clee turned her head away as if this conversation was too boring to endure.

"Did he say that?"

"Yeah. What were you wearing?"

"I don't remember." But now that she asked I suddenly did remember.

"Was it something like what you're wearing right now?" She pointed at my pants and tucked-in T-shirt.

"No, this is just to clean in. No, I think it was a long green dress with many buttons down the front. Corduroy." I still had it.

For some reason this was hilarious to Kate; she laughed and looked at Clee with a gaping mouth until Clee finally smiled.

KATE HAD SUCH A GREAT TIME. Kate didn't need her Tupperware back. Kate would text Clee about Kevin and Zack. Kate had trouble loading up the mini ATV. Kate wanted to know where the nearest gas station was. Kate needed to use the bathroom one more time. Kate sat in her truck looking at her phone. Kate finally, finally left.

Clee shut the door and looked right at me—squinting. For a moment I thought she knew what I'd been up to. Then she simply slapped me, as if the whole visit was my fault and could have been avoided. "Fighting from Inside Cars" began with a (simulated) slap, so we continued with that scenario. "Come here, sugar-pie," she recited dourly.

We were back, except it was too late—I was playing something else now. I mimed knee thrusts and elbow jabs, awkwardly wheeling around a phantom erection. At the end I limped to my room, throbbing; shut the door; and slapped her cheek with my giant hairy hand. Just moments after I creamed in her mouth, my phone rang. If it was him I would ask what he did to Kirsten and then I'd do that to Clee. It was just another roiling corner of our journey together; I felt what he felt and it was staggering, tremendous.

But it was Dr. Broyard's office, calling to confirm my upcoming appointment on Tuesday, June 19. I imagined telling him my globus was gone and then trying to explain the cure by referencing his relationship with Ruth-Anne. I could hear her breathing.

"Ruth-Anne?"

"If you need to cancel, please call forty-eight hours in advance."

It was definitely her.

"Would it be possible to talk now? A phoner? I'm in the midst of some complicated new feelings."

She was silent.

"I guess I can wait until tomorrow."

"We'll see you Thursday the nineteenth," she said.

CHAPTER SEVEN

I described tapping into Phillip's lust, his overwhelming appe-
tites and aggressive explosions that convulsed through me. Ruth-
Anne seemed unsurprised, as if I were late to my own party.

"Right. And perhaps we don't even need to call it Phillip's lust?
Maybe it's just lust."

"Well, it's not *mine*. These just aren't the kinds of things I
would think about, on my own, without him."

"So you don't find it arousing when she attacks you?"

"Everything she does to me, I pretend I'm doing to her, as
Phillip."

"I see. And how does Cheryl Glickman feel?"

"Me?"

"Yes, what do you feel?"

Me, I thought. *Me. Me. Me.* Nothing specific came to mind.

"Are you masturbating yourself to orgasm?"

I smiled at the floor. "Yes?"

"Are you asking me?"

"*Yes*. I am. But that's just, you know, behind the scenes."

Ruth-Anne nodded as if I had just said something very astute.
Maybe I had. I wondered if I was her favorite patient, or at least
the only one who could talk on her level.

"Can I ask you something that's a little bit related to this?"

"Of course," she said.

"Remember when you called yesterday, about my appointment with Dr. Broyard?"

Her face changed.

"Well, I'm not sure I should keep seeing him—it might feel funny now."

"Funny how?"

"Not funny, more like uncomfortable. To see you in your receptionist role. And him. Now that I know."

She stared at me for a long time and I wondered if I was her least-favorite patient.

"Well, it's up to you," she said finally. "But I believe you've missed the forty-eight-hour cancellation window."

CLEE THOUGHT HER PINK BOXERS covered her but they didn't. If she was sitting cross-legged I could see the edge of her dark blond pubic hair and sometimes more. One morning I saw a flash of labia, pink and hanging loose. Not the tidy, concealed meat that I had been imagining. With this new information Phillip had to go back and redo all the sex he had already done. He really wanted to see her anus, though he wouldn't have called it that. I reread all his texts but didn't find a word for it. I went with *pucker. I'LL ADMIT IT,* he might have written, *I WANT TO RAM MY STIFF MEMBER INTO HER PUCKER.*

When he was mentioned at work, usually in terms of fundraising, I felt a shiver of invisibility—not that I *was* him, but it was strange to hear him talked about so freely.

"Phil Bettelheim's donation was on the smaller side this year," said Jim, "but it's only June, he might give again. Has anyone walked him through the high-risk outreach initiative?"

We hadn't spoken since I gave him my blessing; I guessed he was busy actually doing all the things I was pretending he was. The thought gave me a sad ache, and even this ache was arousing. I felt so close to him. It could never be proven, but I suspected we were becoming stiff at the same time, possibly even ejaculating in unison, the way women's menstrual periods sometimes become synchronized. I wondered where Clee was in her cycle.

"Cheryl." I looked up. A face so like and unlike hers. "How's my daughter? Is she behaving?"

"Oh yes," I said, too quickly. "Absolutely." Suzanne crossed her arms, waiting. She knew everything.

"Be honest. I know how she is." She looked me dead in the eye.

"She watches a lot of TV," I whispered.

Suzanne sighed. "She takes after Carl's mother—not a ton up here." She tapped her forehead. For an uncomfortable moment I felt almost protective of Clee.

"She's more instinctual," I said.

She rolled her eyes. "But thank you. Carl and I are thinking of some way to repay you. Not—I don't mean money."

HER COWLIKE VACUOUSNESS DIDN'T REALLY bother me any-more. Or it didn't matter—her personality was just a little piece of parsley decorating warm tawny haunches. Clee was bouncing up and down on Phillip's stiff member every day, many times a day, and at first it seemed he would never get tired of creaming in her puss winged by the dark blond pubic hair. But now, ten days later, I had a problem. He wanted it just as much, even more, but it took longer and longer to get there—sometimes as many as thirty minutes. Sometimes never. I tried unusual positions, new locations. One fantasy involved Ruth-Anne observing the intercourse, admiring and applauding with clinical approval. It was so unlikely that it worked, for a short time. But the smallest thing could stymie Phillip's release.

Clee's foot smell. Before it was the least of my problems; now it was a real turnoff. Phillip sometimes put plastic bags on her feet, trapping in the smell with rubber bands just so he could become stiff.

Cream in my puss, she begged. *In me! In me!* her puss whined, through aching mushy lips.

Not until you get your feet taken care of, he barked. *I know a chromotherapist who specializes in this, best on the west side. Tell him I sent you.*

I waited for a neutral moment to bring it up, then I plopped down on the arm of the couch. She was slurping ramen from a cup.

"Good stuff?" She stopped eating and frowned distrustfully. We hadn't exchanged unscripted dialogue since Kate's visit. "First of all: peace. Okay?"

She furrowed her brow and looked at the V my fingers were making. I had no idea what I was doing.

"Okay," I continued. "We live together, we are sometimes . . . physically close?" My voice rose to a question here; it was an insane thing to say given that I plowed her many times a day as Phillip. But I meant the fight scenarios. She nodded, putting her soup down. She was listening with an almost disconcerting level of attentiveness. I fingered the Post-it in my back pocket.

"Look, I don't want to be too forward here, or say something that you're going to take offense to." Clee shook her head like *No, no, I won't be offended.*

"I can speak candidly, then?"

She actually laughed, and her mouth broke into a smile, a real smile. I'd never seen that before. Her teeth were huge.

"I've been hoping that you would," she said, now pressing her lips together as if there was an ocean of other smiles and more laughter on the other side and she was trying to hold it back for just a few more seconds. She nodded for me to go ahead, to say it.

My hand had been waiting for its cue and I watched with a distant horror as it came forward with the Post-it. She peeled it off my palm and studied Dr. Broyard's address and the date of my appointment with soft, quizzical eyes. Thursday, June 19, tomorrow. There was nothing to do but continue with the plan.

"The situation with your feet—the odor, I mean—"

I'd never seen a face change shape like that. It dropped: every feature fell. I hurried on.

"My friend Phillip swears by Dr. Broyard for athlete's foot. When you get there, tell the receptionist I sent you—I'm giving you my appointment." I pointed at the paper.

Now her face was red, about to explode. Her eyes were watering. Then she took a breath and all at once she was perfectly calm. More than calm—blank.

THE LAST THING I EXPECTED was that she would go. But Friday morning there was a sundrop crystal hanging from the lock on the bathroom window and a tiny glass bottle next to her toothbrush. WHITE. Was that even a color? But I could see it just looking at the back of her blond head; she was subtly but utterly different. It was impossible to put a name on it. Not happier or sadder or less foul-smelling. Just whiter. Paler. I couldn't wait for therapy; Ruth-Anne had actually seen her now. Which maybe was the whole point.

I leaned back in the leather couch. "So. What did you think of Clee?"

"She seemed young."

I nodded encouragingly. Ideally she would say "shapely" or "curvaceous" in a clinically approving way. But Ruth-Anne seemed finished with her appraisal.

"Would you say she's what you pictured?"

"More or less, yes."

"Any man would become stiff looking at her, right?" I had hoped I would be brave enough to use one of Phillip's words in front of Ruth-Anne, and I was. It was working; my groin felt warm and full of cream. As soon as I got home I would use the Ruth-Anne–watching fantasy.

Suddenly Ruth-Anne stood up.

"No," she barked, slapping her hands together violently. "Stop immediately."

My blood went cold. "What? What?"

She crossed her arms, walked once around her chair, then sat again.

"*Not* okay. Not okay to do with me. Okay with Phillip, okay with a janitor, or a fireman or a waiter. Not okay with me."

She was talking to me like I didn't understand English. I felt like a gorilla. My finger went to my eye; maybe she had made me cry. No, she hadn't.

"I don't want to be a part of it." Her voice was a little softer now; she gestured toward the window. "There's a whole world of people you can use, but not me. Do you understand?"

"Yes," I whispered. "Sorry."

MY EMBARRASSMENT SHADED THE REST of the morning. I tried to involve a pair of her thong underwear but it only made things worse, my fingers became clumsy and pruned as Phillip pounded away. We gave up. I tried to work. I took a shower. Because of Clee's long hairs the drain had gradually become clogged to the point that the water filled the stall like a tub and I had to hurry to finish before it overflowed. Clee came home and put on her labia-revealing boxer shorts. I was furious and the bathroom was a mess and I was always stiff but could no longer achieve cream.

I called the plumber. Hurry, I said. We are completely clogged up over here. He was a chubby Latino man with no chin and eyes that grew sluggish at the sight of the juggy woman on the couch. I couldn't even wait; I gestured toward the shower as I hurried to my room. "Knock when you're done." It was better than Ruth-Anne; it was like the first time with Phillip. The plumber's eyes were wide with amazement when she entered the bathroom with her shirt off. He wasn't sure at first, he didn't want to get in trouble. But she begged and tugged at the wide, matronly front of his pants. In the end he was not as polite as he seemed. No sirree. He had quite a bit of pent-up rage, possibly from racial injustice and immigration issues, and he worked through all of it. Then he fixed the drain and to test it they did mutual soaping. The repair was two hundred dollars. I showed Clee the mesh hair-catcher and how to empty it; she looked right past me. Was she still mad about the foot thing? I didn't have time to wonder; there was suddenly so much to do.

A thin, nerdy lad I saw in Whole Foods: Clee followed him out to his car, begged him to let her hold his stiff member for one to two minutes. An Indian father who politely asked me directions with his shy wife in tow: Clee rubbed her puss all over his body and forced stiffness out of him, he was whining in ecstasy when his wife walked in. Too nervous to say anything, she waited silently until her husband creamed on Clee's jugs.

Old grandfathers who hadn't had sex in years, virginal teenage boys named Colin, homeless men riddled with hepatitis. And then every man I had ever known. All my teachers K through twelve and college, my first landlord, all my male relatives, my dentist, my father, George Washington so hard his wig slipped off. I tried to work Phillip in here and there, for example, inviting him to enter her from behind while I was an old man in her mouth—but this was just out of guilt, it didn't really add anything. Perhaps we were both sowing our wild oats. Or maybe Kirsten, being real, outweighed my hordes of imaginary men. Mostly I was too busy for guilt; there was almost no time that I wasn't rubbing myself. The postman delivered a box and before I could open it Clee had to unzip his government-issued pants; I helped him push his little nub into her. The penises were getting more abstract and unlikely—I couldn't rein them in. Some were slightly pronged, some pointed and willowy at the end like a wild yam, or serrated like a fleshy pinecone. I took the box into the kitchen and opened it with a butter knife. What could it be, what could it be? Right as I pushed my hand through the flaps I realized, with horror, what it was. Rick's snails. One hundred of them, all with their butts high in the air. They crawled upon broken pieces of each other, watery yellow guts smeared on brown shells. The inside of the box was thickly encrusted with layers of snails moving over each other, hundreds of blindly reaching antennae, and the smell—a rotten tang. My phone was ringing.

"Hello?"

"Cheryl, it's Carl calling from the cell phone store. I'm testing out a phone. Free call! How do I sound?"

"You sound very clear."

"No noise? No echo?"

"No."

"Let's try the speakerphone function. Say something."

"Speakerphone. Speakerphone." A snail was on my hand; I knocked it back into the box.

"Yep, that works. It's a nice little phone."

"Should I hang up?"

"I don't want you to feel like I just called to test the phone."

"It's okay."

"Hang on, lemme ask this guy if we can talk a little longer."

I listened to him ask if there was a time limit on the free call. An aggressive-sounding man said, "Talk all day if you want to." Clee was on her knees and my hand was back down my pants before I even knew what happened. It smarted; whatever was on my fingers from the snails was stinging my privates. Just an aggressive voice wasn't enough, though—she couldn't suck a voice. Carl was standing by to watch but I couldn't pull the picture together. Clee shuffled around the store on her knees, mouth open like a fish's.

"We can talk all day!" Carl said.

Clee was making a beeline for her father. *No, no*, I thought. *Not him.* But my fingers were already accelerating, zeroing in.

"How's tricks? How's Clee doing?"

Clee latched on to him just as he said her name. Needless to say, he was shocked.

"She's doing great." It was hard not to sound breathless. "She loves her job."

Shocked but not displeased. There was something that felt very right about this, wrong of course, but right. He put his hand on the back of her familiar head and pushed down a few times, helping her find the right rhythm.

"I'm coming down on Friday—how about I take you two out for a fancy dinner?"

Everyone else in the cell phone store was transfixed; someone whispered something about the law but the man with the
aggressive voice pointed out that the law's hands were tied because no nudity was involved. He was right—the bottom of
Carl's dress shirt parted around his member and was stuck to
Clee's lips, so each time she pulled her head away this curtain
came with her. Forward and back, forward and back. Carl suddenly made a warrior noise to indicate he was about to shoot.
He had wanted to last longer but his paternal pride had en-
gulfed him.

"That would be great," I said fervently.

"I'll pick out a nice place," he said. And then he creamed, not
into his daughter's mouth, which really would be against the
law, but up inside his own shirt. Clee's hand was under there, discreetly milking out the last drops. A flood of nausea and sadness
washed over me. I missed Phillip's familiar member. Where was
I now and where was he? The snails were everywhere. Not only
underfoot and glued to the kitchen walls, but all over the rest
of the house. They weren't the slow kind. One was procreating
asexually on a lampshade. I watched two disappear under the
couch. Was this the bottom or would my problem get worse? It
was a problem. I had a problem.

SOMETHING LIKE THIS HAD HAPPENED to me once before.
When I was nine a well-meaning uncle sent me a birthday card.
It wasn't really an appropriate card for a young girl; a group of
rough-looking birds in rakish hats were playing cards with cigars
in their beaks. It said something I can't remember, but on the
inside was a phrase like a virus or a self-replicating parasite waiting for a host. When I opened the card it flew out, gripping my

brain with merciless talons: "Birds of a feather flock together."
It couldn't be said just once, only repeated and repeated and repeated. *Birdsofafeatherflocktogether, birdsofafeatherflocktogether.* Ten
million times a day: at school, at home, in the bath, there was no
way to hide from it. It receded only as long as I was distracted; at
any given moment a bird or flock of birds or a cigar or playing
card or anything could bring it on. *Birdsofafeatherflocktogether-
birdsofafeatherflocktogether.* I wondered how I would live a full
and normal life, how would I get married, have kids, hold a job
with this handicap. I was under this spell, on and off, for a full
year. Then, quite unknowingly, the same uncle sent a card for my
tenth birthday. This one had a Norman Rockwell painting of a
girl covering her eyes on the front. It read: "Another year older?
I can't bear to see!" And then on the inside: "Because what's
happening to you, is happening to me." It worked like a gunshot.
Each time a flock of grimy birds began to descend, I incanted
What'shappeningtoyouishappeningtome and they immediately dispersed. The uncle is dead, but the card is still on my dresser. It
hasn't failed me once.

"Until now," I finished gravely, leaning forward on the leather
couch. "It doesn't work on this new spell."

Ruth-Anne nodded compassionately. We were moving past
my inappropriate behavior in last week's session.

"So we need an antidote," she said. "A corrective, like the card,
for this particular spell. But not *What'shappeningtoyouishappeningtome*, it's too short."

"That's what I thought, that it might be too short."

"You need something that will take a little time."

We tried to think of a longish antidote.

"What songs do you know? 'O Come, All Ye Faithful'? Do you
know that?"

"I really can't sing. I can't hold a tune," I said.

"I don't think that's a problem, you just have to know the words. 'Mary Had a Little Lamb'?"

I bleated out "Mary Had a Little Lamb."

"What do you think?"

"Well . . ." I didn't want to disparage her idea. "I'm not sure I want to sing 'Mary Had a Little Lamb' all day."

"Of course you don't. That'll drive you crazier than the blow jobs. What's a song you love? Is there a song you love?"

There was a song. A girl in college played it all the time; I was always hoping to hear it on the radio.

"I'm not sure I can sing it."

"But you know the words?"

"Yes."

"Just say them. Chant it."

I felt hot and cold. I was shaking. I put my hand on my forehead and began.

"Will you stay in our Lovers' Story?"

It sounded terrible.

"It's by David Bowie."

Ruth-Anne nodded encouragingly.

"If you stay you won't be sorry
"'Cause weeeee believe in youuuu"

I kept gasping; the air wasn't going in and out of my throat in the regular way.

"Soon you'll grow so take a chance
"With a couple of Kooks
"Hung up on romaaaancing"

"That's all I know."

"How do you feel?"

"Well, I know the tune wasn't right, but I think maybe I captured some of the energy of the song."

"I mean about Clee."

"Oh."

"You got a little break."

"I guess I did."

The next morning I rose early, awaiting my first chance to test the song. I took a shower, gingerly. The spell kept its distance. I dressed and waved to Rick—he was looking at the snails with distress.

"Good morning!" I stepped outside with a hearty mug of tea.

"This situation is out of control."

"Yes, I know. I ordered too many."

"I will deal with four of them. That is the number of snails I am prepared to supervise. I don't have the training to care for a herd."

"Perhaps you can call them? Round them up?"

"Call them? How?"

"A snail whistle?"

The words were hardly out of my mouth when Clee began sucking on the tiny snail whistle between Rick's legs. He was shocked and so forth, etc.

"Rick, I'm going to sing a song now."

"I don't think that will work. They have no ears."

"*Will you stay in our Lovers' Story . . .*" Rick politely lowered his eyes. He'd seen crazier things living on the streets. "*If you stay you won't be sorry, 'cause weee belieeeve in you.*"

It sort of worked. It wasn't like saying *abracadabra* to make a rabbit disappear, poof. It was like saying *abracadabra* billions of times, saying it for years, until the rabbit died of old age, and then continuing to say it until the rabbit had completely decomposed and been absorbed into the earth, poof. It took dedication, which I had when I first woke up—but my resolve decayed with the day. Faced with the option of singing or rubbing her warm puss through her jeans, I always decided tomorrow was the day to begin.

CARL WAS WEARING DRESSY LOAFERS that clicked on the sidewalk like tap shoes. There was some confusion about who should sit in the front seat—me, because I was older, or Clee, because she was the daughter. I sat in the back. We drove in silence.

The wine tasted off to Carl; he asked for another bottle.

"That's why they let you try it," he said. "They want you to be happy."

Clee seemed bored but I knew her well enough to know this was just a look. Like me, she was wondering why we were here. What didn't look bored were her nipples; they sat upright, attentive in a stretchy green tube dress. It was very hard to hum the song and make polite conversation at the same time.

Carl showed me his new cell phone and I felt a little sick. What if he was here because I had summoned him, given him an overwhelming and inappropriate desire to see his daughter? But he wasn't looking at her. He took a long sip of wine, watching me over the rim of the glass.

"How many years have we known you, Cheryl?"

"Twenty-three."

"That's a lot of years. A lot of commitment, a lot of trust."

When he said *trust* he gestured to Clee; she was wide-eyed and chewing on a hangnail. He knew. Kristof had told him about the old videos I had borrowed. He had figured out the rest. Bruises. The missing pummel suit.

"I think you know what I'm about to say."

His face was stern. My chest heaved.

"Suzanne wanted to be here too, by the way. So this comes from both of us." He raised his spoon in the air. "Cheryl, would you do us the great honor of joining the board?"

Clee shut her eyes for a moment, recovering. Carl watched a redness sweep over my face; luckily the rash wasn't subtitled or waving any explanatory signs. I bowed my head.

"Carl and Suzanne and Nakako and Jim and Phillip can be on the board alone," I began, "they are the best at being on the board, I am joining them even though I'm not much help, because I'm not good at being on the board."

Carl dinged each of my shoulders with a spoon, not something we did in the office and probably not done in Japan either. Then he raised his glass.

"To Cheryl."

Clee raised her glass, and maybe it was just our shared relief but I suddenly felt almost tender toward her. I hadn't really considered her recently, apart from trying to mentally push tubers and polyps into her vagina or mouth. How was she doing these days? The wine was quite strong; its vapors expanded behind my forehead. Carl refilled my glass.

"Phil Bettelheim is stepping down. So we had an opening to fill."

My face didn't change, I made sure of that.

"But there's no hard feelings. He made a major donation when he left."

I smiled at my napkin. Of course the point of being on the board was to be near him, but taking his place was interesting too. Almost better. For the first time I understood cigars and the urge to light one up and lean back.

Clee and I had both ordered the Mandarin beef; mine was placed in front of me at an ordinary speed but Clee's was lowered in slow motion. I looked up at the waiter's long, red gullet as he swallowed drily. It had been a little while since I'd seen this kind of thing happen in reality and suddenly it didn't seem like such a fantastic idea for her to hold this man's stiff member for one to two minutes. Especially since Phillip's was right there, swelling under the table. I shot the waiter a look to let him know she was spoken for; he hurried off.

Three minutes later he was back to ask how everything was. He used the question to lick Clee's jugs with his doglike eyes.

"That waiter was way out of line," I said after he left. This accidentally came out in a low, brusque voice, Phillip's voice. It was a subtle thing; Carl didn't notice. But Clee cocked her head, blinking. She shot her hand into the air, signaling the waiter.

"I think there's something wrong with my chair."

"Oh no," he said, stricken.

"Yeah, I think it's snagged my dress." She stood up and the waiter examined the chair.

"I don't see anything, but let me get a new chair."

"Are you sure? Is there a snag on my dress?"

The waiter paused and then cautiously leaned down and studied Clee's derriere.

She turned and smirked at him and his sly goatee came to the fore; their energies interlocked like a handshake, an agreement to have intercourse very soon.

"I'm Keith," he said.

"Hi, Keith."

I put my glass down with a bang and Keith and Clee exchanged looks of pretend fear. He thought I was her mother. He didn't have enough experience to guess I might be stiff and shaking with violence. How shocked he would be when I bent her over the dinner table, pushed up her dress, and jimmied my member into her tight pucker. I'd thrust with both hands high in the air, showing everyone in the restaurant, including the chefs and sous-chefs and busboys and waiters, showing all of them I was not her mother.

With each course they grew more comfortable with each other's bodies. He recited the dessert selections while giving her a shoulder massage.

"Do you know him?" Carl asked, confused.

"His name's Keith," she said.

But when Keith followed Clee out the door and asked for her number she said, "Why don't you give me yours?"

She was silent on the ride home.

And the moment I shut the front door, she grabbed my hair and jerked my head back. A silly gasping noise escaped me. No scenario; she was fighting the old way. It took a moment to reorganize—to switch places with her and become Phillip. He shoved her against the wall. Yes. It had been a while since we'd given it any gusto; this was just the release I needed. She deserved it for her loose behavior. She slapped my breasts around, something she had never done before and not part of any simulation I had watched. It took a lot of concentration to experience what hitting hers would feel like. Maybe because of this I had an aggressive or manly facial expression, I don't know. I don't know what she saw.

"What are you doing?" she said, stepping back.

"Nothing."

She took a few heavy breaths. "You're thinking shit stuff."

"No I'm not," I said quickly.

"Yes you were. You were shitting on me. Shitting on my face or something."

While I totally wasn't, in general terms I guessed I was. I guessed I had been shitting on her unceasingly for the last month. She was waiting for me to say something—to explain, to defend myself.

"It wasn't"—I was loath to say the word—"shit."

"Shit, piss, cum, whatever. It was all over my—" She gestured to her face, hair, bosom. "Right? Am I right?"

"I'm sorry," I said.

She looked utterly betrayed, as betrayed as the most betrayed person in Shakespeare.

"I thought *you*, of all people, would"—her voice dropped to a whisper—"know how to be nice."

"I'm really sorry."

"Do you know how many times this has happened to me?" She pointed to her face as if she was actually covered in something.

I thought of different numbers—seventy-three, forty-nine, fifty.

"Always," she said. "This always happens."

She turned away, and because she had no room of her own she went into the bathroom, locking the door behind her.

The map of the world detached from the wall and slid noisily to the floor. I hung it back up slowly. Her feelings. I had hurt them. She had feelings and I had hurt them. I stared at the bathroom door, one hand against the wall to steady myself.

RUTH-ANNE SAID TO JUST stick with it. To not worry if the song was working or not working—just sing it. I'd have a few chaste and hopeful days, but something always pulled me down again.

Once I began dreaming Clee was in Phillip's shower, mutual soaping, and when I woke up I pretended I was still asleep while I creamed. Another time I shoved his stiff member into her mouth for a second just to prove I was the boss of me and I could do it once without falling back under the spell, but it turned out I was not the boss of me, the spell was, and doing it once meant doing it fifteen more times over the next two days, swiftly followed by a bog of shame. And she knew—now she could somehow tell when I had recently creamed on her. She talked with Kate on the phone about how much more money she needed to get her own place; it wasn't much.

Sometimes I could only mumble, *"Will you stay in our Lovers' Story?"* but it worked best if I really gave it my all, belting it out with full deep breaths, either mentally or in my car at full volume, *"If you stay you won't be sorry!"* If she wasn't home, I did it with some tai chi–like movements that seemed to bring the practice into my consciousness more deeply. Some work was being done on the sewer lines out front; they sawed the pavement with a deafening screech, and each time their yellow vehicle backed up it had to beep, beep, beep, beep. It took incredible concentration to mentally sing and maintain the rhythm of the song against the opposing rhythm of the beeps. I sang over the beeps three days in a row, five to seven hours a day, before finally marching out of the house. The yellow machine was quite formidable up close; its claw dwarfed me. And the man it belonged to, its master, was proportional to the claw. He was drinking Gatorade in big gulps; his head was tilted back and sweat was running down the sides of his enormous, meaty face. This was exactly the sort of man whose member I loved for Clee to suck.

"Excuse me," I said. "Do you know how much backing up you'll be doing today? I live in that house. The beeping is very loud."

"A lot." He looked behind himself. "Yeah, a lot of backing up today."

A cool breeze moved past and I knew how nice that must feel on his sweaty face, but that was all. I didn't know how anything else would feel to him.

"Sorry for the noise," he added.

"Don't be," I said. "I appreciate everything you're doing."

He straightened up a little and I waited to see if his embarrassed dignity, so ripe with potential, would stir Clee. But no, nothing—the spell was broken. I had sung the song hard enough and often enough: now I never had to sing it again. I walked back to the house, noticing the neighbor's orange tree for the first time. It almost didn't look real. I breathed in the citrus, the ocean, the smog—I could smell everything. And see everything. My breath caught in my throat. I dropped down to the curb, bludgeoned by the vision of a middle-aged woman who couldn't keep her hands off herself. Cars passed, some fast, some slowing down to stare and wonder.

CHAPTER EIGHT

She didn't attack me for the entire month of July. Or talk to me. Or look at me. *I* was the vulgar one, I had dirtied *her*, not the other way around. How had it come to this and how could I clear my name? I was ready to throw myself into penitent acts as soon as an opportunity arose, but none did. Instead the hours limped by and each working day she was a little closer to moving out of my house. This would probably be for the best, though the thought was gutting, absurdly so.

On the last day of the month a blanket of heat descended in the middle of the night, waking every living thing and setting them against each other. I stared out the kitchen window into the moonless night, listening. An animal was being mauled in the backyard, possibly a coyote attacking a skunk—but not well, not deftly. After a few minutes Clee padded out from the living room and stood a few feet away from me. We listened to the squeals change as the animal approached death; the pitch had entered the human register, every exertion contained a familiar vowel. If words began to form then I would go out there and break it up. Words, even crudely formed ones, would change the game entirely. Of course they would be accidental—the way a tortured human might accidentally make sounds that were meaningful to a pig—but I would still have to step in. We both listened for a word. Maybe *help*, maybe a name, maybe *Please no*.

But the thing died before any of that, an abrupt silence.

"I don't believe in abortion," whispered Clee, shaking her head ruefully.

It was an unusual way to think about it, but no matter: she was talking to me.

"I think it should be illegal," she added. "Do you?"

I squinted into the dark corners of the yard. No, I didn't. I had signed petitions making sure of that. But it seemed like she was referring to what we had done just now, or hadn't done.

"I'm definitely on the side of life," I said, meaning not that I was pro-life, just that I was one of life's fans. She nodded several times in full agreement. We walked back to our beds with a formal feeling, like two diplomats who had signed a treaty of historical import. I wasn't forgiven, but the air in the house had changed. Tomorrow I'd ask for directions. *Do you know where the drugstore is?* I saw her smiling with relief, as if I'd asked her to dance. Everything forgiven.

TOMORROW BEGAN WITH A PHONE CALL. Suzanne was outraged.

"I want no part in it. And I don't feel guilty about that. Did I wake you up?"

"No." It was six A.M.

"If she was keeping it, I would be mad but I would feel I had to participate. But according to Kate's mom that's not the plan. It's just false stupidity. She's doing it so she can feel like a trashy Christian girl, like Kate, like all of them."

There was a little tickle in my brain, like the feeling of being about to remember the word for something. I knew I would understand what she was talking about in just a second.

"You have my permission to kick her out immediately—in fact, I insist on it. She needs a taste of reality. Who's the father? She can live with him."

The father. Father Christmas? Feather, farther, fallow? Was there liquid running out of my ear? I looked in the mirror; no liquid. But it was interesting to watch my face as it happened. It gave a very large, theatrical performance of a person being stunned: the mouth fell open, the eyes widened and protruded, color vanished. Somewhere a large soft mallet hit a giant cymbal.

The word for the thing we were talking about was *pregnant*.

Clee was pregnant.

Were there many ways to get pregnant? Not really. Could you get pregnant from a water fountain? No. My ear was being so loud I could barely make out Suzanne asking if I knew who the father was; even my own reply was hard to hear.

"No," I yelled.

"Kate didn't know either. Is Clee there?"

I cracked my door the tiniest bit. Clee was sitting up in her sleeping bag. Her face looked blotchy from crying or maybe just from being pregnant.

"She's here," I whispered.

"Well, please tell her she's on her own. I'd tell her myself but she's not answering my calls. Actually, you know what? Don't talk to her. Just make sure she doesn't leave. I'll be there in an hour and a half."

She broke the contract. It didn't cover this, of course it didn't, why should it? What did I care? What contract? We didn't have one. I pressed my face into the bed, smothering myself. Was it the plumber? Of course it couldn't be the plumber; that was imaginary. But something unimaginary had happened, probably not just once, more likely many times, with many people. That's who she was. Perfectly fine. Not my business. She could have as much unimaginary intercourse as she wanted. Of course, she would need to leave immediately; our contract was terminated. What contract? Where did they do it? In my bed? I would throw her garbage bags onto the street myself. I put on exercise clothes for swift movement.

Suzanne's Volvo rolled up silently; she must have cut the motor for the last block. I tried to give her a thumbs-up through the window but she didn't see me. She was also wearing athletic clothes and she looked as if she had been battle-crying for the whole drive and now was ready for the kill. There was a sharp rap on the door, a metal beak or her keys. I rolled my shoulders back and came out of the bedroom, stone-faced.

Clee was peeking through a crack in the living room curtains. She looked from her mother's wrathful face to mine, from my exercise clothes to her mother's. With her arms folded across her stomach she stepped back until she was against the wall with her garbage bags. Rap, rap, rap went the beak. Rap, rap. My eyes fell on Clee's bare feet; one was on top of the other, protecting it. Rap, rap, rap. We both looked at the door. It was shaking a little. Suzanne began to pound.

I swung it open. Not the big door, but the tiny one within it. It was just big enough to contain all of my features. I pressed them against its rectangle and looked down at Suzanne.

"Is she still in there?" she mouthed, pointing at the windows conspiratorially.

"I don't think she wants to see you right now," the door said.

Suzanne blinked; her face sank with confusion. I pressed myself against the oak door. *Stay oaken.*

"No one home. Keep out."

"Okay, Cheryl, ha ha. Very theatrical. Let me talk to Clee."

I looked at Clee. She shook her head no and gave me a tiny grateful smile. I redoubled my efforts, retripled them.

"She doesn't want to talk to you."

"She doesn't have a choice," Suzanne snapped. The door handle rattled desperately.

"Double dead bolt," I said.

She slammed her fist against the small iron grate that covered my face. That's what the grate was there for. She examined her fist and then gazed at her parked car and Clee's car behind it, her old car. For a moment she just looked like a mom, tired and worried with no graceful way to express herself.

"It'll be okay," I said. "She'll be okay. I'll make sure."

She squinted at me; the rectangle was starting to cut into my face.

"May I at least be granted permission to use the bathroom?" she asked coldly.

I shut the tiny door for a moment.

"She wants to use the bathroom."

Clee's eyes were shining.

"Let her in," she said with careful magnanimity.

I unlocked the door and swung it open. Suzanne hesitated, eyeing her daughter with a last-ditch harebrained scheme. Clee pointed to the bathroom. We listened to her pee and flush and wash her hands. She exited the house without looking at either of us; the Volvo rumbled away.

Clee took a long swig of old Diet Pepsi and tossed the empty bottle in the general direction of the kitchen trash. It bounced on the linoleum a few times. I understood. She had temporarily forgiven me in the heat of the moment without really meaning it. With all the fuss I had forgotten to make my bed; I headed to go do that.

"So," Clee said loudly. I stopped. "I don't really know a lot about health and stuff? But I figure you probably know what I should be eating. Like vitamins or whatever."

I turned and looked at her from my bedroom door. She was standing on the moon and if I responded I would be on the moon too, right next to her. With her and away from everything else. It looks so far away, but you can just reach your hand out and touch it.

"Well," I said slowly, "for starters you should take a prenatal vitamin. And how far along are you?" The phrase *far along* just fell out, as if it had been waiting in my mouth this whole time.

"Eleven weeks, I think. I'm not totally sure."

"But you're sure you want a baby."

"Oh no." She laughed. "It'll go up for adoption. Can you imagine? *Me?*"

I laughed too. "I didn't want to be rude, but . . ."

She mimed cradling a baby, rocking it frantically with a manic grin.

IN WEEK TWELVE IT WAS just a neural tube, a backbone without a back; the next week the top of the tube fattened into a head, with dark spots on either side that would become eyes. I read these developments aloud to her each week from Grobaby.com.

"All clogged up? Those pesky pregnancy hormones are to blame. Time to fixate on fiber." She was constipated, she admitted, starting this week. The website had an uncanny ability to predict what she was about to feel, as though her body was taking its cues from the weekly updates. With this in mind I often reiterated parts that seemed important. ("Paddle-like hands and feet emerge this week. Hands and feet: this week. They should be *paddle-like*.") When I accidentally skipped a week the cells twiddled their thumbs, waiting for further instructions. She took the vitamins and ate my food but the idea of a prenatal checkup sickened her.

"I'll go when it's closer," she said, hunched over her sleeping bag. I dropped it for the moment. Talking to her this way felt like a role—not unlike "Woman Asks for Directions." "Woman Takes Care of Pregnant Girl."

"I don't want anyone from the medical establishment touching me," she added a few hours later. "It has to be a home birth."

"You still have to get checked, though. What if there's a problem?" Somehow I knew just the right thing to say, as if I had watched Dana say it in a video.

"There won't be a problem."

"Hopefully you're right. Because sometimes it just never comes together—you think there's a baby in there but it's just unconnected bits and when you push it all comes out like chicken rice soup."

When Dr. Binwali showed us the fetus with the sonogram I was sure Clee would weep like every astronaut who has seen the earth from space, but she turned away from the screen.

"I don't want to know the gender."

"Oh, don't worry, it's too early to tell," said the doctor. But her eyes held fast to the ceiling, avoiding the sight of her own splayed legs. She meant ever. She hoped to never see it.

"Grandma might be curious to see the last bit of the tail," he said, tapping the screen.

Neither of us corrected him. We were rolling on rails now; the good people of the world glided around mothers and daughters, opening doors and carrying bags, and we let them.

HER SHAPE SHOULD HAVE LENT itself to a fertile appearance, but it was her biggish chin that I noticed now, and her burly way of moving. Together with the swollen stomach it created a peculiar picture, almost freakish. The more pregnant she became, the less like a woman she was. When we were out in public I tried to see if other people flinched or did a double take. But apparently I was the only one who could see this.

"'Week seventeen,'" I read, "'This week your baby develops body fat (join the club!) and his or her own unique set of fingerprints.'" It was hard to tell if she was listening. "So, make fat and fingerprints this week," I summarized. She pulled a snail off the coffee table and handed it to me. I dropped it into the covered bucket by the front door; Rick was collecting them.

"'Your baby weighs five point nine ounces and is about the size of an onion.'"

"Just say 'the baby,' not 'your baby.'"

"The baby is the size of an onion. Do you want me to read 'A Tip from Our Readers'?"

She shrugged.

"'A Tip from Our Readers: No need to splurge on maternity wear, just borrow your husband's button-down shirts!'"

She looked down at her stomach. It looked like a beer belly peeking out under her tank top.

"I have a shirt you could borrow."

Clee followed me to my closet. The clothes were all clean but collectively they had an oily, intimate smell that I had never noticed before. She began sliding hangers around. Suddenly

THE FIRST BAD MAN

she pulled out a long green corduroy dress and held it up.

"It's the lesbo dress," she said.

The dress I'd worn on the date with Mark Kwon, Kate's dad. She'd found it awfully quickly. It was long sleeved with tiny buttons running the whole length of it, from the edge of the calf-skimming skirt to the high collar. Thirty or forty buttons.

"It probably still fits you."

"I don't think so." An older, blue-blooded woman with white hair and real pearl earrings could have been elegant in it. Anyone younger or poorer would look like a soldier from one of those countries where women hold automatic weapons. I pulled out my pin-striped men's shirt. She took it into the bathroom with her but when she came out she was still wearing her tank top.

"It's not my style," she said, handing it back.

"Does it feel natural to you?" I asked. "To be pregnant?"

"It is natural," she said. "It's the medical establishment that makes it unnatural."

Her friend Kelly had given birth at home in a bathtub. Same with her friend Desia. There was a whole group of girls in Ojai who had put their babies up for adoption through a Christian organization called Philomena Family Services. All of them home-birthed with midwives.

"But here, in LA, the hospitals are really good, so you don't need to do that."

"You don't need to tell me what I don't need to do," she said, narrowing her eyes. For a split second I thought she was going to push me against a wall. But no, of course not. That was all over.

EVERYONE AT OPEN PALM KNEW and thought it was big of me to take her in like this.

"She was already in—I just didn't kick her out."

"But you know what I mean," said Jim. "Risking your job." My job was in no danger; Suzanne and Carl routinely sniffed out news of Clee from my coworkers. After each prenatal checkup I made sure to circulate the update. Everyone assumed I knew who the father was, but I didn't. I didn't know anything. It seemed impossible to broach the subject without also recalling *our* past, the scenarios, my betrayal. The unspoken agreement was we wouldn't look back.

In the middle of the second trimester I saw Phillip. He was parking his Land Rover just as I was leaving the office. I ducked into a doorway and waited for twenty minutes while he sat in his car, talking on the phone. Probably to Kirsten. I didn't want to think about it. Everything was in delicate balance and it needed to stay that way. When I finally walked to my car my legs were shaking and I was drenched in a foul sweat.

Each night I listened as she stumbled to the bathroom, bumping into the doorway and then hitting it again on the way back. It was torture.

Finally one night I yelled out from bed. "Careful!"

She stopped abruptly and through my half-open door I watched her stand in the moonlight and touch the swell of her stomach with a look of shock, as if the pregnancy had just come upon her right then.

"Was it Keith?" I called out.

She didn't move. I couldn't tell if she was awake or had fallen back asleep, still standing.

"Was it one of the men from the party? Did it happen at the party?"

"No," she said huskily. "It happened at his place."

He had a place called his place and it happened there and it was sex. This was both more and less than I wanted to know.

"It's a nightmare," she said, holding her stomach.

"Is it?" I was desperate to know more. She lurched back to bed. "Is it?" I cried again, but she was done, already half-asleep. It could only be a nightmare, someone growing inside you who you hoped never to see the face of.

IN THE MORNING I TRIED for a more hard-nosed approach.

"I think for safety's sake I should know who the father is. What if something happens to you? I'm responsible."

She looked surprised, almost slightly moved.

"I don't want him to know about it. He's not a good person," she said quietly.

"Why would you do that with someone who's not a good person?"

"I don't know."

"If it was nonconsensual then we should call the police."

"It wasn't nonconsensual. He's just not the type of person I usually go for."

How did they form the consensus? Did they vote? Did everyone in favor say *aye*. Aye, aye, aye. I went into the ironing room and returned with a pen, a piece of paper, and an envelope.

"I won't open it, I promise."

She went into the bathroom to write the name. When she came out she slid the envelope between two books in the bookshelf and then carefully placed the tab from a soda can in front of the books. As if it would be impossible to re-create the position of a soda can tab.

I ACTED QUICKLY, SETTING UP an emergency therapy appointment before Clee had a chance to think harder about trusting me. Once I was behind the pee screen I asked Ruth-Anne to look in my purse.

"There's a sealed envelope and an open empty envelope," I said. "Open the sealed one."

"Rip it open?"

"Open it the way you would normally open an envelope."

A clumsy ripping sound.

"Okay. It's open."

"Is there a name on a piece of paper?"

"Yes, do you want me to read it to you?"

"No, no. It's a man's name?"

"Yes."

"Okay." I shut my eyes as if he was standing on the other side of the screen. "Write that name down."

"On what?"

"On anything, on an appointment card."

"Okay. I'm done."

"Already?" It was a short name. It wasn't an unusual, long, foreign name with many accents and umlauts that one would have to double-check. "Okay, now put the paper back in the unsealed envelope and seal it."

There was a complicated rustling of papers and some banging.

"What are you doing?"

"Nothing. I dropped them. I hit my head on the table picking them up."

"Are you okay?"

"A little dizzy, actually."

"Is the envelope sealed?"

"Yes, now it is."

"Good, now put the envelope in my purse and put the card with the name somewhere safe that I can't see."

She laughed.

"What's funny?"

"Nothing. I hid it in a really good place."

"It's done then? I'm gonna come out. Okay?"

"Yes."

Ruth-Anne stood wide-eyed and smiling with her hands behind her back. The envelope was in many torn pieces strewn all over the rug. When you get something notarized, there is a dignified feeling about the proceedings, even if the notary is just a stationery store clerk. I had expected this to be more like that.

"What's behind your back?"

She opened her empty hands in front of herself. Now she was rolling her eyeballs to the side of the room in a strange way.

"What are you doing? Why are you looking over there?"

Her eyes jumped back. She pressed her lips together, raised her eyebrows and shrugged.

"Is the card over there?"

She shrugged again.

"I don't want to know where it is." I sat down on the couch. "This is probably unethical." I waited for her to draw me out. There were still ten minutes left in the session. Ruth-Anne sat down and rubbed her chin, holding her elbow and nodding significantly. She seemed to be acting out the role of a therapist in a mocking way, like a child pretending to be a therapist. "I don't want to break my promise to Clee," I continued, "but I also want the option of knowing. What if there's a problem? What if we need his medical history? Do you think that's wrong?"

Something slid down the wall. Ruth-Anne's eyes grew wide but she made a great show of ignoring it.

"Was that the card?"

She nodded vigorously. She had hidden it behind one of her diplomas. It now lay on the floor. I averted my eyes.

"It doesn't need to be hidden like an Easter egg. Just put it in your desk drawer." She leapt to the card and rushed it not to her desk but out the door to the receptionist's desk, slamming the drawer as if the card was a rascally character, prone to escape.

"Where were we?" she said, returning breathlessly and folding herself back into the therapist pose.

"I asked if you thought this was wrong."

"And I've been telling you." She was suddenly herself again, dignified and intelligent.

"What do you mean?"

"You wanted to play like a child, so we played."

I slumped back into the couch and my eyes ached with dry tears. This is why she was so good, always finding a way to take it right to the edge.

"You can throw out the card," I said, winded.

"I'll keep it there as long as you want. Our lives are filled with childish pranks, Cheryl. Don't run from your playing, just notice it: 'Oh, I see that I want to play like a little girl. Why? Why do I want to be a little girl?'"

I hoped she wouldn't make me answer this question.

"Have you ever considered being birthed for a second time?" she asked.

"Like born again?"

"Rebirthing. Dr. Broyard and I thought it might be a good idea."

"Dr. Broyard? You talk to him about me?"

She nodded.

"What about patient confidentiality?"

"That doesn't apply to other doctors. Would a pulmonologist withhold information from a neurologist?"

"Oh, right." I hadn't realized I was such a serious case.

"We're certified"—she gestured to a certificate on her wall—"to work as a team."

I squinted at the certificate. TRANSCENDENTAL REBIRTHING MASTERS CERTIFICATION II.

"Do you really think it's necessary?"

"Necessary? No. All that's necessary is that you eat enough to survive. Were you happy in the womb?"

"I don't know."

"After a session with us you *will* know. You'll remember being a single cell and then a blastula, violently expanding and contracting." She grimaced, contracting her upper body with a tortured shiver and then groaning with expansion. "All that upheaval is inside you. It's a heavy load for a little girl."

I pictured lying on the floor with Ruth-Anne's groin against the top of my head. "Why does Dr. Broyard need to be there?"

"Good question. The baby may have consciousness even before fertilization, as two separate animals—the sperm and egg. So we like to begin there."

"With fertilization?"

"It's just a ritual symbolizing fertilization, of course. Dr. Broyard would play the role of the spermatozoa and I would play the ovum. The waiting room"—she pointed to the waiting room—"becomes the uterus and you come through that door to be born."

I looked at the door.

"He's here with his wife this weekend, a special trip. How's Sunday at three?"

"Okay."

She glanced at the clock; we were out of time.

"Should I—?" I pointed to the scraps of paper on the floor.

"Thank you." She checked her phone messages while I knelt down and gathered the pieces of envelope. I carried them out with me, not wanting to clutter her wastepaper basket.

After slipping the envelope back between the books and repositioning the soda can tab, I clicked back through Grobaby.com. Nothing about the blastula expanding and contracting. I stared at a cartoon fetus, biting my fingernail. This website was not a how-to guide. If the thing in Clee was in any way relying on my narration, there would be major gaps in its development. I saw a lazy, text-messaging, gum-chewing embryo, halfheartedly forming vital organs.

Embryogenesis arrived the next day; I splurged on expedited shipping. Its nine hundred and twenty-eight pages weren't neatly divided into weeks, so it seemed safest to start at the beginning. I waited until Clee was done eating her kale and tempeh. She settled on the couch and I cleared my throat.

"'Millions of spermatozoa travel in a great stream upwards through the uterus and into the Fallopian tubes—'"

Clee held up her hand. "Whoa. I don't know if I want to hear this."

"It already happened, I'm just recapping."

"Do I have to listen?" She picked up her phone and headphones.

"Music might be confusing—it has to hear my voice."

"But my head is way up here."

She scrolled through her phone, found something with a thumping beat, and nodded at me to go on.

"'The successful sperm,'" I orated, leaning toward her round belly, "'merges with the egg and its nucleus fuses with the egg's nucleus to form a new nucleus. With the fusion of their membranes and nuclei the gametes become one cell, a zygote.'" I could see it so clearly, the zygote—shiny and bulbous, filled with the electric memory of being two but now damned with the eternal loneliness of being just one. The sorrow that never goes away. Clee's eyes were shut and her brow was sweaty; it wasn't so long ago that she was two animals, Carl's sperm and the ovum of Suzanne. And now the same thing was happening inside her, a new sorrowful creature was putting itself together as best it could.

The next morning I greeted my bosses with empathy; you would think a thing made of you would at least remain on speaking terms. Suzanne and Carl hadn't heard from Clee in months. They sat as far away from me as possible, hands folded on the tabletop, a demonstration of civility. Jim smiled encouragingly; it was my first meeting of the board. Sarah took notes in my old chair, off to the side. I was formally welcomed and Phillip's resignation was acknowledged.

"He's not in great health," Jim explained. "I vote for sending him a basket of mixed cheeses." More likely he was too ashamed to show his face—and he should have been. Sixteen! A sixteen-year-old lover! When Suzanne argued against retirement benefits for Kristof and the rest of the warehouse staff, I found myself rising from my seat and jabbing my fist in the air like a person who knew something about unions. Taking Phillip's place was wonderfully emboldening. When the vote fell in my favor, Suzanne mouthed "Touché." She was studying my hair and clothes, as if I was someone new. I called Sarah *Miss* Sarah—like a servant.

Suzanne laughed at this and asked Miss Sarah to bring us more coffee.

"You can sit down, Sarah," Jim said. "Those two are just playing around." I felt drunk with camaraderie. All these years I'd been looking for a friend, but Suzanne didn't need a friend. A rival, though—that got her attention. When the meeting adjourned we both went to the staff kitchen and made cups of tea in silence. I waited for her to begin the conversation. I sipped. She sipped. After a while I realized this *was* the conversation; we were having it. She was giving me her blessing to care for her young and I was accepting the duty with humility. When Nakako came in, Suzanne walked away. For honor's sake we would keep our distance.

RUTH-ANNE HAD WARNED AGAINST parking in the garage; there was no attendant on the weekend. I parked on the street. An elderly woman was cleaning the elevator as I rode up. She quickly Windexed the door when it shut behind me and then began cleaning the buttons, illuminating each one as she polished it, but politely focusing on the numbers above my floor.

The door was locked; I was early. I turned off my phone so it wouldn't ring during the rebirthing. I sat in the hall. They were almost fifteen minutes late. Apparently they weren't as professional about their side work—it was a more casual affair. Well, wasn't I the fool for being exactly on time. After a while I remembered that the appointment was for three o'clock, not two o'clock; I was forty minutes early. I wandered around. No one worked on the weekends; the building was silent. Ruth-Anne's office was at the end of a long corridor connected to another long corridor by a long corridor. An H formation. That was useful to know—I had never been totally clear about the floor plan of the building. *How else can I use this time constructively?* I asked myself. *What can I do that I need to do anyway?* I jogged back to the door, turned, jogged down each of the corridors—it was a terrific workout and no small distance. Thirty or forty H-reps probably equaled a mile, two hundred calories. After seven Hs I was covered in sweat and breathing heavily. As I jogged past the elevator it dinged. I accelerated, rounding the corner just as the doors swished apart.

"But the parking attendant doesn't work on the weekends," Ruth-Anne was saying. "He never has." I ran past the door of her office and turned the corner. I needed a moment to catch my breath and wipe off my face.

"Oh no," she said.

"What?"

"The key's on my other ring. I just got a new fob and . . ."

"Jesus, Ruth-Anne."

"Should I go back and get it?" Her voice was strangely high, like a mouse on a horse.

"By the time you get back here the session will be over."

"You could work with her alone until I get back."

"In the hallway? Just call her and cancel."

It took her a moment to find my number in her phone.

"Straight to voice mail. She's probably parking. I'm sure she'll be up in a minute or two."

My panting was hard to control and my nose was whistling. I should have gone farther down the hall but it was too risky to move now.

Dr. Broyard sighed. "This never really works out," he said. It sounded like he was unwrapping a candy. Now something was clacking around in his mouth. "For one reason or another."

"Rebirthing?"

"Just—these things you cook up so you can see me when I'm with my family."

Ruth-Anne was silent. No one said anything for a long time; he started biting the candy.

"Is she even coming, or was this your plan, that we would stand in the hallway together and—what? Fuck? Is that what you want? Or you just want to blow me? Hump my leg like a dog?"

A confusing high-pitched noise seemed to descend from the vents, then broke into a mass of wet, convulsive gasps. Ruth-Anne was crying. "She's coming, I promise. It's a real session. It really is."

He crunched his candy angrily.

I tucked my hair behind my ears and smoothed my eyebrows—it would be embarrassing for everyone but at least he would know she wasn't a liar. I took a deep breath and stepped boldly around the corner.

"Did you—" Her crying was so violent that she could barely talk. "Did you say that because you want me to"—the last part came out in a shrill chirp—"blow you?"

My backward steps were silent and swift. No one had seen me.

"No, Ruth-Anne. That's not why I said that." He sighed again, louder this time.

"Because," she said, "I might be willing to do that." I could hear her attempt at a coy smile through her stuffy nose and running mascara.

In the very beginning she didn't even like him. She could see his arrogance and his tendency to ignore what was inconvenient to him. The doctor was surprised, taken aback, when she pointed out these flaws. It made him want to have intercourse with her, just to put her in her place. But he was married and it wasn't worth it. She wasn't his physical ideal—a little too old, a little manly around the shoulders, horsey in the jaw. She knew this; it was as clear as if he had said, "You're a little too old, a little manly around the shoulders, horsey in the jaw." The insult kept her interested, this and the fact that he was married. Nothing inspired her like the thought of wifely Mrs. Broyard, obsessed with making dinner and the consistency of her children's stools. Finally she broke him down. One night after rebirthing class he wept into his wineglass and admitted that he and his wife were going through a rough patch. It was on this night that she suggested the arrangement; she described it as a form of therapy. He said he trusted her and for the first few months this trust was the basis of their dynamic. She was his new receptionist but it was as though he was working for her. She guided him into each thing he did to her. It was sweet, and he actually loved her a little bit. She felt satisfied and at peace. Gradually he gained confidence and the game heated up. It was aerobic and exhilarating for him; in their finest moments he admired her athletic build and the broadness of her shoulders. A smaller woman would have been more quickly exhausted, but she had a brute endurance.

But eventually she wanted it more than he did, and this made her lower than him. There was no way to knock down a woman who was already lying on the ground. Their intercourse continued for a while, ritualistically, then dwindled to a pat on the rump in passing. And then finally nothing, for years now.

"Where are you going?" she sniffed.

He was walking straight toward me. His arm extended around the corner as he used the wall to stretch out his shoulder, one hand resting just a few inches from my forehead. I stared it down and it withdrew. He groaned and walked back to Ruth-Anne.

"Let me pay you a normal rate. My secretary in Amsterdam makes three times what you do."

"But she's a real secretary."

"You're a real secretary."

Like a person slapped, she said nothing.

"How are you different from a real secretary? Tell me. It's been years, Ruth-Anne. Years."

The contract, I thought. *Refer to the terms of the contract.*

She was silent.

"If you won't take a normal salary, then I'll hire a secretary who will."

Ruth-Anne cleared her throat. "Okay. Hire another secretary." Now she sounded like herself again, calm and astute.

"Yes, I will. Thank you. I think it's best for both of us," he said. "Shall we go?"

"You go. I'll wait a bit longer."

Dr. Broyard laughed tiredly. He still didn't believe I was coming. "Are you sure?"

She wasn't at all sure, this was plain as day. She was giving him one last chance to choose her, to stay, stay forever, to honor all her complications and live with her in a new world of love and sexuality.

"Yeah, I'm sure." I could hear the smile she was using. Last chance, it said. Last chance forever.

"Well, I might not see you before Helge and I take off. Let's have a phone call when I'm back in Amsterdam, okay?"

Maybe she nodded. He walked to the elevator. He pressed the button and we both listened, my therapist and I, and waited for this part to be over—the part where he had already left but was still with us. We listened to the elevator rush upward, the doors opening and shutting, and then a long descent, which got fainter and fainter but never seemed to end. She slid to the floor, sobbing. Something in the building shut off, the heating or cooling; it became even quieter. I tried not to listen to her choking, wet gasps. After a while she blew her nose, hard and loud, gathered her purse, and left.

It was a wonderful feeling to be back in my warm car, driving home to Clee. I turned on the phone; there was one new message.

"Hi, Cheryl, it's Ruth-Anne, it's three forty on Saturday afternoon. You missed your three o'clock rebirthing appointment. Because you didn't cancel twenty-four hours in advance you will have to pay in full. Please make the check payable to me. See you at our regular time on Tuesday. Be well."

There was no way around it. I called back and made an emergency appointment. I would have to tell her what I had done and admit that I was struggling with my conception of her. She seemed pathetic and desperate to me now. Obsessed.

"Good, good," she would probably say. "Keep going." It would turn out that this was the key, witnessing this exchange between the primordial mother and the primordial father.

"But I eavesdropped!" I would cry.

"It was essential that you perform the role of a spy, a naughty child," she would say, excited because for the first time in her twenty-year practice a patient had shifted the field—this was a psychiatric term, *shifting the field*. It meant everything could be exposed for what it really was, every question answered, total clarity for both doctor and patient, leading to a true friendship inaugurated by the therapist reimbursing all her fees in one lump sum. Dr. Broyard would now come out wearing a mask that was a crude drawing of his own face and it would be revealed that the entire exchange in the hallway was a farce—it *was* the rebirthing.

"You witnessed the reverse conception and survived it. That's very powerful."

"But how did you know I would be early?" I would say, incredulous, almost dubious.

"Look at your watch," Dr. Broyard would say. My watch was one hour behind. Dr. Broyard would take off his mask, revealing a very similar face, then Ruth-Anne would pretend her face was a mask and because her skin was a little on the loose side it would look for a moment as if she really might be able to peel it off. But she couldn't, luckily. We would all laugh and then laugh about how good it felt to laugh. A massage for the lungs, one of us would say.

Now I almost felt like I didn't need to go to the emergency appointment, but I went anyway. I was curious if I would really get all my money back in one lump sum; it seemed unlikely, but if I had really shifted the field then I guessed it was only fair. If shifting the field was a real thing, which, as I sat on the leather couch, I remembered it wasn't. I explained about arriving early and hearing their entire exchange.

Ruth-Anne's eyes widened. "Why didn't you say anything?"

"I don't know. I really don't know. But do you think maybe it was important that I perform the role of a naughty"—I could see already that she didn't—"child? A spy?"

"I just don't understand how you could do this." She put her face in her hands. "It's such a violation."

Unless this was also part of the farce? I smiled a little, experimentally.

"For the record, I think you did the right thing," I said. "By quitting."

Ruth-Anne stood up, took a moment to put her long hair in a ponytail, and told me our work was done.

"We've gone as far as we can go together. You broke the patient confidentiality agreement."

"Isn't that to protect the patient?"

"It's a two-way street, Cheryl."

I waited to see what would happen next.

"So, goodbye. I'll prorate today since it wasn't a full session. Twenty dollars."

It seemed like she meant that so I fished out my checkbook.

"You don't have cash?"

"I don't think so." I looked in my wallet, all ones.

"How much do you have?"

"Six dollars?"

"That's fine."

I gave her the cash, including both halves of a dollar bill that I had been meaning to tape together for a few years.

"You can keep that one," she said.

As I drove out of the parking garage I could feel her watching my car from her window on the twelfth floor. I marveled at the therapeutic process. This was bringing up a lot for me, being abandoned like this. Our most potent work to date.

CHAPTER NINE

All the women in Clee's birth class were in their twenties or thirties, except the teacher, Nancy, who was my age. Whenever Nancy referred to what obstetricians were like twenty years ago, when *she* had *her* children, she would look at me; it was impossible not to nod in agreement, as if I were remembering. Sometimes I even chuckled ruefully with Nancy, and all the young couples would smile respectfully at me, a woman who had been through it and now was supporting her striking but sadly single daughter. We were given color-coded handouts to refer to during the birth in case we forgot how to time contractions or what to visualize for relaxation. We learned how to push a baby out (like urinating), what to drink in labor (Recharge and honey) and eat after birth (your own placenta). Clee seemed to be feverishly recording every little detail, but a closer look at her notebook revealed pages of bored loop-di-loops.

In the last trimester the musculoskeletal and hematopoietic systems completed themselves and Clee stopped moving. She lowered her immense body onto the couch and stayed there, wanting everything to be brought to and taken from her. Princess Buttercup.

"Remember what Nancy said in birth class," I warned.

"What?"

"About how important it is to stay active. I'm sure the baby's parents would appreciate you not watching TV every second of the day."

"Actually, this is their favorite show," she said, turning up *America's Funniest Home Videos*. "So I should get the baby used to it."

"Whose favorite show?"

"The baby's parents. Amy and Gary."

She laughed at a dog walking around with a can stuck on the end of its nose.

"You've met them?"

"What? No. They live in Utah or somewhere. I just picked them off the website."

It was called ParentProfiles.com; a woman from Philomena Family Services had sent her the link a few months ago.

"Why Amy and Gary?" I clicked through pages and pages of clean, desperate couples. "Why not Jim and Gretchyn? Or Doug and Denice?"

"They had good favorites."

I clicked on their favorites. Amy's favorite food was pizza and nachos, Gary's was coffee ice cream. They both liked dogs, restoring classic cars, and *America's Funniest Home Videos*. Gary liked college football and basketball. Amy's favorite holiday tradition was baking gingerbread houses.

"Which favorite was your favorite?"

She looked over my shoulder.

"Was there something about ducks? Scroll down." She squinted at the screen. "Maybe that was someone else. Gingerbread houses—I like those."

"That was the deciding factor?"

"No. But look at that barn." She touched the image in the masthead.

"That's a stock photo—it's on every page."

"No, that's their barn." She tried to click on the barn. "It doesn't matter, they're already official."

"You e-mailed them?"

"Carrie did, from PFS. I don't have to ever meet them."

She'd really done it. Forms had been filled out.

"Did you go to an office and sign papers?"

"Carrie e-mailed me a thing. I did it all online."

A snail was crawling up the bookshelf. I put it in Rick's bucket.

"Did you put who the dad is?"

"I said I didn't know. There's no law that says I have to say."

I clicked on Amy and Gary again. They looked nice, except for Gary. Gary looked like he was wearing sunglasses even without them. A cool customer. I clicked on "Our Letter to You." "We realize this must be a tremendously difficult time in your life. The love and compassion you are showing for your child are immeasurable." I looked at Clee.

"Would you say this is a tremendously difficult time in your life?"

She looked around the room, checking to see if it was.

"I think I feel okay." She nodded a few times. "Yeah, I'm doing all right."

I frowned with pride. "That's the hormones."

I was good at this. I was a good mother. I wanted to tell Ruth-Anne—it was agonizing that she didn't know. But maybe she did. Maybe I was still under her gaze somehow. I tucked my hair behind my ears and smiled at the computer.

"Go to Grobaby.com," said Clee.

I fingered *Embryogenesis*. "We should get through the musculoskeletal system. Wouldn't want to skimp on that." But she was due in three weeks. Even with no guidance her body could probably finish it off from here. I clicked on Grobaby.com.

" 'Talking, singing, or humming to your baby is a fun way to bond during pregnancy. So warm up those pipes and get your Broadway on!' "

"What if you don't want to bond with the baby?" she said, staring at the TV.

I hummed a little, clearing my throat. "Do you mind if I give it a try?"

She changed the channel on the remote and lifted her shirt.

It was really huge. There was a disturbing dark line coming down from her belly button. I put my lips close enough to feel its radiant heat, and she flinched a little.

I hummed high and I hummed low. I hummed long, sustained notes like a wise person from another country who knew something ancient. After a while my deep tone seemed to split and harmonize with itself and I thought for a moment that I was doing that beautiful throat singing the people of Tuva do.

Her eyes were on the TV, but her lips were pressed together and she seemed to be trying to match my pitch. And she was scared, that was suddenly obvious. She was twenty-one and any day now she would give birth, in this house, probably on this couch. I tried to hum reassuringly. Everything will be fine, I hummed, nothing to worry about. Clee's stomach lurched against my lips—a kick; we raised our volume in surprised unison. I wondered if there would be an awkward confusion about how to end this but the hum simply grew fainter, as if it were leaving on its own, like a train.

IN BIRTH CLASS WE LEARNED that her face would swell up when the time was near. Or she might begin scrubbing the walls with a fierce nesting instinct. That one was hard for me to picture—how would she know where I kept the sponges?

She rose at dawn, certain a cat had pissed in the house.

"Smell over here," she said, sniffing my bookshelves. I couldn't smell it. She followed the invader's invisible tracks around the house. "It must have come in, peed, and left." She whipped aside the shower curtain. "All we can do is look for the hole it came in through." So we spent the earliest hour of the day searching for the hole, until she suddenly sat down on the couch with a gasp. She put both hands under her stomach and looked up at me with amazement. A contraction.

"Maybe there's no cat?" I said.

"Yeah, no cat," she said quickly, as if I was way behind.

I called the midwife immediately, describing the cat pee, the hole, and now the contractions. All the information was valuable, not to a doctor, but certainly to our wise midwife, who had fifteen years of experience. "Do you think it's time to come over?" I tried not to sound too desperate. "Or is it too early?"

"I'm in Idaho," she said. "But don't worry, I'm coming back immediately. I'll drive as fast as I can."

"Drive?"

"I'm bringing a friend's car back to Los Angeles for her." Before making a snap judgment, I tried for a moment to put myself in her position. What was she supposed to do, not drive the car back? What kind of friend would that be? The kind of friend who is a midwife.

"I guess we'll go to the hospital."

She laughed. "Don't worry, everyone always thinks the baby is about to come out. That baby isn't going anywhere for at least twelve hours. The good news is, you can call me as much as you want. I'm completely available by phone."

I told Clee not worry, the baby wasn't coming for twelve more hours.

"I can't do this for that long," she groaned. She was scraping the couch with her fingernails. "We should call Carrie from PFS, she has to tell the parents." A weird low noise came out of her chest and her eyes bulged.

"Maybe we should call *your* parents?" I suggested.

"Are you kidding?"

The contractions seemed closer together and longer than they should be, but I wasn't sure we were measuring them right. And you weren't supposed to time them in the beginning anyway; the blue handout from class suggested having friends over, going to a movie or dancing. It would be the first time we'd ever done any of those things, but I mentioned them to Clee.

"Do any of those sound good?"

She shook her head and moaned in a terrifying way. I skipped ahead to the pink handouts. We tried one of the visualizations from class—each contraction was a mountain. "Picture the mountain, you're halfway up, now you're at the top, now you're coming down the other side and it's easier, almost over."

"I can't hold it in my mind," she whispered. "I'm not a visual thinker."

I tried to make it more real, describing the craggy peak, its majesty. "Think of the picture on the one-dollar bill, the mountain." I got out my purse. There was no mountain on the one-dollar bill—it was a pyramid. "Focus on this, you're at the base of it," I said, holding the dirty money in front of her face.

"Okay." She glued her eyes to the tiny pyramid. "It's starting." I used a bobby pin to trace her progress up the steep side. "Too fast," she said. The pyramid was so tiny that it was hard, at first, to go slow enough. But soon we had it down and each time a new one came she would pick up the dollar and thrust it at me and we'd make our way up to the floating eye. It was a tool the government gave out for women in labor; it could be spent again and again but only to buy a contraction.

At seven o'clock Rick let himself in with his key. We were in the middle of the pyramid so I ignored him. He used the bathroom and watched us from the doorway. Once Clee was down the other side she told me to tell him to leave.

"I'll just be in the yard," he said, trying to slip back out.

"I don't want him to hear me," Clee whined. "Or see me through the windows."

Rick crumpled and shuffled away. My cell phone rang.

"It's me," said the midwife. "How's she doing?"

"Okay. We're using visualization."

"That's good, that's perfect. The flower opening?"

"No, the mountain."

"There's a lot of great mountains around here. Have you ever been to Idaho?"

"You're still in Idaho?"

"It's beautiful but not in an obvious way, you know?" It sounded like she was trying to open a package of chips with her teeth. "I once had a boyfriend who lived out here. Much too rural for me. I wonder what ever happened to him."

She was bored. She was calling because she was bored.

Clee thrust the dollar at me and I hung up. The journey was getting slower and harder.

"I can't do it anymore," she said.

"Just make it to the eye. See what it says at the top? 'Annuit Coeptis.'"

"What's that?"

"'He favors our undertaking.' God does."

She breathed out fiercely. "I'm not kidding, I really can't."

Her face looked crazy and swollen. Her blond hair had darkened with sweat and was sticking to her face. She clumsily pulled off her shorts; I looked away and spied Rick tiptoeing into the bedroom. Why was he still here? I skipped through the pink handout to the white ones.

"You're in transition," I said. The teacher had told us about this—it was a good sign.

"What do you mean?" It was almost like she hadn't attended the class with me.

"This is the worst you'll ever feel."

"Ever?"

"Well, maybe not ever in your whole life. We don't know how you're going to die—that might be worse." I had veered off course. I put my face right in front of hers. "You can do this," I said. She looked at me like I knew everything. She was hanging on my every word.

"Okay," she said, suddenly clamping her hands to my forearms. "It's starting."

Now the dollar was cast aside, spent. For the length of each contraction she lived in my eyes, never blinking, never looking away, gripping my arms like they were steel supports. I wasn't strong enough for this but that was a problem for later.

"Shouldn't she be here?" Clee wheezed. I had been telling her the midwife was on her way, which wasn't untrue. I was waiting for a break, during which I would explain the situation, we would calmly discuss the options, and then we'd go back to having the baby.

"She's driving her friend's car from Idaho to California. She won't make it in time. We have to go to the hospital."

"Really? Is that really true?"

I nodded.

She was crying, and now another contraction was starting.

"They'll cut me open, I don't want to be cut." She began to pee. Then, with the pee still running down her thigh she lowered her head to the floor and threw up. She was exploding and disintegrating. I tried to clean her off but she rolled against the wall. "If we don't go, does it mean the baby will die?"

"No, no. Of course not." She said thank you; the only thing she cared about was not going to the hospital. If I had it to do over again I would have said *Probably. It might live, but probably not.* Also, I would have dragged her to Dr. Binwali the moment the midwife said *Idaho.* Because now it was getting away from us; the hospital seemed like a rest stop we had missed hours ago. Clee let out a bellow. "Should I push?"

"It feels like you want to push?"

"I have to."

"Okay, just a little. Let me call the midwife."

But she wouldn't let me leave until the push was done. The midwife had the radio on very loud—a country song, it sounded like.

"What do I need for the delivery?" I yelled.

"She's progressed? You need to go to the hospital."

"She's pushing. We're having it here. Do I need to boil water? What do I do?"

She turned the radio off.

"Shit. Okay. Bare minimum, you need three clean towels, some olive oil, a bowl of hot water, some sanitary sharp scissors, and a clean piece of string."

I was running through the house, grabbing the things as she said them. Rick was in the kitchen, pouring boiling water into a mug.

"I need that water!" I yelled.

He bent down and calmly unlaced his tennis shoe. "There's already hot water in the bedroom," he said, dropping his shoelace in the mug. "I don't think you have any string, but this will do." He was rolling up his dirty sleeves and washing his hands at the kitchen sink with brisk authority.

Clee bellowed in the other room.

"Do you really know how to do this?"

He nodded modestly. "I do."

I studied his face. It was not soft or deranged; his eyes were clear, his brow almost hawklike, though overly tan from outside living. A fine surgeon who fell from grace—malpractice, destitution, homelessness. I didn't verify any of this, just followed him into the bedroom. He gently placed the mug on my dresser, beside a steaming bowl. The scissors and olive oil were waiting, and a stack of towels. The floor was covered with black plastic garbage bags. I smiled weakly with relief.

"You've done this before."

His brow furrowed and he started to speak, a response that already sounded terrifyingly longer and more complicated than *Yes*. Clee screamed, crawling into the bedroom on her hands and knees.

She was yelling that its crown was showing. A royal baby. She meant he was crowning, but he wasn't.

I explained about how we were in Rick's hands and also how he had washed his hands. I hoped she wouldn't notice the swarm of doubt flying around the room. But she was past all that.

"Can I really push now? I want to get it out."

My heart jumped. It. I had forgotten about the baby. Until then she had been giving birth to birth—to contractions and noises and liquids. There was someone in there.

We gave her water and Recharge energy drink and a little bit of honey. I had forgotten these things earlier but with Rick here it was easier to think. He suggested I wash my hands before the next contraction. But it was too late. She squatted and with an unearthly scream her legs slowly split apart to reveal a perfect wedge of head. Clee reached down and touched it.

"There's no face," she said.

Rick took my palms and squirted Purell into them. He waved his hands in the air to indicate I should do the same. We flapped our hands. Clee suddenly reclined and seemed to fall asleep. I raised my eyebrows at Rick and he made a smooth gesture with the flat of his hand, indicating that this was normal. He put his face in front of her and in a low, unfamiliar voice he said, "It comes out on this push." Clee opened her eyes and nodded obediently, as if they shared a long history.

"Big breath in," said Rick. She took a big breath in. "Release it with noise and push. Harder."

It came out with a gush of fluids and Rick caught it. A boy. He looked dead, but I knew from the birth videos we watched in class that this was normal. The silence was terrible, though. And there was a foul smell. Rick tipped the baby to the side and he coughed. And then he squawked. Not like a person making his first sound ever, but like an old crow—a bit tired, a bit resigned. Then silence again. Rick lay the baby on the floor and cut the umbilical cord with a seasoned swipe of my nail scissors. He tied his sanitized shoelace onto the baby's stub. Clee tried to stand and fell into a convulsive squat. A pile of gizzards dropped from between her legs. The placenta. She leaned back against the bed. "You take him."

He weighed almost nothing. His legs were covered in green slime, like pea soup, and his eyes rolled upward like a drunk old man trying to get his bearings. A pale, drunk old man with floppy arms and legs.

"He's pale, isn't he?" I said.

I looked at Clee's skin, tawny even now.

"You're not pale. Is his dad pale?"

I tried to think of all the very pale men in Clee's world. The baby was so fair it was almost blue. Who that we know is blue? Who, who, who do we know that's blue? But this question was just a funny costume, a silly clown nose on the real thought I was having.

"Call 911," I said.

Clee lifted her sleepy head and Rick froze.

The phone was by his knee; he picked it up slowly.

"Pea soup. We learned that in class. It means something bad. Call 911."

The baby was darker blue now, purple almost. *Seconds*, I was thinking, *we're down to seconds.* Suddenly there was a feathery sound like giant wet wings unfurling—it was Clee's body unsticking from the plastic garbage bags. She was standing. Her big hand tore the phone away from Rick. She dialed and said the address, she knew the zip code, she knew the cross street, the dispatcher was giving instructions, she clearly relayed each one—"wrap him in a towel," "cover the top of his head," and I completed each task with an unusual fluidity, as if we'd been working on this scenario for years, this baby-saving simulation, and now was our chance to perform it. Rick watched from the corner, disheveled and shrunken; he was the homeless gardener again.

The ambulance people yelled and threw equipment around like a swat team. A beige blanket was wrapped around Clee. An athletic-looking older woman was counting over the baby. Maybe keeping track of how many seconds it had been since he'd died. She would never stop, she would count forever if that's how long he was dead for.

Rick handed me a Tupperware container just before I got in the ambulance.

"I washed it off," he cried. "It's clean."

Spaghetti, I thought. *Kate's spaghetti in case we get hungry.*

CHAPTER TEN

Something huge was inserted into his tiny throat. A cord was implanted in his raw belly button. He was covered in white stickers. A net of cables and tubes was woven between him and many loud, beeping machines. There was hardly enough baby to accommodate all the things that had to go into him.

"Do you think they know?" Clee whispered from her wheelchair.

We were gripping each other's hands between the folds of our white hospital gowns—a small hard brain formed by our interlocking white knuckles. I peeked around at the nurses. Everyone knew that this baby was up for adoption.

"It doesn't matter. As long as *he* doesn't know."

"The baby?"

"The baby."

But there was no thought more horrible than this baby fighting for his life not knowing that he was completely alone in the world. He had no people, not yet—legally we could walk out the door and never come back. We stood there like mesmerized criminals who had forgotten to flee the scene.

My own brain and its thoughts were just distant noise. What mattered was that every few seconds she or I would tighten the fist, which meant *live, live, live.* A bag of blood was rushed in;

it was from San Diego. I'd been to the zoo there once. I imagined the blood being pulled out of a muscled zebra. This was good—humans were always withering away from heartbreak and pneumonia, animal blood would be much tougher, *live, live, live.* A beefy man in scrubs motioned us over.

"He's critically stable. If he starts to desaturate you'll need to leave him alone."

He showed Clee how to put her hands through the holes in the clear plastic incubator. The baby's palm miraculously curled around her finger. That's just a reflex, the man said. *Live, live, live.*

Clee was mumbling a rolling chant that I could barely hear; at first it sounded like a prayer, but after a while I realized it was just "Ohhh, sweet boy, oh, sweet baby boy," over and over again. She only stopped when the head doctor came over, a tall Indian man. His face was gravely serious. Some people's faces always look this way, it's just how they're raised. But as he talked it became clear he wasn't one of these people. *Meconium* was repeated several times; I remembered the word from birth class: excrement. Meconium has been *aspirated* leading to *PPHN.* Or *PPHM.* He was talking slowly but it wasn't slow enough. *Nitric oxide. Ventilator.* We nodded again and again. We were actors nodding on TV, bad actors who couldn't make anything look real. He finished with the words *closely monitored.* We forgot to ask if the baby would live.

A toothy young nurse with glasses suggested Clee lie down in a receiving room on the Labor and Delivery floor. Clee said she was fine and the nurse said, "Actually, you're bleeding a lot." The back of her gown was soaked through. She fell back into the wheelchair, suddenly not fine at all. Her eyes were strangely sunken. They would call us, the nurse said, if anything changed.

We looked at each other darkly. If we didn't leave, then we couldn't get a terrible phone call.

"I'll stay," I said, and Clee was rolled out the door.

I was afraid to look at him. There were ten or fifteen other babies, each one hooked up to a beeping machine that regularly burst into alarm; the alarms overlapped, creating an undulating chaos. On the other side of the NICU another team of doctors and nurses surrounded something small and unmoving. Its parents stood apart from each other to let all of us know the other one was to blame and would never, ever, be forgiven, for all eternity. Their prayer was rage. The mother looked up at me; I looked away.

Without Clee's hand to hold, my thoughts were terrifyingly unbound. I could think anything. I could think: *Why am I here?* And: *This is going to end in tragedy.* And: *What if I can't handle this, what if I lose my mind?* I started crying giant wet tears.

Ha. I was crying.

It was easy now, stupidly easy. I wiped my nose on my hands, contaminating them. I went back out to the foyer and washed them again; the hot water on my skin made me homesick. This time I was asked to sign in. For *Relationship to the baby* I wrote *grandmother* because that's who everyone thought I was.

I forced myself to look at the tiny gray body. His eyes were shut. He didn't know where he was. He couldn't deduce, from the beeps and the sound of feet on linoleum, that he was in a hospital. He didn't know what a hospital was. Every single thing was new and made no sense. Like a horror movie, but he couldn't even compare it to that because he knew nothing about the genre. Or about horror itself, fear. He couldn't think, *I'm scared*—he didn't even know *I.* I shut my eyes and started humming. It was easier to do back at home, when he was still inside her. That time now seemed like a silly TV show, the three of us floating in a daze, believing we would always be safe. This here was real life. I hummed for so long I started to get dizzy. When I opened my eyes, he was looking right at me. He blinked, slowly, tiredly.

Familiarly.

Kubelko Bondy.

I smoothed my hospital gown and tucked my hair behind my ears.

I'm embarrassed to admit I didn't know it was you until now, I said. He gave me the same warm look of recognition that he'd been giving me since I was nine—but exhausted, like a warrior who has risked everything to get home, half-dead on the doorstep. Now it was unbearable that he should be lying untouched except by needles and tubes. I opened the circular doors and carefully held his hand and foot. If he died he would die forever; I would never see another Kubelko Bondy.

See, this is what we do, I began, *we exist in time. That's what living is; you're doing it right now as much as anyone.* I could tell he was deciding. He was feeling it out and had come to no conclusions yet. The warm, dark place he had come from versus this bright, beepy, dry world.

Try not to base your decision on this room, it isn't representative of the whole world. Somewhere the sun is hot on a rubbery leaf, clouds are making shapes and reshaping and reshaping, a spiderweb is broken but still works. And in case he wasn't into nature, I added: *And it's a really wild time in terms of technology. You'll probably have a robot and that will be normal.*

It was like talking someone off a ledge.

Of course, there's no "right" choice. If you choose death I won't be mad. I've wanted to choose it myself a few times.

His giant black eyes strained upward, toward the beckoning fluorescent lights.

You know what? Forget what I just said. You're already a part of this. You will eat, you will laugh at stupid things, you will stay up all night just to see what it feels like, you will fall painfully in love, you will have babies of your own, you will doubt and regret and yearn and keep a secret. You will get old and decrepit, and you will die, exhausted from all that living. That is when you get to die. Not now.

He shut his eyes; I was wearing him out. It was hard to lower the pitch of my mind. The Asian nurse with the glasses went on her lunch break and was replaced by a pig-faced nurse with short hair. She looked me over and suggested I take a break.

"Get something to eat, walk around the block. He'll be here when you get back."

"He will?"

She nodded. I didn't want to push it by asking if he was going to live in general, or just until I got back. And if I didn't go would he still live?

I'm going away, but just for a short time. It was impossible to leave him.

I left him.

My guilt was cooled by relief: it was good to be out of that terrifying, earsplitting room. I followed the signs to Labor and Delivery, dazed by the calm hallways filled with business as usual.

There was some confusion at the nurses' station.

"What did you say her name was again?"

"Clee Stengl."

"Hmmm. Hm, hm, hm, hm, hmmmm." The chubby nurse clicked around on a computer. "Are you sure you have the right hospital?"

"They told her to come down here, in the NICU, she was—" I

gestured to the back of my pants to indicate bleeding. I remembered her sunken eyes and suddenly felt that Clee was in great danger, fighting for her life at this very moment. An older nurse was reading a magazine and watching from a distance. I leaned my body over the counter.

"Are you searching . . . widely?" What I meant was maybe she was in an emergency operating room, or the ICU, but I didn't want to say that. "Stengl. You might be adding a vowel between the g and the l? There's no vowel there, she's part Swedish. Very blond." And just in case it would help, I added, "I'm her mother."

The older woman put her magazine down. "Receiving," she said quietly to the other nurse, standing behind her. "Two oh nine, I think. Home birth."

The door to 209 was half-open. She was in a mechanical hospital bed, wearing a smock. A tube ran from her arm to a hanging bag of liquid. She was asleep, or not asleep—her eyes were fluttering.

"Oh good," she said when she saw me. "It's you."

I sat next to her, feeling strangely meek and nervous. Her hair was in two braids—I'd never seen it like that. I thought of Willie Nelson or a Native American person.

"I guess he's okay for right now. A nurse said I should go."

"They told me."

"Oh."

It seemed like she had been in this room forever and knew everything about the hospital whereas I had been staggering around like a beggar.

"What's that bag?"

"It's just saline, I was dehydrated. Dr. Binwali checked me. He said I'll be fine."

"He said that?"

"Yeah."

I looked at the ceiling for a minute. Now that crying was easy, it was too easy.

"I thought maybe"—I laughed a little—"you were dying."

"Why would I be dying?"

"I don't know. You wouldn't be."

It wasn't an exchange we would have had before, but now we'd ridden in an ambulance together, listening to the siren from the inside. That's when she'd first grabbed my hand.

A nurse came in.

"You pressed the call button?"

"Can I have some more water?" Clee asked.

The nurse went off with the pitcher, leaving a weird metallic smell.

I felt we couldn't say anything, knowing she'd be back. She banged in again with the pitcher, her coppery smell redoubled. I waited, first for the nurse to leave and then for her scent to follow her.

"Can you get me something?" Clee asked. "That Tupperware?"

Kate's spaghetti. It was on a plastic chair.

Clee peeled the lid off and lowered her head, sticking her mouth down into the container. She made her hand shovel-like and started pushing the food into her mouth. It wasn't the spaghetti. Of course it wasn't—Kate's visit was months and months ago. I stood up and faced the window so I wouldn't have to look at it. I could still see her in the reflection but not the bloody thing she was eating. What happens when you eat that much of yourself? She was leaning back now, just chewing, chewing, chewing. She had gotten too much in her mouth and now she had to catch up with it. The glass had an amber tint or film that made her look old-fashioned. It was mesmerizing, how different this woman was from Clee. Now she carefully shut the container, click, wiped her hands on a napkin, drank a glass of water, and leaned her head back on the angled bed. Her braids lay on her chest and she looked leaden with sorrow, like a picture from the Dust Bowl. You just knew her whole life was going to be hard, every second of it.

"If he lives," she said, "will he be messed up?"

"I don't know."

"Amy and Gary won't want him," she said slowly. "What happens to babies like that, if they're not adopted?"

She was looking at me now, in the glass. I was the same sad sepia color.

I sat with Kubelko Bondy through the evening, staring at his miniature fingers wrapped around my thumb. I knew it was a reflex—their hands would curl around a carrot—but I had never been held so steadfastly for so long. He grabbed at the air when I gently pulled away. *I'll be back in the morning.* For now this was true.

I slept on a metal cot between Clee's bed and the window. A baby cried in the night, on and on without stopping, and then was abruptly silent. A cart rattled down the hall and someone said, "Who?" and someone replied, "Eileen." An alarm rang and was shut off and rang again before it was finally shut off for good. I slept for a minute or two and woke up as the old me, untroubled and dumb, until it came back like a floating carcass. Leaving him would be like killing someone and getting away with it. I'd be haunted forever. What was this life even for? It was over.

He was up there, alone. Maybe not even alive. I wanted to wail. Where was the real grandmother, the pastor, the chieftain, God, Ruth-Anne? There was nobody. Just us.

The cot was impossible. I sat up and put my feet on the floor; the mattress made a V shape around me.

"Are you leaving?" she whispered. "Please don't go."

"I'm not leaving."

She raised her bed up. The motor sound was too loud.

"I've been having some bad thoughts," she said.

"I know. Me too." It was not a scenario where something comforting could be said, like *Everything will be okay*. Nothing would be okay, that was the problem. I stood up and reached for her hand; maybe we could make the fist again. She grabbed my whole arm.

"Really, don't leave me here."

Her eyes were huge, her teeth were chattering. She was in a mad panic. I pulled the blanket off my bed and draped it around her shoulders, turned the thermostat up though I wasn't sure it was connected to anything. I filled the pitcher with hot water from the bathroom and made steamy compresses with the white hospital washcloth.

Clee wondered if she should call her parents.

"I think that's a good idea."

"You do?"

"Their daughter had a baby. They'll want to know."

"They're not like that."

"It's biological, they won't be able to help it."

"Really?"

I nodded knowingly.

She dialed. I began to tiptoe out but she shook her head violently and pointed at the chair with a sharp finger.

"Mom, it's me."

The cadence of Suzanne's voice was abrupt; I couldn't make out actual words.

"In the hospital. I had the baby."

"I don't know, we don't know yet. He's in the NICU.

"I didn't have a chance to, everything was crazy.

"I said I didn't have a chance to. I haven't called anyone.

"No, Cheryl's here.

"I don't know, it just worked out that way. She came in the ambulance."

Suzanne became loud; I moved to the window so I couldn't hear her.

"Mom—

"Mom—

"Mom—"

Clee gave up and held the phone straight out in front of her; the shrieking distorted violently, crackling in the air. Was she holding the phone like that to be funny and rude? No. She was hyperventilating. Her hand was gripping her stomach; something was seizing up in there. I leaned toward the phone—the sarcastic voice taunted, ". . . apparently I'm not your mother anymore; I've been replaced . . ." I wanted to punch Suzanne, to strangle her and drag her to the floor and bang her head against the linoleum again and again. Your (bang) daughter (bang) is in hell (bang). Be gentle with her.

I motioned for Clee to hang up and she looked at me with feral, uncomprehending eyes.

"Hang up," I whispered. "Just hang up."

Her hand obeyed me; the phone went silent.

I apologized for encouraging the call. She said she'd never hung up on her mom before.

"Really?"

"No."

We sat in silence. After a moment she poured herself some water and drank the whole glass.

"Do you want more?" I rose to take the glass. "Should I call the nurse?"

"Will it be the same one from before?"

"She had a funny smell, didn't she?"

"She smelled like metal," Clee said gravely.

I laughed.

"She did," she said. "The smell made my teeth hurt!"

This seemed funny too. I gripped the bed rail, giggling; I felt slightly hysterical. Clee's laugh was an unflattering guffaw; her mouth became huge. There was that smile I'd seen once before. She was looking at my lips; I brushed them off as I finished chuckling. We were done laughing. She was still looking at my mouth; I kept my hand over it. She quietly moved my fingers away and kissed me softly. She pulled back, swallowed, and then began again. We were kissing. For a while I kissed thinking that this was not that kind of kissing. I kissed her unfamiliarly soft, full lips again and again and reasoned that there were plenty of families who kissed easily and on the lips, French people, young people, farm people, Romans . . . After a while the hypothesis fell away; her palms were rubbing my back, my hair, she held my face. I stroked her braids again and again, as if I had wanted to touch them for a million years and would never tire of it. After a long time, ten or fifteen minutes, the kissing slowed. There were a series of closing kisses, goodbye kisses, kisses placed like lids on boxes—then the lid would pop off and need to be replaced. There, *this* is the final kiss—no, *this* is the final kiss. This one is, it really is. And now I'm just kissing that kiss good night.

She turned out the light by her bed. I stepped backward and crouched onto my cot. She lowered her mechanical bed; the noise of the motor filled the room. Then silence.

I had never been so awake in my life. What did it mean? What did it mean? I hadn't kissed anyone in years. I'd never kissed a person with silky lips. Did I even like it? It was a little sickening. I wanted to do it more. It probably wouldn't happen again. We were in a crisis. It was the kind of thing that happens for no reason in a crisis in the middle of the night. What did it mean? I blushed thinking of the starved way I had acted. As if I had been dying to do that. When really it was the furthest thing from my mind. I raised my pointed finger in the air—Furthest thing from my mind!—but the jury was inscrutable. How would we be in the morning? Kubelko Bondy. Somehow it was hard to believe he would die now, since he was a part of this. *Soft* was the wrong word. *Satiny? Supple?* A new word, I would come up with it right now—which letters would I use? S, for sure. Maybe an O. Was this how words were made? How would I announce the word? Who would I contact about that?

IN THE MORNING HER BED was empty. I hurried into my shoes and took the elevator up to the NICU. The linoleum hallways were endless and fluorescent and the kissing episode was remote, just one of yesterday's many dramatic events. Today was day two of his life, hopefully. I washed my hands and put on the gown. Clee was hunched over the glass case, chanting her "sweet baby boy" hymn. Her braids were gone. Without looking at me she stepped back, so I could have a turn.

The tube down his throat looked huger today, as if he'd shrunken in the night. His tired black eyes had just opened when the tall Indian doctor appeared behind us.

"Good morning." He shook our hands. "Please come with me."

His face was grim and it occurred to me that we would now

be told the baby wasn't going to make it. Maybe he had already technically died and it was just the machines giving the illusion of life. Clee gave me a stricken look.

"Can she stay with the baby?" I asked. "He just woke up."

I followed the doctor across the room. I yearned for a lawyer and the right to make a phone call. But those rights were for arrested people. We got nothing. Whatever he told me would be the new reality and we'd just have to accept it. The doctor parked me in front of a skinny woman with a folder.

"This is Baby Boy Stengl's grandmother," he said, introducing me.

"I'm Carrie Spivack," said the woman, sashaying forward.

"Carrie is from Philomena Family Services."

And the doctor turned to leave, just like that. I grabbed him. "Shouldn't we wait to see if—"

He looked down at his pocket; my hand was in it. I took it out.

"If what?"

"If he lives?"

"Oh, he'll live. That's a tough kid. He just needs to show us he can use his lungs."

Carrie from Philomena Family Services brought out her hand again. I hugged her, brittle reed that she was. *He'll live.*

She stepped backward out of my arms; she wasn't that kind of Christian.

"I'm here to talk with your daughter—is that her over there?"

"No."

"It's not?"

"Now wouldn't be a good time."

"Of course it wouldn't."

"It wouldn't?"

"She's saying goodbye," Carrie said.

"Which might take a little while."

"You're right. There's an arc to adoption."

"An ark?"

"A beginning, a middle, and an end. The end is always the same."

"Well, I don't know."

"That's because she's in the beginning. Nobody knows in the beginning. She's right on track."

"How long does it take?"

"Not too long. I like to give a lot of space and let the hormones do the work."

"But approximately."

"Three days. In three days she'll be herself again."

Carrie said she would be back tomorrow and not to worry about a thing. Amy and Gary were on their way.

"They're coming here?"

"She won't have to meet them. Here's my card, just let her know she's not alone."

"She's *not* alone."

"Great."

CLEE'S FOREHEAD WAS AGAINST THE ISOLETTE. His eyes were shut again.

"Who was that?"

"The doctor said he'll live. He said he's a tough kid."

She straightened up. "A tough kid?" Her chin was trembling. She unclicked one of the circular doors and put her mouth into the arm hole. "Did you hear that, sweet boy?" she whispered. His skinny, mottled arms lay limply against his tiny torso. "You're tough."

I glanced across the room—did three days include today? Or

was yesterday the first day and today was already day two? Was she factoring in that we had kissed and kissed and kissed last night? I winced with embarrassment.

A nurse hurried past. "Excuse," she said, too busy for the *me*. I looked across the room at the parents who would blame each other for all eternity. They belonged here, both of them equally, as did the nurses and the doctors and Clee. None of them recognized the interloper among them, but they would soon. I'd gotten swept up in the drama of the situation and mistakenly involved myself.

It was time to go home.

He was going to live, Carrie Spivack was here, in three days from either yesterday or today Clee would be discharged without the baby. I would clean up, get the house ready. I pictured myself taking off my shoes and putting them in the rack on the porch. Funny how up until a few minutes ago I thought this incoherent fear, this limbo, was going to last forever. I tried smiling to see if it really was funny, ha ha. My hand went to my throat as it seized violently. Globus hystericus. I had thought it was gone for good but of course it wasn't. Nothing ever really changes.

I bent over the opposite side of the case. His fingers wiggled like underwater plants. How would I recognize him if we crossed paths later in life? These seaweed hands would be buried inside normal man hands. I wouldn't even be able to know him by name, because he didn't have one.

Almost! I said. There was no good way to be, so I was being cavalier, lancing my own heart. *We came pretty close. See you next time!*

Kubelko Bondy looked at me with disbelief, speechless.

I turned and walked out of the NICU before Clee looked up. I went down the elevator and into the lobby. I walked out of the lobby into the street. The sun was blinding. People were striding past thinking about sandwiches and feeling wronged. Where was I parked? Parking garage. I searched for my car, floor by floor, row by row. Ambulance. I'd come by ambulance. I'd have to call a cab. I didn't have my cell phone. It was in the room. Fine. Go back and get it. In and out again. I took the elevator back up to the seventh floor. Everything looked the same, the pig-faced nurse still had that face. How good this world was, with its large and real concerns. There was the couple who blamed each other—they were holding hands and smiling tenderly. I was a ghost, spying on my old life without me. Room 209. Clee would be making her way back from the NICU any second now. My cell phone, grab it and go.

She was sitting on the edge of her bed, crying. Something terrible had happened in the short time I was gone. She glared at me and made a shapeless angry sound.

"I couldn't find you. I looked all over."

Nothing terrible had happened.

"I was just trying to make a call." I patted my phone in my pocket to show her. My phone was actually in my pocket; it had been there all along. I'd come back for something else.

The last of her crying came out in a clotted sigh after the first kiss. We began a series of impatiently off-center ones, as if we were too hurried to land them properly; then our mouths became fingertips, moving blindly over the bumps and hollows of each feature. She stopped, pulled her head back a little and looked at me. Her mouth hung open and her eyes were slow with thought. She was studying my face like she was trying to break it down, find some appeal in it—or maybe figure out how she got here, how this could be happening.

"Come in here," she said, lifting the starched white sheet.

"There isn't enough room." I sat carefully on the edge of her bed. "Just come in."

I took off my shoes and she slowly, painfully scooched to one side of the twin bed. The combined width of our bottoms just barely fit inside the guardrails.

We began again, slowly this time. And deep. Her bosom, loose beneath the hospital smock, pressed against mine; she pushed her tongue into me with strong, mature movements and I held her face, that soft, honeyed skin. It was nothing like the things I had once done with her in my head. Phillip and the plumber and all the other men had missed the point completely. The point was kissing. Suddenly she froze, wincing.

"Are you in pain?"

"I am, actually," she said, a little curtly. It was startling how quickly she changed.

"Maybe you need more fluids?" I looked at her saline bag. "Should I call the nurse?"

She laughed hoarsely. "Let me just think about something else for a minute." She exhaled a long, controlled breath. "I guess I'm not ready to have these kinds of feelings."

"Which feelings?" I said.

"Sexual."

"Oh."

At eleven I brought us lunch from the cafeteria in the basement; she ate the minestrone soup and the crackers and the yellow cake and the orange juice and then she needed to take a nap. But only after kissing my neck while running one hand through my short hair. It was like a dream, where the most unlikely person can't get enough of you—a movie star or someone's husband. How can this be? But the attraction is mutual and undeniable; it is the reason for itself. And like a surprise on the moon or a surprise on the battlefield, astonishment was native to these parts. The climate in 209 was fetid, breeding an exotic flower instead of the natural thing that Carrie Spivack had described. Or maybe she would say that things often became very sensual right before the release of the baby on the third day; maybe this was part of the arc. Tomorrow was day three.

I waited for her to wake up and when she didn't I went up to the NICU by myself. A couple was taking off their gowns as I was putting on mine. They were talking about used cars.

"You would never buy a car without kicking the tires first," he said, balling up his gown and throwing it in the recycling by mistake.

"You would if you were taking a leap of faith and trusting that God knew what you could handle."

"I'm pretty sure God would not want you to buy a falling-apart old junker."

"Well, it's too late now," she said, making a fist around her purse strap. She looked older than her picture on ParentProfiles.com, both of them did. They reeked of their house back in Utah, its old carpets suffused with cigarette smoke. This would be the smell of his life, of him.

"Is it?" Gary said. "Is it too late—legally?" He was scared. He really did not want the car they had bought. "Yes, it is," she said. Then she gave him a look like *Let's not talk about this in front of that woman.* They were terrible people, even slightly worse than most. I stalled, fumbling with the sleeves of my gown. Should I introduce myself or try to kill them? Not violently, just enough that they wouldn't exist. Amy gave me a polite nod as they exited. I nodded back, watching the door swing shut. It occurred to me that the doctor had said only that the baby would live. Not that he would run, or eat food, or talk. Living just meant not dying, it didn't necessarily include any bells and whistles.

Kubelko Bondy's eyes were wide open and waiting.

Every single thing about you is perfect, I told him.

You came back, he said. I bowed my head and tried to come up with a promise that would allow for nothing being in my control.

I love your dear little shoulders, I said. *And I always will.*

Clee slept until noon and then we went back up together. She put her arm around me in the elevator and kept it there as we walked down the hall. Our hips bumped together in a difficult syncopated rhythm. We passed the couple who used to blame each other and they nodded without flinching. I thought to myself that these would always be the first people I came "out of the closet" to. They seemed very accepting. A few of the nurses looked silently startled by our new intimacy. Maybe because they had thought I was Clee's mother. Or maybe because they were now dealing with two sets of parents and we weren't the real ones. Clee gave me a peck on the lips in front of the Isolette. In this quiet way we came out to the baby.

Carrie Spivack had been here too; her Philomena Family Services card was sticking out of the plastic name tag that said Baby Boy Stengl. I palmed it like a magician and moved it into my pocket.

"We can't keep calling him 'the baby,'" I whispered.

"Okay. Do you have a name?"

This moved me, that she thought I had any right to name him. I pictured trying to explain the name Kubelko Bondy.

"It should come from you, you're his mom."

She laughed, or I thought it was a laugh—it ended in a gasping kind of swallow. We noticed a strange red mark on his tiny arm. I waved over a nurse with bleached-blond hair.

"Hi, little dude," she croaked, checking his monitor. "It's a big day for you." She reeked of perfume, perhaps to cover the smell of cigarettes. The mark: a cigarette burn. I felt alive with anger. But I was a manager and knew how to handle this; I could already picture her crying after what I was about to say.

"He comes off the ventilator later today," she continued. "So we hope he's a good little breather."

Clee and I glanced at each other with alarm. Breathing. That was on the top of our list of things we hoped he would be able to do.

"Will you be involved in taking it out?" I said nervously. *Please no.*

"Yep. We'll put him on CPAP—continuous air—and see how he adapts." She winked. It wasn't a kindly wink, it was a wink that said all the other nurses and all the employees at Open Palm have told me about you, and now—wink—we get our revenge. I looked at her name tag. CARLA. It was too late to buy Carla a gift certificate or a Ninja five-cup smoothie maker. Maybe some candy or a coffee.

She looked at the mark on his arm and made a clicking noise.

"Sometimes when they take the IV out it leaves a mark. But if I'd done it"—she winked again—"there wouldn't be a mark."

The wink was a tic. It wasn't cruel or conspiring, it was just a thing she did. Obviously smoking wasn't allowed in the Neonatal Intensive Care Unit. I watched her arrange the cords around his body so they wouldn't poke at him. Her fingers were quick, like she'd done this nine hundred times before.

Clee asked what time the ventilator would come out.

"It's scheduled for four o'clock. You can visit him afterward—he'll be sedated, but he should be much more comfortable."

"Thank you, Carla," I said. "We appreciate everything you're doing." It wasn't enough, it sounded fake and silly.

"You're welcome." The nurse smiled with her whole face; she didn't think it was silly.

"We do," I repeated vehemently, "we really appreciate everything you're doing."

AT FOUR THIRTY WE CALLED the NICU from the floor below.

"It's taking them a little bit longer than expected," said the receptionist. "The doctor's still with him. We'll call you when it's done."

"Is it the tall Indian doctor?"

"Yes, Dr. Kulkarni."

"He's good, right?"

"He's the best."

I hung up.

"He's with the tall Indian doctor and they said he's the best."

"Dr. Kulkarni?"

I asked Clee to recite all the names of the nurses and doctors while I wrote them down. The short, beefy male nurse was Francisco, the toothy Asian one with glasses was Cathy, Tammy was the pig-faced one.

"How do you know all of this?"

"They have name tags."

The room grew dark and we didn't turn on the light. We would turn on the light when good news came and if it never came we would live in the dark like this forever.

FIFTEEN MORE MINUTES PASSED. AND then another five. I got up from my cot and turned on the fluorescents.

"Let's name him," I said.

Clee blinked in the light.

"Did you think about a name?"

She put a finger in the air and took a sip of water. *She forgot to think of a name. She's making one up on the spot.* My old disgust for her was just right there.

"I have two names," she said, and cleared her throat. "The first might seem kind of like it doesn't fit him right now, but I think it will later." I felt shame for my disgust. The shame felt like love.

"Okay."

"I'll just say it," she said, hesitating.

"Just say it."

"Little Fatty."

I waited with no expression, to see if this was really the name.

"Because"—her eyes suddenly filled with tears, her voice cracked—"he *will* be fat one day."

I put my arm around her. "It's a really nice name. Little Fatty."

"Little Fatty," she whispered tearfully.

"I don't think I've ever known anyone named that." I rubbed her back. "What's the other name?" I asked nonchalantly, knowing this other name would be his name, no matter what it was.

She took a deep breath and on the exhale said, "Jack."

AT FIVE THIRTY THEY CALLED to tell us that the ventilator was out and he was breathing well on CPAP. We hurried upstairs.

He looked completely different without a big tube in his mouth. He was a baby, a cute little baby with a plastic prong in his nostrils.

"Hi, Jack," whispered Clee.

Jack is your name now, I explained. *But Kubelko Bondy will always be the name of your soul.* I took a breath and forced myself to add: *You will also have a third name, the one Amy and Gary give you. It might be Travis, it might be Braden. We don't know yet.*

We stood on either side of the incubator and each put a hand in. He squeezed Clee's finger in his right hand and my finger in his left. He thought they were fingers from one person, a person with one old hand and one young hand. We stood like this for twenty-five or thirty minutes. My back ached and my hand was numb. Every once in a while Clee and I would look over the plastic case at each other and my stomach would go tumbling backward. A chaplain came in and began blessing babies. I looked around to see if this was legal. What about the separation of church and state? No one cared. Eventually he paused in front of Jack and before I could shake my head no, Clee nodded. His prayer swept across the three of us; my face tingled and my head spun dizzily. I felt holy, almost married.

As we walked arm in arm back to 209 I became aware that the woman clicking down the hall in front of us was Carrie Spivack. I subtly slowed our gait and waited for her to peel off to the left or right. But of course she did not, because she was headed for our room. It was day three. Up ahead was a fire extinguisher and a window. I chose the window. Speaking was risky so I just gestured, making an expansive motion toward the view. Clee peered down at the parking lot. The couple who'd once blamed each other ambled toward us, stopping with bemused smiles to see what we were looking at. The four of us peered out the window. A middle-aged man was helping an elderly woman out of a wheelchair and into the front seat of a station wagon.

"That'll be us one day," said the wife of the couple who'd once blamed each other. "Me and Jay Jay." Her husband squeezed her shoulder. I guessed Jay Jay was the name of their baby.

The elderly woman's legs didn't work at all, so her son was lifting her from the wheelchair to the passenger seat in one prolonged and unwieldy motion. His mother's hands were clasped around his neck, holding on for dear life. Amy of Amy and Gary would hang on to Jack's neck like this one day. Right now it was much too tiny but one day he would be a sturdy middle-aged man, maybe even brawny or burly. He would move his mother with a much swifter motion than this man was able to, saying *There you go, Ma, lemme buckle you and we'll be set to go.* My jealousy overwhelmed me; I had to look away.

Carrie Spivack straightened up as we approached, sharpening the corners of her smile and swinging our door open like a hostess. Clee walked right in, thinking she was just another nurse wanting to check her blood pressure.

"I'm sure you don't mind giving us a moment alone," Carrie Spivack said to me. She'd figured out I wasn't the grandma. Or anyone. Behind her Clee gave me a confused shrug and a little half smile. The same half smile the passengers on the *Titanic* gave to their loved ones on the pier as the boat pushed away. Bon voyage, Kitty! Bon voyage, Estelle!

I floated back down the hall to the elevator.

"Going down?" It was a young Latino couple holding a newborn baby. Blue balloons bobbed from the wheelchair handle.

"Okay, I'll go down."

The couple was vibrating; this was the most incredible moment of their lives. They were about to take their baby into the world, the real world. The baby had lots of wet-looking black hair and was fatter than Jack. When the doors opened, the young father glanced back at me and I gave him a nod to say, *Yep, your life, here it is, go into it.* And they went.

I walked around the lobby. I scrolled through the numbers in my phone; there was no one to call. I mechanically deleted all my saved messages, except the one I'd left myself last year. The ten maximum-loud NOs sounded like wails, an inconsolable woman howling in the street, NO NO NO NO NO NO NO NO NO NO.

No one was in the cafeteria except a cashier. I ordered some hot water; it came with a slice of lemon and a napkin. I sipped it very slowly, burning my mouth each time. Three of the walls were white, and the fourth was painted in pinks and oranges. It took a little work to see it was a mural of a sunset in a place like Tuscany or Rhodesia. The door I had come through was in the beach part; to the left of the sun an empty paper towel dispenser hung open like a slack jaw, dumbfounded. Not a single thought could be had about what was happening upstairs. It was unthinkable. A railing had been painted along the bottom of the wall, placing the viewer on the terrace of a villa or maybe a palazzo. The salt air filled my nose; giant waves crashed on the rocks below, one after another after another. I cried and cried. Seagulls keened near the ceiling. Far in the distance a figure walked up the beach. He or she was clothed in a flowing white gown. Golden hair and warm Mediterranean smile. She waved. I wiped my face with the backs of my hands. She dropped into the chair next to me.

"I looked in the lobby first," she said.

"I was there for a while." I blew my nose on the paper napkin.

She glanced around. "Not very crowded, is it?"

"No."

She pressed on my lemon slice and licked her finger.

"I didn't realize that place was so Jesusy."

"What place?"

"Philomena Whatever. If Amy and Gary hadn't wanted him he would have gone to some other gross Christian family."

A weird thing began to happen with the mural. The sun started rising, very, very slowly.

"The lady was okay, though—she didn't try to hard-sell me or anything. I just said my situation had changed." She picked up my hand.

Or maybe it had always been rising; maybe it was a mural of a sunrise, not a sunset. *Oh, my boy. My sweet Kubelko Bondy.*

"I'm not wrong about that, am I?" Clee said, sitting up. "This thing between us?"

"No, you're right," I whispered.

"I thought I was." She settled back in her chair, extending her legs in a wide V. "But communication . . . you know. I believe in communication."

I said I did too and she said she thought Jack was a pretty cool baby and while she hadn't planned on being a mom, it didn't seem that hard unless your kid was a jerk, which she was 100 percent sure Jack wasn't. "Plus," she added, "I thought you'd be psyched."

I said I was psyched. Eight or nine immediate questions came to mind vis-à-vis her relationship to me and my relationship to the boy but I didn't want to undo anything by overwhelming her. She rubbed her thumb deep into my palm and said, "I need a nickname for you."

"Maybe Cher?" I suggested.

"*Cher?* That sounds like an old man's name. No, let me think for minute."

She thought with her knuckles against her head and then she said, "Okay, I've got it. Boo."

"Boo?"

"Boo."

"Like a ghost?"

"No, like Boo, like you're my Boo."

"Okay. That's interesting. Boo."

"Boo."

"Boo."

CHAPTER ELEVEN

Once the nurses heard that Clee was keeping Baby Boy Stengl, they gave her a breast pump and told her to pump every two hours.

"Even if nothing comes out, just keep pumping," said Cathy. Carla nodded in agreement. "Don't look at the bottles, just relax. It'll come. Bring us every little drop, and we'll give it to him when he's off the IV."

Clee chuckled nervously, holding the pump at arm's length. "I don't know. Yeah. No. I don't think so." She handed it back to Cathy. "It's not my thing."

That evening a barrel-chested old woman named Mary wheeled a pump into our room. "I'm the lactation consultant for this hospital and for Cedars-Sinai. I can get milk out of a fly." I explained Clee wasn't going to nurse; Mary retorted with a short speech about breast milk decreasing the baby's risk of diabetes, cancer, lung problems, and allergies. Clee unbuttoned her shirt, blushing, with her head down. Her breasts hung long and pink. I'd never seen them before. Mary pressed different cones over the nipples with a brusque efficiency.

"You get me, you get properly sized. You're a size large."

Clee's lowered head was motionless, her face completely curtained by her hair.

Mary attached the bottles to the cones and turned on the ancient machine. *Shoop-pa, shoop-pa, shoop-pa.* Clee's nipples were rhythmically sucked in and out.

"Just like a cow. Ever been on a farm? No different from a cow. You hold these now." Clee held the cups against her own chest.

"Anything coming out?" Mary peered at the bottles. "No. Well, stick with it. Ten minutes every two hours."

As soon as Mary left I turned off the machine.

"That was awful, I'm sorry."

Clee clicked it on again without looking up.

Shoop-pa, shoop-pa. Her nipples became grotesquely elongated with each suck.

"Can you give me a little space?" she said.

I quickly walked to the other side of the room.

"I don't like my chest looked at. I'm not into it."

"Sorry," I said. "I wish I could be the one who did it."

Shoop-pa. Shoop-pa.

"Why's that?"

"I just don't think I would mind it."

Shoop-pa.

"You don't think I can make milk?"

"No. I didn't mean that."

"You think a cow can do it but I can't?"

Shoop-pa, shoop-pa.

"No, of course you can do it! *And* a cow can! You both can."

NOTHING CAME OUT THAT NIGHT. She set the alarm on her phone for two A.M., four A.M., and six A.M. Nothing. At eight A.M. Mary came by and checked.

"Anything? No? Keep going. Think about your baby. What's your baby's name?"

"Jack."

"Think about Jack."

Clee tethered herself to the machine. She didn't want to go to the NICU with no milk so I went up alone and told Jack how hard his mom was working to make him a delicious meal. When I got back she was pumping. Empty bottles.

"I told him how hard his mom was working."

"You called me Mom to him?"

"Mommy? Mother? What do you want to be called?"

Shoop-pa, shoop-pa. Her eyes seethed with frustration.

"Fucking shit." She banged on the pump with her fist, knocking a cup and a fork off the table with an incredible clatter.

Shoop-pa, shoop-pa, shoop-pa.

IT WAS DAWN AND SHE was touching my ear. I was dreaming that the pump was on, but it wasn't, everything was very quiet, it was dawn, and she was touching my ear. Tracing its perfect edges with her finger. The first light of the day was creeping into the tiny room. I smiled at her. She smiled and pointed at her bedside table. Milk. Two bottles, each with an eighth inch of yellow milk in them.

Clee was discharged the next morning. But Jack, of course, was not. Dr. Kulkarni said he would be released when he was able to drink two ounces of milk and digest them properly.

"I'm guessing two weeks," he said. "Or less. Or more. He needs to show us he can nipple his own feeds; suck and swallow."

He started to move away. Clee was waiting with her purse and street clothes on. I grabbed his sleeve.

"Yes?" said the doctor. I hesitated; it was taking me a moment to draw together all the facets of my question. I was wondering if my life, the life in which I had a son and a beautiful, young girlfriend, could exist outside of the hospital. Or was the hospital its container? Was I like honey thinking it's a small bear, not realizing the bear is just the shape of its bottle?

"I can guess what's on your mind," Dr. Kulkarni said.

"Really?"

He nodded. "It's too early to tell but he's recovering beautifully so far."

We told Jack we would be back in the morning and then we left and then we doubled back because I hadn't said I love you—*I love you, my sweet potato*—and we left again, walking shakily out the front doors and into the sunlight. We held hands in the back of the cab. My street looked the same. My neighbor two doors down was wheeling in her trash cans and watched us hobble to the door. Clee started to slip off her shoes.

"You don't have to do that."

"No, I want to."

"It's your house as much as mine now."

"I've gotten used to it."

Everything was as we had left it. There was dried blood all over the bedroom. Snails were clustered on the kitchen ceiling. Towels lay in strange places. Rick's bowls of hot water were waiting on the dresser, cold. I cleaned quickly while Clee pumped, whipping her sleeping bag off the couch and stuffing it into the linen closet.

Before she climbed into my bed for the first time she mumbled an apology about the way her feet smelled.

"The color therapy didn't work."

"It didn't work for me either."

"Did you know Dr. Broyard's wife is the famous Dutch painter Helge Thomasson?"

"He told you that?"

"No, someone in the waiting room did."

"The receptionist?"

"No, another patient."

We got under the covers and held hands. Cheating on a housewife was understandable, he might have done it for the intellectual stimulation alone—but shame on Dr. Broyard for not rising to the challenge of Helge Thomasson. I had never heard of her but she was obviously a formidable woman. Clee put her hand on my stomach for a moment and then took it off.

"Dr. Binwali said I could have sex in eight weeks."

I smiled like someone's nervous aunt. The topic hadn't come up since that first day. Some women just kiss and give back rubs and leave it at that. I wondered if her old aggression would come back. Perhaps it would be like a simulation. We might begin on the "park bench"—she grabs my breast. But instead of fighting her off I just let her rape me. Would we need to buy a rubber penis? I had seen a store for things like that next to a pet store in a strip mall on Sunset.

"The muscles," she said. "They won't contract."

An orgasm. That's what she couldn't have for eight weeks.

"But I could, you know, for you. If you want."

"No, no," I said quickly. "Let's wait. Until we both can." I liked this way of talking where the verbs were left out. Maybe we would never say them.

"Okay, good." She squeezed my hand. "I hope I can wait that long," she added.

"Me too, it's so hard to wait."

I WOKE WITH A START like a passenger on an airplane—for a moment I could feel how high I was and had an appropriate terror of falling. It was three A.M. We had just left him there. Tiny him. He was alone in the NICU, lying there in his plastic box. Oh, Kubelko. A howl was curdling inside me; the ache felt inhuman. Or maybe this was my first human feeling. Would I put on my clothes and drive to the hospital right now? I waited to see if I would. I looked at her yellow hair spread across the pillow that I usually wedged between my legs. None of this would last. It was all a preposterous dream. I pushed myself out of consciousness.

The radio and the sun were blaring. "What kind of music do you like?" Clee said, rolling through some staticky stations. I rubbed my eyes. I had never used my clock radio as anything but a clock.

"I bet you like this." She paused on a country music station and looked at me. "No?" She scrolled, watching my face. Different kinds of jangly and upsetting music passed by.

"Maybe that."

"This?"

"I like classical."

She turned it up and lay back down, putting her arm around me. I didn't have a favorite kind of music. Eventually I would have to tell her that.

"This can be our song," she whispered. She couldn't wait to get started on having a girlfriend.

We listened until the end to get the name; it was unendurably long. Finally a snobby British man came on. It was a Gregorian chant from the seventh century called "Deum verum."

"This doesn't have to be our song."

"Too late."

WE VISITED JACK EVERY MORNING and evening. Each time we entered the NICU in our gowns and clean hands I dreaded the news, but he was getting stronger every day. Clee thought we were out of the woods and it seemed like we probably were; all the nurses said he was the toughest white baby they'd ever seen. We converted the ironing room into a nursery and bought onesies and diapers and wipes and a crib and a changing table and a changing pad and a changing pad cover and a soft tray called a "sleeper" and a first-aid kit and a whale-shaped bathtub and baby shampoo and baby washcloths and towels and swaddling blankets and burp cloths and squeaky toys and cloth books and a video baby monitor and a diaper bag and a diaper pail and an expensive personal breast pump with its own carrying case. It would still be at least a week before Jack could nurse but he was drinking her milk handily through a feeding tube.

"It has a really powerful motor," Clee said admiringly. "It's the same motor that's in power tools and the blenders professional bakers use to make dough. Same exact motor." She wore the strap of the case diagonally across her chest like a bike messenger bag.

BEING IN STORES TOGETHER WAS a new pleasure, as was being in the car, or a restaurant, or walking from the car to the restaurant. Each time the scenery changed we were brand-new all over again. We strolled around the Glendale Galleria mall, arm in arm, chins held high. I liked to watch men ogle her and see the way their faces changed when I put my hand in hers. Me! A woman who was too old to qualify and in fact had never qualified, not even at her age. Anyone who questions what satisfaction can be gained from a not-so-bright girlfriend half one's age has never had one. It just feels good all over. It's like wearing something beautiful and eating something delicious at the same time, all the time. Phillip knew—he knew and he'd tried to tell me, but I hadn't listened. I couldn't help but wonder if he'd heard the news about me and Clee.

She was more than young, she was chivalrous: holding doors open, carrying bags—not paying for things, because she didn't have any money, but pointing out what she thought would look good on me. She steered me into a lingerie store so I could get some "curtains," as she called them. The stuff she picked out was frilly and girlish looking, totally inappropriate for someone my age, with my body. Wiry salt-and-pepper pubic hairs poked through the sheer pink panties, but she never saw—she just asked me to wear them out of the store.

"You've got the curtains on?"

"Yes."

She threw her arm over my shoulder.

WHEN TAMMY THE PIG-FACED nurse asked us if we'd started skin-to-skin yet we both went red. We had never even been naked together.

"Skin-to-skin helps to regulate the baby's heart rate and breathing, and of course it's great for the mother-baby bond."

"No," I whispered, catching up. "We've haven't held him yet."

"Who wants to go first?"

"Cheryl," said Clee quickly. "Because I really have to go to the bathroom."

Tammy glanced at me. She had thought I was Clee's mom right up until the moment she saw us kissing by the elevator. I took off my blouse and bra and hung them on the back of a chair. Tammy wrangled Jack's lines and tubes, carefully lifting him out of his case. He grimaced and twisted in the air like a caterpillar. She placed him between my breasts and adjusted his limbs so that his skin and my skin were touching as much as possible, tucking a thin pink cotton blanket over the two of us. And then she left.

I looked behind me. Clee was in the bathroom. Jack's little chest pushed in and out; his machines were quiet. He made a snuffling noise and his enormous black eyes lurched upward.

Hi, he said.

Hi, I said.

We'd been waiting for this since I was nine. I leaned back and tried to relax with my hand cupping the whole of his legs and bottom. I felt like a statue of something virtuous. *Here we are. Here we really are.* It was hard to stay present, the moment kept jumping around like a sunspot. Across the room Jay Jay was settled on his mom's chest in the same position covered by the same pink blanket. We smiled at each other.

"What's his name?" she whispered.

"Jack," I whispered.

"Really?"

"Yeah."

"That's *his* name," she said, pointing to Jay Jay.

"You're kidding."

"No."

"What are the chances?"

"Don't move." It was Clee; she took a picture on her phone and then kissed my ear.

"Guess what that baby's name is?" I said.

"Jack, I know," she said. "That's where I got the idea."

"You named our baby after their baby?"

Clee looked annoyed. "We don't know them—we're never going to see them again. I thought it was a nice name."

The other Jack's mom looked both flattered and offended. Clee patted our Jack right on his soft spot, undeterred. Was all this real to her? Did she think it was temporary? Or maybe that was the point of love: not to think.

CHAPTER TWELVE

She behaved a little more like a guest now, folding her clothes and putting them in a careful stack on my dresser while inadvertently knocking over all my lotions and jewelry. For the first few days back we tried to eat at the kitchen table and have conversations, but I could tell it just wasn't her thing, so I sat with her on the couch and we watched TV during dinner. I even ate microwave meals sometimes; they all had the same brown sweetness, even the very salty ones. I washed her breast pump parts and helped her label the bottles with the date; she took pictures of us and decorated them with an app called Heartify. We were kids playing married—it was exciting just to brush our teeth side by side, pretending we were used to it. She may have thought I'd done all this before because I had a late-blooming flair for cohabitation—ideas just came to me. The first weekend I bought a chalkboard and hung it next to my calendar, above the phone.

"For phone messages. The chalk is in this dish. There's all the colors plus white."

"Everyone calls me on my cell," she said, "but I can write your messages there. If you want me to answer. Usually I just let it go to voice mail."

"You can really write anything on the chalkboard. It could be for encouraging sayings, like each Sunday we put a saying for the week." I wrote DON'T GIVE UP in blue chalk and then erased it. "That was just an example. We can alternate weeks."

"I don't know that many sayings."

"Or tally marks—like if you need to keep track of anything, you can do it here."

She looked at me for a moment and then picked up the purple chalk and made a little mark in the upper left-hand corner of the chalkboard.

"Exactly," I said, putting the chalk back in the dish.

"Do you want to know what it's for?"

"What's it for?"

"Each time I think: *I love you.*"

I straightened all the chalks so they were in a row before I looked up. Not smiling, no, she was serious and excited. I could tell this was the kind of thing she'd been planning to say to a woman for a long time.

"See how it's up in the corner like that?" Her lips against my ear. "I left lots of room for the future."

TAMMY SAID IT WAS TIME to try nursing. "Come back for his four o'clock feeding. First child, right? The nurse on duty will help you get the hang of it."

I looked at Clee. She was squinting at the ceiling.

At four there was a new young nurse with short hair, Sue. She looked at her clipboard.

"So it looks like the mother"—her eyes moved back and forth between us—"will be nursing for the first time?"

"Actually, no," said Clee firmly. "I've decided to stick with the pump."

"Oh," Sue said. She was looking around the room hoping another nurse would be interested.

"Is Lin your married name?" Clee asked, touching the nurse's name tag with a roguish frown.

Sue Lin smiled at the clipboard, adjusting the pen on it until it dropped to the floor.

"No, I mean it is, I'm not—I guess it's okay if you give a bottle."

I watched Clee swagger over to the Isolette.

"Isn't it important that she nurses?" I said. "For bonding?"

Sue blushed. "Yes, of course. Next time she should breastfeed."

But she didn't, she dodged it every time. I learned to hold the tiny bottle like a pencil, tease his lips until they opened, point the nipple at the roof of his mouth.

This is Clee's milk, not mine.

It was important to give credit where it was due. He sucked and swallowed with his eyes locked on me.

THE PICTURE CLEE CHOSE FOR the birth announcement was the one of me and him she'd taken with her phone. She kneaded my shoulders while I designed it on my laptop.

"Can the writing be a little more fun?" she said.

"You mean a different font?"

"Maybe."

I put everything in chubby cartoon letters as a joke.

"That looks good," she said. She was right. The cartoon letters had a love of life in them, and wasn't that what we were celebrating here?

JACK STENGL-GLICKMAN
BORN 3-23-2013
5 LBS. 6 OZ.

We sent it to all of Clee's friends, her parents, Jim and all the other Open Palm employees, both our relatives, and everyone else we could think of except for Rick, who we had no way of reaching. Rick probably thought Clee and I were lesbians together all along. To everyone else it had to be a shock, but they all replied with the same appropriate word: *congratulations*. Some people, like Suzanne and Carl, did not respond at all. When Clee was asleep I quietly addressed an e-mail to Phillip and pasted in the announcement. Surely he had heard about my very young girlfriend by now. I stared at his name on the screen. Of course, there's young and then there's young. Sixteen was too young. Improbably young. I picked up my phone and scrolled until I found the picture of the girl in the Rasta alligator shirt. Who was she? Because she wasn't K-ear-sten. There was no Kirsten; that was suddenly obvious. No sixteen-year-old girl yearns for a man nearing seventy. I gasped quietly and smiled. The texts were a game! A little game between consenting adults. What a saucy flirt he was. I erased the birth announcement and then, command-V, pasted it in again. How to put it? What to say? Or was it better to call? Or text? Or just come over?

I looked down at my hands; they were clasping each other like two giddy bridesmaids.

What was I thinking?

I deleted the e-mail, closed the computer, and turned out the light. Clee was spread across the bed like a person falling; I folded myself around her.

NEAR THE END OF THE week we stopped by Open Palm together. Clee passed her phone around and Nakako and Sarah and Aya cooed over the pictures of Jack and told her how thin she looked.

I had missed a lot of work. Jim said not to worry, I had six weeks' maternity leave plus my sick days—but he had trouble looking me in the eye.

"Want to see the new Kick It banner?" He unfurled it on the floor and I called Clee over.

"What do you think, hon?"

"I don't know anything about this stuff, Boo." She rubbed the small of my back. I covertly scanned the room to see the reaction. Michelle was red-faced. Jim kept his eyes on the floor. Everyone else was working.

"But that's what's great, hon, you have fresh eyes."

Jim took me aside.

"You know I have no problem with it. I'm happy for you."

"Thank you."

"But I'm not the one who calls the shots around here."

"What are you saying?"

"Carl and Suzanne are here—they're with Kristof in the ware-house."

"They're in the warehouse right now?"

"They're waiting for you to leave."

I went outside and walked down the block to the warehouse. They were peering out the big windows but quickly turned away as I approached. I asked Kristof to take a ten-minute break.

"Actually, Kristof, you can stay," Suzanne said. "Stay right where you are." Kristof froze between us, one foot poised in midstep.

I held up my phone. "Your grandson is beautiful. Would you like to see?"

"Do you know what a *persona non grata* is?" Carl said.

"Yes."

"It's Latin for *person not great*."

Kristof started to say something and then stopped himself. Maybe he knew Latin.

"For Clee's sake we're not going to fire you, but you're a persona non grata. And you're not on the board anymore."

Kristof looked at me, waiting for my reaction. I put my phone away. It wasn't hard to see the situation from their point of view; they'd trusted me and look what happened.

"It was her decision to keep Jack," I said.

Kristof looked at Suzanne and Carl.

"It's not about the baby. It's about your inappropriate relations with our daughter."

Kristof whipped his head back to me.

Jack. Your grandson's name is Jack.

"You don't know what our relations are."

"We have a pretty good idea."

"We haven't had sex."

"I see."

Kristof didn't seem to believe this either.

"Her doctor said she can't have sex for eight weeks."

"Eight weeks from when?" Kristof asked.

"From the birth."

Suzanne and Carl exchanged a look of relief.

"That's May eighteenth," I continued. "You might want to mark your calendars. That's the day we're going to have intercourse." I realized that was probably the wrong word for it but I forged on. "And then every day after that. Many times a day, in every position, all over the place, probably even in here."

Kristof let out a Swedish whoop of excitement and then caught himself. Too late. Suzanne fired him on the spot—her face shaking with regret about things she had not nipped while they were still in the bud.

WE HAD A REAL RHYTHM GOING. We slept in, visited Jack for two hours, then did errands and went out to lunch, came home and took a nap, visited Jack for one more hour, home by eight, watched TV until twelve or one and went to bed. We slept a lot because we had this great position—Clee held me from behind and our bodies interlocked like two Ss.

"Not many people could do this," I said, squeezing her arms. "Everyone does this."

"But not fitting together so perfectly the way we do."

"Any two people can do it."

Sometimes I looked at her sleeping face, the living flesh of it, and was overwhelmed by how precarious it was to love a living thing. She could die simply from lack of water. It hardly seemed safer than falling in love with a plant.

After two weeks it felt like this was the only way we had ever lived. We still kissed frequently, usually a cluster of short pecks. An acronym for our early deep kisses. Which in a way was more intimate, because only we knew what it stood for.

"We shouldn't pressure them to let us bring him home," said Clee. A peck.

"No, of course not." A peck back. Another peck. A third. She pulled her head back.

"You were being a little bit pressuring this morning."

"I was? What did I say?"

"You said 'We can't wait.' But we can wait. We can wait forever if that's what's best for him."

"Well, not *forever*. He can't be an old man in the NICU."

"He can if that's what's best for him. When they say he's ready to go, we'll say 'Are you one hundred and twelve percent sure?'"

But it wasn't like that; it wasn't a conversation. Jack had an MRI, it came back normal. The next day he drank two ounces of milk, passed a healthy stool, and was declared fit for discharge. There were forms to fill out; he was given shots. As he signed our outtake papers, Dr. Kulkarni said Baby Boy Stengl had made a complete recovery—"It doesn't take much to be a baby, though. You'll know more in a year."

Clee and I exchanged a look.

"But he made a complete recovery," I said, keeping my voice very even.

"Right, but as with any child, you won't know if he can run until he runs."

"Okay. I see. And besides running? Should we keep an eye out for anything in the future?"

"Oh, the future. I see." A shadow fell over the doctor's face. "You're wondering if your son will get cancer? Or be hit by a car? Or be bipolar? Or have autism? Or drug problems? I don't know, I'm not a psychic. Welcome to parenthood." He swiveled and walked away.

Clee and I stood with our mouths agape. Carla and Tammy looked at each other knowingly.

"Don't worry," Tammy said, "you'll know if something's wrong. A mother knows."

"Just make sure he hits his milestones," said Carla. "Smiling is the first one. You want to see a smile by"—she counted on her fingers—"the fourth of July. Not a gassy smile, a real one." She threw open her mouth, producing a daft, infantile grin, and then reabsorbed it. Tammy handed Clee and me each a baby doll with a movable jaw and guided us into a room with a TV. We sat down in a daze, holding the dolls.

"Infant CPR," the nurse whispered, pressing play on the remote. "Just come out when you're done." She tiptoed away, gently shutting the door behind her.

We sat side by side and watched a mother come upon her unbreathing baby. "Maria?" She shook the baby. "*MARIA!*" Her face was gripped with terror. She called 911 and then, because she didn't know infant CPR, she waited, howling, while her baby probably died in front of her.

We breathed desperately into our dolls' mouths and pushed on their chests in dirty, well-worn spots. Never before had we simulated with such passion. I looked sideways at Clee, wondering if she was reminded of the how-to videos we had both watched long ago. This was self-defense too, in a way. Now poor Maria choked on a grape.

"I don't know if I can do this," Clee said, pushing her doll aside.

"You can," I reassured her. "It's almost over." But she stared at me, intent with some unspeakable, specific meaning. Motherhood. She didn't know if she could do it. I looked away, pounding on my baby doll's back, one, two, three times, then I put my ear to his mouth, listening for a breath.

CHAPTER THIRTEEN

There were no machines at home. If Jack's blood pressure or heart rate or oxygen intake went up or down there was no way to know. He ate every hour around the clock; Clee was almost never not pumping and I was always warming, washing, or holding a bottle. She moved back to the couch and Jack slept in the bed with me in the sleeper tray. Every few seconds I had to put my hand on him to calm him but I couldn't fall asleep that way because the full weight of my palm would crush him. I lay with my hand hovering for hours. This led to an excruciating shoulder and neck problem that normally would have been my top concern. I ignored it. He was colicky—after each bottle he writhed and bucked in agony for hours at a time. "Do something do something," screamed Clee. He stopped moving his bowels. I massaged his stomach and cycled his legs. Clearly, something was very wrong with him; a smile by the fourth of July seemed unlikely at best, since he was hardly more than a pile of guts. His face was covered in scratches, but neither of us felt confident enough to cut his nails. My shoulder worsened. After the first week I moved Jack's tray to the floor and slept beside him there. I didn't bathe him because I was too afraid he would slip out of my hands or his belly button would open. Then one night I woke at three A.M. certain he was rotting like a chicken carcass. Only as I lowered him into the sink did I realize this was a crazy time to wash a baby and I began to cry because he was so trusting—I could do anything and he would go along with it, the little fool.

Clee only pumped. Sometimes she slept while she pumped. Mostly she watched TV on mute. If I couldn't find her, she was outside, sitting on the curb. When I complained that she wasn't helping, she said, "Do you want him to drink formula?" As if she really wanted to help but couldn't. She was the worst possible person to do this with—that was evident now, but what could I do? There was no time to get into it and Jack still hadn't had a bowel movement. It had been twelve days. All the dishes were dirty and Clee tried to wash them all at once in the bathtub—she said she'd done it before. The drain clogged immediately, and the fat plumber came, the same one; Jack took one look at him and had a massive bowel movement that exploded his diaper; yellow cottage cheese was everywhere. I cried with relief, kissing him and wiping his skinny bottom. Clee said I'm sorry and I said No I am and that night I moved back to the bed, wondering why I had ever thought sleeping on the floor would help anything. Clee stayed on the couch. That was fine, we still had four weeks left until the consummation date set by Dr. Binwali.

Besides pooping and eating and sleeping, he hiccoughed and made sticky pterodactyl sounds, he yawned and experimentally pushed his clumsy tongue through the small O of his lips. Clee asked if he could see in the dark like a cat and I said yes. Later I caught my mistake but it was five A.M. and she was asleep. The next day I forgot. Each day I forgot to tell her he couldn't see in the dark like a cat and each night I remembered, with increasing urgency. What if this continued for years and I never told her? My body was so tired that it often floated next to me or above me, and

I had to reel it in like a kite. Finally one night I wrote "He can't see in the dark" on a slip of paper and put it by her sleeping face.

"What's this?" Clee asked the next day, holding the slip.

"Oh, thank God, yes. Jack can't see in the dark like a cat."

"I know."

Suddenly I was unsure how this had begun. Maybe she had never asked. I dropped the subject with dark thoughts about my own mind. The following night I was overwhelmed with the suspicion that this baby wasn't Kubelko Bondy at all, that I'd been duped. An hour later I decided Jack was Kubelko Bondy's *baby*—he had given birth to the tiny thing and we were just babysitting until Kubelko Bondy was old enough to look after him.

But if you're Kubelko Bondy's baby, then where's Kubelko Bondy?

I'm Kubelko Bondy.

Yes, you're right. Good. That's easier.

I curled my arm around his swaddled shape. Trying to cuddle him was like trying to cuddle a muffin, or a cup. There just wasn't enough acreage. Very carefully I kissed each blotchy cheek. His vulnerability slayed me, but was *love* the right word for that? Or was it just a very feverish pity? His terrible cry tore through the air—it was time for another bottle.

The night feeds were at one A.M., three A.M., five A.M. and seven A.M. Three A.M. was the bad one. All the other hours retained some elements of civilization, but at three A.M. I was staring at the moon cradling someone else's child who had stolen my one life. Every night my plan was to make it to dawn and then feel out the options. But that was just it—there were no options. There had been options, before the baby, but none of them had been pursued. I had not flown to Japan by myself to see what it was like there. I had not gone to nightclubs and said *Tell me everything about yourself* to strangers. I had not even gone to the movies by myself. I had been quiet when there was no reason to be quiet and consistent when consistency didn't matter. For the last twenty years I had lived as if I was taking care of a newborn baby. I burped Jack against my palm, supporting his floppy neck in the crook of my thumb. Clee's pump started up in the living room. Not the benign *shoop-pa* of the hospital pump; this new one was shriller, it sounded like *hutz-pa, hutz-pa*. A perpetually building condemnation—who did we think we were, taking this child? Such *hutz-pa, hutz-pa, hutz-pa*.

But as the sun rose I crested the mountain of my self-pity and remembered I was always going to die at the end of this life anyway. What did it really matter if I spent it like this—caring for this boy—as opposed to some other way? I would always be earthbound; he hadn't robbed me of my ability to fly or to live forever. I appreciated nuns now, not the conscripted kind, but modern women who chose it. If you were wise enough to know that this life would consist mostly of letting go of things you wanted, then why not get good at the letting go, rather than the trying to have? These exotic revelations bubbled up involuntarily and I began to understand that the sleeplessness and vigilance and constant feedings were a form of brainwashing, a process by which my old self was being molded, slowly but with a steady force, into a new shape: a mother. It hurt. I tried to be conscious while it happened, like watching my own surgery. I hoped to retain a tiny corner of the old me, just enough to warn other women with. But I knew this was unlikely; when the process was complete I wouldn't have anything left to complain with, it wouldn't hurt anymore, I wouldn't remember.

Clee never touched Jack unless I handed him to her, and then she held him away from her body, legs dangling. Little Dude is what she called him.

"Do Little Dude's hands seem funny to you?"

"No. What do you mean?"

"He has no, like, control over them. I've seen people with that—adults, you know, in wheelchairs."

I knew what she meant, I'd seen people like that too. We watched him flail erratically.

"He's just young. Nothing counts until he smiles. July fourth."

She nodded doubtfully and asked if we needed anything at the store.

"No."

"Maybe I'll just go anyway."

Now that she'd completely healed she went out often, which was sometimes a relief; I only had to take care of him instead of him and her. This made me smile because I was so like a housewife from the 1950s; she was my big lug. Could that be a nickname?

"You're my Big Lug."

"Yeah."

"And I'm your Boo."

"Right."

Except she wasn't like a husband from the 1950s, because she didn't bring home the bacon. She tried to get her job at Ralphs back, but there was a new person in charge of hiring now—a woman. Put out feelers, I said. Just put them out, you never know. She put out one feeler, a text to Kate: *Know of any jobs?????????*

DESPITE MY EXHAUSTION I SHAVED off all my pubic hair on May 17th, the night before the last day of the eighth week; I was pretty sure she would prefer this to my salt and pepper. Suzanne remembered the special day too and sent me a text in its honor: *Please reconsider.*

On the night of the 18th I put Jack in the carrier and walked him around and around the block until he was solidly asleep. I lowered him into the crib and kept my hands on his head and feet for a count of ten, then lifted them away in one smooth motion and tiptoed out of the ironing room. I brushed my hair behind my ears, put on the sheer pink "curtains," and left my door open.

It was a little bit of a relief when she didn't come in. I didn't want sex to take over our lives—R movies and rubber equipment and all that. Every once in a while I checked the chalkboard to see if there were any new tally marks. None yet, but the little purple one was still there. I flipped through the calendar counting the weeks until July 4. When he smiled everything else would fall into place, tally marks would grow like grass.

AS IT TURNED OUT, KATE'S mother's sister was a party planner with a catering crew.

"It's a real job," Clee said, "not like Ralphs. It's a career."

"So she's Kate's aunt?"

Jack erupted loudly in his diaper.

"It's her mother's sister. My dream is to learn everything and then start my own company."

"A party-planning company?"

"Not necessarily, but maybe. That's one idea. Rachel who's on the crew is going to start a company that does popcorn in flavors. She already has all the popcorn. It's in her room."

"Do you want to do it?" I put Jack in her arms.

"What?"

"Change him."

When it had been eight weeks and seven days I shaved again

and put on the curtains. Because if you didn't count the first week, which she probably didn't, then this would be the last night of the eighth week.

After that night I didn't shave again.

FOR THE CATERING EVENTS SHE had to wear a white tuxedo shirt and a caterer's black bow tie. She looked incredible, of course; that's why she'd been hired. The first night she got home at two A.M.

"They made such a mess—I've been cleaning for hours," she moaned.

She noisily unloaded a paper bag full of half-drunk bottles of champagne and cupcakes and a stack of napkins with ZAC & KIM printed on them.

"Shhh." I pointed furiously at the baby monitor. It had taken four laps around the block to get him to sleep.

She dropped the empty paper bag like a hot potato.

"Okay, I have to say something."

Her face was strange and serious. My stomach dropped. She was breaking up with me.

"When I tell you things? You don't always seem very interested. Like, you don't ask questions and that makes me feel like you don't care. Don't smile. Why are you smiling?"

"I'm sorry. I *am* interested. What wasn't I interested in?"

"Well, and this is just one example off the top of my head, when I was telling you about Rachel's flavored popcorn company that she's gonna have? You didn't ask anything about that."

"Right, I see what you're saying. I think maybe in that one particular case you gave a very complete picture so there weren't any questions left to ask."

"I can think of a question."

"What?"

"What flavors? That would be the first question that an actually interested person would ask."

"Okay. You're right."

She shifted, waiting.

"What flavors?"

"See, that's the whole thing: papaya, milk, chocolate milk, gum—all stuff like that. Have you ever had gum popcorn?"

"No. I've had gum and I've had popcorn, but not—"

"Not as one thing."

"Never as one thing."

Two A.M. was early. Sometimes the parties ended at three and she cleaned until five. Once she and Rachel had to drive a marble podium to Orange County at four in the morning so Kate's mother's sister wouldn't have to pay the rental fee for another day. Sometimes she was drunk when she got home, which was just part of the job.

"Because there's so many leftover beverages," she slurred.

She unbuttoned her tuxedo shirt and pumped out the alcoholic milk. *Hutz-pa, hutz-pa, hutz-pa.* I poured it down the drain and she gave me a peck. Then another, longer kiss that tasted funny.

She watched my face. "Tastes like tequila?"

I nodded.

"You like it?"

"I'm not a big drinker."

"Well, we gotta get you drunk sometime, lady."

Lady wasn't really one of her names for me; it made me feel old. She put her hand on my hip.

"Where's that dress?"

"What dress?"

She made a sour face, one of her old mean faces.

"Never mind."

The TV came on; I went into the bedroom and shut the door. Anytime I was alone now I dropped into a stunned stupor, holding my forearms and trying to locate the old me in this new life. Usually I didn't get very far—Jack cried and I streamed into motion, forgetting myself again. If he didn't cry my thoughts became increasingly curly and frantic, which was what was happening now. I realized the dress she meant.

She blushed when she saw me. Her eyes locked onto the pennies in my shoes and slowly crawled up the length of the corduroy dress, button by button. When she got to my face she stepped back and took in the whole picture. Her face was stricken, almost pained. She ran her hand through her bangs and wiped her palms on her sweatpants a couple of times. I had never been looked at this way before, like a fantasy come to life.

She stood up and bowed her head, kissing me on the neck just above the high collar. The way she pushed me down was rough. Not like before, but a little bit like before. Which made me tearful—that was us too. She scooted down to my feet, down to the hem. They were difficult buttons, almost slightly too large for the holes. She grappled with each one as if it were the first, never accruing any tricks or unbuttoning techniques. I thought the chances were very slim that she would make it to my pubic area before Jack cried, if that's where she was headed. When he didn't cry I worried he was dead, but since I didn't want to be the one who found him I stayed on the floor. Her fingers worked their way past my waist. I watched the serious oval of her face as she struggled across my bosom. Her alcoholic breath was quick with anticipation. It was an arousing sound; anyone of any persuasion would have become excited hearing it. When the button under my chin was free, she carefully spread the two sides of the dress apart, like a fish split open. I wasn't wearing the curtains or anything else. She sat back on her heels, locked her eyes on my watery breasts and began mumbling something under her breath.

"Cheryl can do it alone . . . I am joining her even though I'm not much help . . ."

She quickly muttered through the end as if it was the Lord's Prayer. It was hard to bow in acknowledgment while lying on the floor, but the moment I did she pulled off her sweatpants and thong in one swift motion and lowered herself, lining up her dark blond mound on top of my stubbly gray one. I lifted my head to kiss her; she shut her eyes and cleared her throat while shifting her hips a little to one side. With great concentration she began slowly kneading herself on my pubic bone. It was a lot of weight and I wasn't sure where to put my hands. They hovered over the lobes of her bare bottom for a while before landing there. I squeezed. There was no denying that this felt good but it was hard to gather the sensation into any kind of momentum. I shut my eyes and Phillip encouraged me, "Think about your thing." It had been a long time since I'd thought about my thing. I pointed my feet and tried to generate an echo, the fantasy inside the fantasy, but somewhere along the way my eyes had fallen open. Her swollen breasts were pressing against my hard, hairy chest and I felt her actual wet puss sliding against my stiff member. I squeezed her bottom as hard as I could and thrust upward; the sensation was incredible, I had her, I was having her. I thrust again and again until I ejaculated in clenched and thunderous surges, filling her. Clee watched my face contort and sped up, her rubbing becoming embarrassingly pointed. I tried to go with the movement but it was too fast for two people, so I held still like a good post for a dog to scratch against. The smell of her feet rose up in waves, alternating with clean air. I could feel the paunch where Jack used to be. She kept working at it; something was chafing. Finally she shuddered stiffly with a high-pitched moan that almost sounded fake. I knew I would get used to it. Maybe I would even make a sound next time.

She rolled off me and quickly pulled her thong back on and then her sweatpants. She stood up with a big jump and almost fell backward, laughing.

"Oh my god," she said, not to me, just into the air. "Oh my god!"

It looked like that was all, so I got started on buttoning the dress.

"I'm gonna order a pizza right now and eat the whole thing." She was already dialing. "Do you want any? No, right?"

"No."

I turned the baby monitor on and off to make sure the screen wasn't frozen.

"He hasn't moved in a long time."

She looked at the screen. "What do you mean?"

"Just that he hasn't moved."

"Is that bad?"

"Not if he's alive."

"Should you go check?"

"And wake him up?"

I sat by myself with the monitor, putting the edge of my fingernail against his chest to measure any shift that might indicate breathing. The resolution just wasn't high enough. *I'll go screaming into the street, that's the first thing I'll do. After that, no plans.*

When the pizza delivery man rang the doorbell, the baby woke up. She'd eaten it all by the time I'd gotten him back down.

ON JULY 3RD JACK WAILED on and off all day long, as if he knew this was the last day for a smile and it made him terribly sad to miss the deadline.

It's no problem at all, just put it out of your mind.

I feel one coming on, though.

No rush.

Clee spent thirty minutes harassing him with noises and silly faces and then gave up and stomped outside. I watched her pace around, smoking and talking on the phone.

On the fourth we went to Ralphs and Clee got a free employee hot dog even though she didn't work there anymore. The manager held Jack and a woman named Chris held him and the butcher held him and then Clee held him, really cradling him as if she did this all the time. He tried to latch on to one of the buttons of her tuxedo shirt. She wore it every day now, even when she wasn't working. And green pants, army pants. Her personal style had quietly and completely changed over the last month. It suited her. When she started to look antsy the redheaded bagger boy plucked Jack from her arms and rocketed him into the air.

"Careful," I said.

"He likes it," said the bagger boy. "Look!"

Clee and I looked up at our baby and he grinned down at us. We laughed out loud and hugged each other and the bagger boy and Jack. The milestone had been met.

After smiling came laughing, then rolling over. The days and nights began to unwarp; three A.M. became an ordinary time.

The first few months were hard for all new parents, a test, really—and we had passed! And it was summertime. I washed the linens. I opened all the windows and did my best to tidy the backyard, pruning and weeding while Jack rolled around on a blanket. Rick would have to empty the snail bucket if he ever returned; it was almost full. Clee wore jean shorts and used some of her catering money to buy her friend Rachel's old moped because Rachel was getting a new one. They mopeded together on the weekends and were thinking of joining a team.

"Because we're friggin' fast!" she said loudly, taking off her helmet.

"Maybe Jack and I can watch you compete." I saw myself sitting by a cooler, holding the baby and waving a pennant. Suntan lotion.

Her face twisted shut. "It's not like that. There aren't races."

"Oh, okay. You said team, so I thought—"

She grabbed something from the kitchen and went back outside. I stared out the front window with Jack on my hip. She was spraying the wheels of her moped with the hose and scrubbing them with my vegetable scrubber. Most of her baby weight had disappeared. Her even larger new bosom looked almost unreal, but in a wonderful way. She turned the water off and stepped back, admiring the shiny moped. Many people would have had trouble keeping their hands off her. Did she expect that from me? Of course she did.

That night I put on the curtains. It was too embarrassing to strut out half-naked, so I wore my bathrobe and then slid it off once I was beside her on the couch. It took her a moment to pull her eyes away from the TV and then she did. Just for a second.

"I"—she was blinking rapidly—"need advance warning."

I pulled up the robe.

"All right. How much advance warning?"

"What?"

"I just don't know if you mean an hour, or a day, or . . ."

She stared at her knees like a teenager being grilled by a parent. After a while the question evaporated; it couldn't be answered now. I got up and made some tea.

I still gave her a peck now and then but her lips seemed to stiffen, a tiny flinch. Sometimes I wished we could just wrestle it out like in the old days, but that was impossible and we'd have had to get a sitter. And I didn't really want to fight her; she wasn't even being mean. She did her dishes and dutifully mowed the backyard wearing dirty rubber boots that came up to her knees. When did she get those? Or were they Rick's boots, the ones he used to garden in. Melancholy suddenly plumed in my chest, as if I missed the homeless gardener. Or missed the past—the hospital, the nurses, the call buttons, the way she looked in braids and the badly fitting cotton gown. The first purple mark was still high in the corner of the chalkboard but if a person didn't know what it was they might think it was just a bit of something else that hadn't gotten completely erased.

IT WAS AN IDEA I was working on. I'd think about it for just a few seconds, then put it away. A couple days later, when Jack was sleeping, I'd make myself take it out and work on it some more. It was like a big needlepoint; I didn't want to see the finished picture until it was done. The reason being that the finished picture was so sad.

We had fallen in love; that was still true. But given the right psychological conditions, a person could fall in love with anyone or anything. A wooden desk—always on all fours, always prone, always there for you. What was the lifespan of these improbable loves? An hour. A week. A few months at best. The end was a natural thing, like the seasons, like getting older, fruit turning. That was the saddest part—there was no one to blame and no way to reverse it.

So now I was just waiting for her to leave me, taking the boy who was not legally my son. One day soon they would be gone. She would do it abruptly to avoid a scene. She'd go home; Carl and Suzanne would help raise him. They weren't talking to her now, but that would change when she arrived on their doorstep with a baby and a purple duffel bag over her shoulder. With this new understanding of my position came shakiness and a loss of appetite; I held Jack in cold hands, always on the verge of tears. For the first time in my life I understood TV, why everyone watched it. It helped. Not in the long run, of course, but minute by minute. The only food I craved was unreal, unorganic chips and cookies and one especially addictive thing that was both—a fried, salty cookie. When those ran out I left Jack with her while I went to Ralphs.

"If he wakes up and cries, wait five minutes before going in. He'll probably go back to sleep after two minutes."

She nodded like *Yeah yeah yeah I know.* She was pumping. "Can you get me those grapefruit sodas?"

Driving home I realized I had forgotten the sodas. Then I thought: *It doesn't matter. Because she won't be there when I get home. Neither of them will.* Sure enough, her car wasn't in the driveway.

It would be perverse to enter the house only moments after she'd left. I had to let it close up a little, settle. Also I couldn't move because I was crying so hard. Wide ragged howls. It had happened. *Oh, my baby. Kubelko Bondy.*

Suddenly her silver Audi pulled up beside mine, two two-liters of Diet Pepsi in the passenger seat, Jack asleep in his car seat. We both stepped out of our cars.

"I let him cry for five minutes but he wouldn't stop," she whispered over the hood. "So I took him for a ride."

After that I kept Jack with me, always, and I tried to do things that he might remember, on a cellular level, after she took him away. I organized a trip to the boardwalk on the Santa Monica Pier, full of stimulating, indelible sights and sounds.

"Can I bring a friend?" Clee asked.

"What friend?" I said.

"Never mind, it's not a big deal."

The pier was packed with hundreds of obese people eating giant fried dough shapes and neon cotton candy. Clee bought a deep-fried Oreo cookie.

"That'll make some sweet milk," I said, thinking about the inflammatory properties of sugar.

"What?" she yelled over the screaming clatter of a roller coaster. Each time it roared by, a Latina woman lifted her baby high into the air and he wiggled his arms and legs; he thought he was on the ride. The next time it came around I lifted Jack in unison; this he would remember. The woman smiled at me and I made a deferential gesture, letting her know I wasn't trying to take over, she was the leader. We thrust our babies into the air again and again, showing them what it felt like to be a mother, to be terrifyingly in love without the option of getting off. My arms became tired, but it wasn't my place to decide when to end it. How I longed to be any one of these people milling about with such easy freedom. Suddenly the roller coaster stopped with a bang; the doors clanged open and a cluster of men and children stumbled toward my Latina comrade, laughing and weak-kneed from the ride. I barely had the strength to tuck Jack into his sling; my arms hung like noodles.

And Clee was gone.

I held my breath and stood perfectly still as the crowd swirled around us.

She'd waited until I was distracted.

Her friend had picked her up.

They were halfway to San Francisco.

She'd left Jack.

I held his face in my hands and tried to keep my breath even. He didn't know yet. It was awful, a crime. Or maybe this was her plan all along, a generous and mature choice. My eyes welled up. She believed in me, that I could do it. And I could. Relief spun with the shock of being left. I reeled in circles, stumbling toward the exit, then the bathroom, then numbly watching a skinny father as he failed to shoot a rubber duck with a gun, bang, bang . . . bang. She was watching him too. She was standing right there in her tuxedo shirt, eating a giant pretzel. The skinny father gave up and Clee glanced around mildly, looking for the next thing to watch. She saw us and waved.

"Do you think it's rigged?"

"Probably," I said shakily.

"I'm gonna try anyway. Can you hold this?"

Another month went by and I realized she might not know. I might be waiting for years. She might grow old in this house, with her son and the employee of her parents, never knowing she was supposed to abandon me. Her impatience would ebb away, her blond hair would turn white-gray and she'd become portly. When she was sixty-five I'd be eightysomething—just two old women with an old son. It wasn't the ideal match for either of us, but maybe it was good enough. This revelation was a great comfort and I thought it might sustain me indefinitely, a hidden loaf. Then one afternoon Jack and I were returning from the park when we saw something in the distance.

What's that on the curb? he said.

It's a person, I said.

A hunched-over gray person. Clee. Her hair wasn't gray, but her skin was. And her face. Weathered and broken down by a burden so heavy that anyone could see it: here was a woman who hated her life. And this was how she planned to get through it, by sitting on the curb, smoking. How long had she been depressed? Months, that was obvious now. She'd been smoking out here since we brought Jack home. It must happen all the time, a fleeting passion overwhelms someone's true course and there's nothing to be done about it. I looked at Jack; his brow was furrowed with concern.

She can be very energetic, I assured him. *And fun.*

He didn't believe me.

She lifted her head and watched us make our way toward her. No wave, just a tired flick of her cigarette into the gutter.

ONE OF MY FAVORITE TV shows was about a man's survival in the wilderness. In a recent episode part of the man's foot was trapped under a boulder and he had no choice but to cut it off with a tiny hacksaw. He sawed and sawed and then threw the piece of his foot into the bushes. It was black and blue. In our case the foot would have to cut itself off, to free the man. To free Clee. I would do it tenderly, ceremonially, but with the same unflinching determination. I shuddered; a panicky whine escaped me. This wouldn't be like the first time Kubelko's mother had taken him away, I wasn't nine. I would never recover. But I couldn't keep him by keeping her, it wasn't motherly, or wifely, or likely to end well. Pick up the hacksaw. Saw and saw and saw and saw.

Real candles are a fire hazard so I bought electric votives that turned on when you shook them. There were thirty of them; it was a lot of shaking. The Gregorian chant CD was not "our song" but it was very similar to the one we'd heard on the radio that first morning. I turned it on, quietly, and turned off the lights. Jack and I stared at the plastic flames floating in the dark; among them was one real candle, the pomegranate currant column I'd given her almost two years ago. The room flickered and glowed. I tried to cry silently, so the baby wouldn't notice. Mouth contorted and hanging open, tears streaming into it. It was the thought of being one again, after having been three—of silence and perfect order after all the noise.

There were forty minutes to get him to sleep before Clee came home from work. I bathed him as if for the last time. His night-night song came out like a dirge, so I opened *Little Fur Family* but the tale was too devastatingly cozy, given the circumstances. Jack began to squirm and fuss.

Why so little faith? he asked.

I said faith had nothing to do with it, you couldn't always get everything you wanted. But he was right. A real mother throws her heart over the fence and then climbs after it.

I closed *Little Fur Family*, turned out the lights, and held him in my arms.

I've gotten myself all worked up, haven't I? What a silly Milly. We'll say goodbye a million times and hello a million times over the course of your long, long life.

Jack looked up at me; he was wondering what had happened to the bedtime story.

Okay. One day, I began, *when you're all grown up, I'll be waiting for an airplane and you'll be on it. You'll be coming from China or Taiwan and I'll rise to my feet when your flight is announced. Clee will stand too, she'll be there. We'll wait with all the other moms and dads and husbands and wives, down at the end of the long arrivals hall. Passengers will begin to trickle down the corridor. I'll be searching, searching, my heart will be pounding, where, where, where—and then I'll see you. Jack, my baby. There you are, tall and handsome with your new girlfriend or boyfriend. I'll wave wildly. You won't see me, and then you will. You'll wave. And I won't be able to stop myself, I'll start running down the hallway. It's too much but once I've started I can't stop. And guess what you'll do? You'll run too. You'll run toward me and I'll run toward you and as we get closer we'll both start to laugh. We'll be laughing and laughing and running and running and running and music will play, brass instruments, a soaring anthem, not a dry eye in the house, the credits will roll. Applause like rain. The end.*

He was asleep.

THE GREGORIAN CHANT WAS STILL playing when she came home from work. I was waiting in the candlelit bedroom. She poked her head in, bewildered. I poured tequila into the tumbler I only had one of; it had been holding dusty barrettes for the last sixteen years.

"Weird lights," she said, sipping and looking around. The CD was on a different track now, a silencing hymn. Mute, we climbed into bed.

I lay with her and she curled around me in the old way, Ss.

The whole chant played through and then a new one began, one lone voice in an infinite cathedral, climbing and echoing and praising. The singer was lifted up and illuminated with gratitude, not for any one thing, but for the whole of this life, even for the agony. Even in Latin you could tell he was thanking God for the agony in particular, for the way it allowed him to cleave so tightly to the world. I squeezed her arms and she tightened them around me.

"You have to move out."

She froze. I pictured the man cutting off his toe. I shut my eyes and sawed and sawed.

"You need to live in your first apartment, learn to take care of yourself, be free. Fall in love."

"I am in love."

"That's nice. That you would say that."

She didn't repeat it.

Because she was behind me I didn't know what was happening for a long time. Then she breathed in sharply, sucking her tearful snot back into her throat.

"I don't know how I'll"—she sniffled into my neck—"take care of him."

I counted to nine.

"I could—if you wanted—keep him here. I mean just until you got settled."

She cried now in a way I could feel, her whole body shaking.

"I guess I'm pretty much the worst mom ever," she coughed.

"No, no, no. Not at all."

The CD played on and on. Maybe it started over again from the beginning, it was hard to tell. We slept. I got up and gave Jack a bottle. I came back, slipped into her arms, slept and slept. Morning had gotten lost on the way home. We would lie this way forever, always saying goodbye, never parting.

CHAPTER FOURTEEN

Clee thought it would be less hassle if I became a legal guardian. "Because it might take me a while to get set up."

"That makes sense," I said, holding my breath. Now that it was decided, she made plans very quickly, with an unfamiliar momentum. I was informed of an appointment at the courthouse; she drove, chatting all the way. As it turns out, almost anyone can legally kidnap your child, just as long as you stand in front of the judge and tell her you're "totally fine with it." A social worker would check in on me four times in the next year and Clee would get her own place.

"We're more than happy to help out with her rent," Suzanne assured me. "Obviously we should have done this in the first place. All parents make mistakes. You'll see. When are you coming back to work?" She thought she'd won—that we were competing for her daughter and she'd won in the end.

I told Clee she could stop pumping since we'd have to go to formula anyway, but she promised me a month's supply of breast milk.

"And when I come visit on Fridays I can pump."

"You'll be dried up. It's fine—he's seven months old. You're done."

Tears seeped into her eyes. Tears of joy. I hadn't realized she hated pumping so much.

WE DIDN'T SAY THE LAST night was the last night but the next day was the day she would move into her apartment in Studio City and it followed that she would sleep there that night and the night after and for years until she moved, probably into a bigger place, maybe with someone, someone she'd marry, maybe they'd have kids. Eventually she'd be my age and Jack would be in college and this time, this very brief time when we lived together, would just become a bit of family lore about an accident and a family friend and how it all worked out for everyone. The details would be washed away; for example, it would not be told as a great American love story for our time.

The next morning her garbage bags were lined up by the door. Any closer to the door and they'd march out by themselves. The famous Rachel came to help her move.

"I heard you're starting a flavored popcorn company," I said, burping Jack over my shoulder. She winced a little.

"I guess you could call it that. I mean, technically that's what it is."

Clee banged in the front door and grabbed two bags, eyeing our conversation. Rachel was very skinny and Jewish-looking. She wore a blouse with diagonal pastel stripes that looked like it was from the 1980s; it was a joke about how silly the time before she was born was.

"Did I get it wrong? Clee said there would be gum popcorn?"

"It's really hard to explain, because I'm working on a lot of different levels?" She heaved the biggest bag over her shoulder. "I'm surprised she even told you about it."

"Well, she just told me the gum popcorn level of it."

She looked me all the way down and all the way back up, landing not on my eyes but on my neck.

Clee huffed inside, grabbing the last bag. "That's everything!"

"Really?" I looked around. "The bathroom?"

"I checked that."

"All right, then."

She rubbed the top of Jack's head. "Goodbye, Little Dude. Don't forget about your Aunt Clee." Aunt. When had she decided that? He grabbed her hair; she freed herself. Rachel took out her phone and turned away; this was the moment allotted for our goodbye. Clee was looking antsy. I doubted she would come every Friday at ten A.M. She held her arms open like a friendly bear. "Thanks for everything, Cheryl. I'll call you guys tonight."

"You don't have to call."

"I'll call."

We watched them get into her car and drive away and then we walked around the house. The rooms sounded different, higher ceilinged, empty.

It used to always be like this, I explained. This is the normal way the house usually is.

Did she not leave anything? he asked. Nothing?

We searched every room. She had been very thorough. The envelope between the books was gone; so was the soda can tab. We did finally find one thing she'd forgotten.

I carried the sundrop crystal from the bathroom and hung it in the kitchen above the sink. Jack watched it clatter against the glass a few times, then spin silently.

Rainbows. I pointed to a flock of them gliding across the wall. His little mouth hung open in transfixed awe.

This kind of thing is more along the lines of what I was expecting,
he said. *This will for sure be my top interest, my area of focus.*

Rainbows?

And everything else like this.

*There is nothing else like this. Rainbows are alone; they're the only
thing like that.*

The crystal began to wind the other way, sending the bright
fleet back across his body. I could tell he didn't believe me; it
did seem unlikely. I racked my brain for others of the species.
Reflections, shadows, smoke—these things were morose and
distant cousins at best. No, rainbows are in their own class of
spectacularity, every single one of them impressive, never a bleak
rainbow, never with just some of the colors. Always all the colors
and always in the right order. She didn't call.

EVERY DAY I MELTED A milk icicle and watched Jack drink what
Clee had pumped exactly one month earlier, each bottle labeled
with a date. First he drank the day we made love; he gulped it
all down. He drank the day we showed him off at Ralphs. He
drank the cotton-candy milk from the day at the pier. The last
batch was from the morning she left and this milk was full of
plans I didn't know about. When he finished that bottle she was
really gone, every last drop of her. But the habit of remembering what had happened a month ago was hard to let go of, so we
continued. As he drank his first bottle of formula I remembered
our first night alone, the house bitterly quiet until I turned on
the TV. I remembered remembering making love and crying
right onto Jack, right into his eyes. When she had been gone for
a full two months I remembered melting the last of her milk
and thinking she was really gone now, every last drop. I burped

him and that was all—I didn't start over again with triple re-membering.

She missed the first two Fridays, and the one after that. I called several times to issue a gentle reminder, but her phone just rang and rang. I pictured it in a rainy gutter somewhere. She was ex-actly the kind of woman who ends up murdered.

"I don't want to alarm you," I said calmly. "But I thought you should know."

"We just saw her yesterday," Suzanne said.

"Oh. How is she?"

"She's happy as a clam in her new place—you should see it, she and Rachel painted the walls all kinds of crazy colors. Did you meet Rachel?"

"Rachel lives there?"

"Oh yeah, they're inseparable. And I have to say they're real cute together—Clee is just gaga for that girl. Did you know Ra-chel went to Brown? Carl's alma mater?"

"When you say 'gaga,' what do you mean?"

"They're in love."

I PUT AWAY ALL THE dishes except my own set and Jack's tiny plastic spoon. I covered the TV with the Tibetan cloth. I took the cloth off and put the TV on the curb by the trash cans. As everything went back into its proper place, I explained my system to Jack, carpooling and so forth.

See, this way the house practically cleans itself.

He crumbled a rice cake into his lap.

So if you're down in the dumps you don't have to worry about things devolving into filth.

He dumped a box of plastic blocks on the rug.

My plan for toys was to not worry about keeping them in their place, since that would be a never-ending battle, but to approach them like the dishes: less. I threw all of them into a suitcase except a ball, a rattle, and a bear. These were allowed to be anywhere but ideally they wouldn't clump together. Two of them could be in the same room but I liked for the third one to be somewhere else, otherwise it became too chaotic. She wanted a girlfriend. Someone to pal around with. Exploration of the body, womanhood and so forth. It was so ordinary. Jack wondered where all his toys went; he crawled all around the house looking for them. I rolled the suitcase back out and emptied it in the middle of the living room. Stacking cups and blocks, soft cars and stuffed animals, board books and interlocking squeaking rings with googly eyes and textured tails. My system wasn't really applicable to babies. Babies ruined everything. Secret plan to get in bed and never move again? Ruined. Tendency to pee in jars when very sad? Ruined.

Each day I walked to the park with Jack in the stroller. We stopped and watched the men playing basketball, wondering if Clee had ever watched these men and if they had watched her. There was a muscular bald man whose place she could have gone back to. He showed no recognition, but why would he think the child of a woman he'd never met was his son?

Do you feel a kinship with any of these men?

Jack did not. He was getting bigger and on some days he looked much less like Clee and much more like someone else. His expression when troubled was not unusual—I'd seen people, men, with brows that furrowed like that. But I couldn't put a face to the feeling; it was a dissolving thought, like a dream that hurries away when you approach it. We watched people jogging and older children playing on the slide and swings.

A couple stretched on the grass smiled at Jack.

Do they know us?

No. People just smile at you because you're a baby.

Now they were waving. It was Rick and a woman. They walked over to us.

"I was just saying, 'Is that her? No, yes, no.'"

"He was just saying that!" the woman agreed. "He really was. I'm Carol." She stuck out her hand.

I glanced around the park. Did he live here? I didn't see a hovel or sleeping bag nearby. Carol was clean and ordinary; she looked like a college professor.

"This is him?" he asked, eyes moist.

"Jack, yes."

He delivered you.

You're kidding.

"I'll never forget that day. He was blue like a blueberry—didn't I say that?"

The woman nodded heartily. "You came home, dropped your gardening tools, and said, 'Honey, you'll never guess what I just did.'" She swung her hands in the pockets of her skirt and smiled. "But it's not the first time you've helped out in a pinch, hon."

Rick was either the homeless man she lived with and called "hon," or else he was her husband.

"I did a small amount of medic work in Vietnam," Rick mumbled modestly. "He certainly *looks* healthy."

"He's fine now."

"Really?" Rick's eyes were pained and full. "And the mother?"

"She's doing great."

Carol patted his back. "He didn't sleep well for weeks after the birth."

"I should have called," said Rick. "I was afraid of hearing bad news."

Not gardening, he wasn't even dirty. Why had I decided he was homeless? Because he always arrived on foot. No car. I looked at him sideways, wondering if he'd been aware of my mistake. But if you weren't homeless you would never assume someone thought you were. I pointed toward my house and said it was almost time for Jack's nap.

"We were just heading back too," said Carol, pointing in the same direction. "We're a few blocks over."

A neighbor with a green thumb and no yard. That's all. Would this be the first of many awakenings? Was I about to be buffeted with truth after truth? More likely it was just a singular instance.

An isolated case of mistaken identity, I explained.

An honest mistake, Jack agreed.

WE WALKED TOGETHER AND RICK insisted on checking the back-yard.

"What a mess. I shouldn't have let it go like this. How are the snails?"

I couldn't remember the last time I'd seen one. The bucket was empty. It seemed they'd left with Clee.

Carol picked lemons off my tree and made lemonade in my kitchen.

"Never mind me, just go about your business."

I walked Jack around the house, teaching him the names of things.

Couch.

Couch, he agreed.

Book.

Book.

Lemon.

Lemon.

"It's so quiet here," said Carol, wiping her hands on my dish-cloth.

"I like to keep it calm for the baby."

"Do you ever talk to him?"

"Of course I talk to him."

"Good, babies need that."

They left lemonade and promised to return next Thursday with a quiche. I locked the door. *Do I talk to him?* I did nothing *but* talk to him! I laid Jack on the changing table.

All day long! I'd been talking to him for decades.

There we go, that's nice, isn't it? It feels good to be all clean and dry.

Okay, sure, I didn't holler at him like a train conductor. But my internal voice was much louder than most people's. And incessant.

Now let's snap your pants.

I suppose it was possible that to someone on the outside it might seem as if I were moving around in perfect silence.

Snap, snap, snap, there we go. All done.

I patted his tummy and watched his wide-open face. It was a crushing thought, little Jack innocently living in a mute world. And all those words, all the terms of endearment—had he heard none of them?

I cleared my throat. "I love you."

His head shook with surprise. My voice was low and formal; I sounded like a wooden father from the 1800s. I continued. "You are a sweet potato." This sounded literal, as if I was letting him know he was a root vegetable, a tuber. "You're a baby," I added, just in case there was any confusion on that last point. He craned his neck, trying to see who was here. Of course he had heard me talk, but always to another person or on the phone. I put him down on the bed and kissed his fat cheeks again and again. He shut his eyes, gracefully enduring.

"Don't worry, there's not just me. You have other people."

Who? he said. No he didn't. He just waited for whatever was going to happen next.

SUZANNE SALUTED AS SHE TOOK off her shoes, I guess meaning it was fascist of me to insist on this.

"Do you do other Japanese customs or just this one?" asked Carl.

"Just this one."

"We looked high and low for a baby present and then at the last moment we discovered a really incredible hat store," said Carl, ambling around the living room. "I mean these hats were like something from a museum—a jester museum. They could have easily charged hundreds of dollars but most of them were twenty dollars or under."

"But they didn't have them in sizes for babies," Suzanne said.

"They were one size fits all. We thought maybe if he had a very large head . . . an adult-sized head . . ."

Jack smiled shyly as his grandparents looked at him for the first time, appraising his cranium.

"It's too big," Suzanne said, pulling a jingling jangling jester hat out of her purse. Jack lunged for it.

"Bells," I enunciated. "Jingle bells. You've never seen bells, have you? He loves it, thank you." Jack gave up on the bells and tried to put his whole hand in my mouth. He'd been doing this ever since I'd started talking out loud to him. He'd also been grabbing the pages of books, shaking anything that rattled, stacking cups, rolling across the floor, chewing the legs of a toy giraffe, and sweetly reaching for me with whimpering excitement every time we were parted for more than a few seconds. Or maybe none of these things were new. Maybe I was just noticing them more acutely since the veil of my internal dialogue had lifted. He seemed less and less like Kubelko Bondy and more like a baby named Jack.

Suzanne smiled, putting the jester hat on her own head. "Do you want to tell her, hon?"

"We're adding twenty dollars to your next paycheck," Carl announced. "We ask that you cash it and put in an envelope—"

"It's a fund," Suzanne interrupted, jingling. "So one day, when his head is big enough, this money will be waiting for him."

"We thought it was more special this way," Carl said. "Look at her—isn't she like a beautiful little sprite?"

We all stared at Suzanne with the hat on. If anyone looked like a little sprite wouldn't it be the baby among us? But she batted her eyelashes daffily and fluttered her veiny hands like wings.

I gave them a tour of the house. In the nursery Carl whispered something to Suzanne and Suzanne asked if this had been Clee's room.

"This was my ironing room. Clee slept on the couch at first and later we shared my room."

They looked at each other sideways. Carl coughed and picked up a stuffed lamb.

"Lamb," I said to Jack. "Grandpa is holding your lamb."

They both frowned uncomfortably. Suzanne gave Carl a little poke with her elbow.

"We're glad you brought that up," he said.

Suzanne nodded vigorously with her eyes shut; Carl cleared his throat.

"Jack seems like an interesting person and we hope we get the chance to know him. But we'd like that to be on his own terms."

Suzanne jumped in. "Do we share common interests and values? Is he curious about us and the kinds of things we care about?"

"I think he might be," I ventured. "When he's a little older."

"Exactly. Until then it's a forced relationship." Suzanne's vehemence was ringing the bells on her hat. Jack shrieked; he thought this was the most fun thing that had ever happened. "We're supposed to play the part of the 'grandparents' [*jingle jingle*] and he's supposed to enact the 'grandson' [*jingle jingle*]. That just feels empty and arbitrary to us, like something Hallmark came up with."

Carl chuckled at the Hallmark line and rubbed Suzanne's neck as she continued.

"Interesting young people come into our lives every day and we adore them, they're engaging, they ask questions. Maybe down the road Jack will be one of these kids."

"We might not even know it's him," Carl murmured.

"We won't know it's him and he won't know it's us—we'll just be people who genuinely like each other."

Suzanne folded the jester hat [*jingle jingle*] and put it back in her purse. She seemed relieved to have the speech out of the way.

"Do you want to hold him?" I said.

Her hands fit around Jack very easily. He looked up at her, wondering if the bells were coming back.

CHAPTER FIFTEEN

One Friday at ten o'clock there was a knock at the door and I thought, *Well, what do you know, maybe she hasn't completely forgotten us.* I wiped Jack's nose and tucked my hair behind my ears. My heart raced as I neared the door. Rachel had broken up with her. She had nowhere else to turn. I ran my fingers across my lips to make sure there was no gunk on them. She was probably a full-blown lesbian by now. If she tried to kiss me I would stop her and say *Let's consider this choice, what does it mean? What are we saying about who we are and who we want to be?* Maybe she was more verbal now; Rachel might have brought that out in her. I couldn't wait to talk to another adult, out loud.

It was a skinny, redheaded young man with a Ralphs name tag: DARREN. The bagger boy.

"Is Clee here?"

Jack tried to pull off the name tag.

"She's not. She doesn't live here anymore."

"Really?" He looked past me into the house. I stepped aside so he could see she wasn't in there.

"Just us."

He regarded Jack and me, brushing his fingers along the white tops of the many tiny pimples that bearded his chin and pink cheeks. Fourth of July. He was the one who made Jack smile.

"Okay," he said. "Bye, Jack, bye, Jack's mom." He darted off the porch, bounding past the TV on the curb. I watched him run down the street. Jack's mom. No one had ever called me that before. But from Jack's point of view no other person was more his mother. I looked at his small hand so confidently wrapped around my upper arm. It was a very ordinary thing to be but I felt suddenly breathless, like I had just made it to the top of something tall. Motherhood. He fussed; I went inside and gave him a plastic spatula. He slapped it on the counter, smack, smack, smack. I stood, holding his warm body, watching his concentrating face. It was too pink, he needed more sunblock. Smack, smack. And more reading—I read to him, but not every night. And we had only spent a few hours a day in the NICU with him. That wasn't enough. It was enough for us at the time, but now it haunted me. Twenty hours a day he'd lain there alone. There would be other unpardonable crimes, I could feel them coming— things that in retrospect would become my greatest regrets. I'd always be catching up with my love. How terrible. Jack flung the spatula onto the ground and wailed. I picked it up, smack, smack. He laughed, I laughed. Terrible. I kissed him and he kissed me back with a wide-open drooly mouth. Terrible.

"Ah, my boy," I said. "My boy, my boy. I love you so. This can only end in heartbreak and I'll never recover."

"Ba-ba-ba-ba," he said.

"Yes. Ba-ba-ba-ba."

TWO DAYS LATER DARREN BOUNCED on the top step of my porch like a runner stretching out his calf muscles.

"I thought I'd leave my number, for the next time you talk to her."

I asked him to come in while I finished feeding Jack in his high chair.

"Have you tried calling her?"

"It's okay," he said too quickly. He had called her many times. I wondered if I should tell him about Rachel.

"Do you need a TV?" I pointed to the curb. "The trash people won't take it."

"I have a flat-screen. You should get a flat-screen."

"I keep meaning to take it to Goodwill."

He scrunched up his face. "I'll take it to the Goodwill for you."

"Really?"

"Of course." He gestured to Jack in a way that made me feel uncouth, as if Goodwill were a house of ill repute.

He sat in the kitchen with Jack while I gathered a few more things for him to take. "Goo goo goo," Darren said, making a silly face. "Ga ga ga."

THE NEXT DAY HE BROUGHT me the receipt from Goodwill in a little envelope.

"For taxes. It was a tax-deductible donation." He leaned on the door frame, waiting. I invited him in. The truth was, he explained while I did the dishes, he felt bad for me and Jack. "All alone and everything. If you want, I can check in on you. I don't mind."

"That's very generous, Darren. But we're really doing fine."

Tuesdays were his usual day; he came after Rick left. He broke down boxes and put them in the recycling, he helped me reach tall things. He said I should see the top of his mom's refrigerator—it was clean like a plate.

"You could eat off it. In fact, that's a good idea—I'm gonna eat off it tonight. I'll just put my spaghetti right on it."

While he installed my tiny new flat-screen he told a long story about his cousin's car. He didn't seem at all worried that the story would bore me; he just went on and on, not even utilizing basic storytelling skills to make it interesting. Sometimes he played with Jack while I went to the bathroom or made food for us. He had to be careful because the baby was fascinated by his pimples. Once his grabbing little hand knocked the top off a ripe whitehead and puss and blood spurted out. Underneath the acne were good bones. Not great bones, but perfectly fine, serviceable bones. Tall too.

I remembered exactly where Ruth-Anne had put the card: the center drawer of the receptionist's desk. If she was seeing a patient I could possibly slip in and get it without her even knowing. Jack looked at himself in the mirrored ceiling of the elevator, leaning his head back in the carrier. My heart was skipping beats as we made our way down the long familiar hallway. *Ruth-Anne,* I would say, *can we put the past behind us?* Better not to phrase it as a question. *The past is behind us.* That was good. Who could argue with that?

I swung open the door. The front desk was empty. I went straight for the middle drawer; it was an awkward reach with Jack in the carrier and the card wasn't where I thought it was. And suddenly I realized I wasn't alone—a young woman was reading a magazine in the corner. She smiled at us and said the receptionist had just stepped out. "I think she went to the bathroom. Dr. Broyard might be running late." I nodded thank you and chastely sat down as if I hadn't just tried to rob the place. Dr. Broyard. Had I unconsciously timed my visit to avoid Ruth-Anne? Ruth-Anne would say I had. I stared over Jack's head at a new painting of a Native American weaver. Maybe it was by Helge Thomasson. The weaver was weaving a rug. Or unweaving it. She might have been taking the rug apart as a nonviolent act of resistance. I wondered if the new receptionist was very pretty. Poor Helge.

The young woman slowly turned the pages of *Better Homes and Gardens*. She kept glancing up at Jack in a way that reminded me of me—as if they shared a special understanding. It was sort of sickening. She put the magazine down and picked up another one.

It had taken a moment.

But now I recognized her.

She wasn't wearing the shirt with the Rasta alligator on it, but the fluorescent lights were glinting off her John Lennon–style glasses, and her hair, though longer than in the photo, was blond and stringy. I wondered who she was—a friend's daughter? His niece?

"Kirsten." I said it to Jack, just in case it wasn't even her name.

She whipped her head around. For a moment it seemed miraculous, like a doll or a cartoon come to life.

"We might have a friend in common," I said. "Phillip?"

She wrinkled her forehead.

"Phil? Phil Bettelheim?"

"Oh. Phil. Yeah."

Her face slowly tightened and she looked me up and down.

"Are you . . . Cheryl?"

I nodded.

She tilted her face up to the ceiling and took a long, dramatic breath. "I can't believe I'm really meeting you."

I smiled politely. "I guess we both learned about this place from Phillip. Phil."

"I told *him* about Dr. Broyard," she said. I rubbed Jack's back to let her know I didn't really care. She seemed like a very bitter and unappealing young lady.

"Phil didn't say you had a baby, but I guess I haven't seen him in a while. Not since you-know-what, actually." She grinned a little, like she had a mean secret.

"I don't think I do know what."

"Not since you told him to"—she made a tube with her fingers and jammed another finger into it—"me."

My eyes widened and I glanced around to be sure we were alone.

"I was so surprised"—she leaned forward—"that you did that. What woman would tell an old man to have sex with a child?"

It was like being accused of a crime committed in a dream.

"I'm so sorry," I whispered. "I didn't think you were real." Or I did. And then I didn't.

"Well"—she extended both her arms—"I am."

It was hard to know what to say to this. Surely the receptionist would be back any moment. Kirsten quietly bumped the back of her head against the wall a few times.

"I hope it wasn't too awful," I said, finally.

"It wasn't a big deal. He had to watch something first, on his phone. That took a long time."

I had no idea what this meant, but I nodded knowingly.

"Hey." She snapped her fingers. "Let's send him a picture of us together. It'll freak him out."

"Really?"

She held her phone out at arm's length and leaned stiffly toward me. Her hair smelled like chlorine. Jack lurched toward the lens with his wet mouth, blocking both of us.

The flash popped, the door opened, and the receptionist returned to the front desk. It was Ruth-Anne. She froze when she saw me, just briefly.

"The doctor is ready for you, Kirsten."

Kirsten swept past me without a glance.

We were alone.

"Hi, Ruth-Anne." I stood up and went to the counter.

She raised her eyebrows, as if she wasn't going to deny that was her name but she wasn't going to confirm it either.

"I'm just here for that card. Remember? The one with the name." I pointed at Jack and she blinked, seeming to notice him for the first time.

"Do you mean a business card?" She gestured to Dr. Broyard's cards in their Lucite display, right beside her own.

"No, the card I asked you to keep. You put it in there." I pointed to the middle desk drawer.

"I'm afraid I can't help you, but you're more than welcome to take several business cards."

Her big-boned androgyny was gone. She had carefully tipped a million tiny details in the girlish direction. The long hair was pulled back by a tartan headband. Her tight-fitting blouse was designed to minimize her broad shoulders and it did. Her whole body appeared shrunken. Sitting down, she actually seemed to be petite, a delicate woman.

Dr. Broyard popped out holding a file folder. As she looked up at him her whole bearing shifted; she became luminous. Not with the light of life, but like a husk lit electrically from within. She reached for the folder and he let it go—just shy of her fingers. It floated to the ground. Ruth-Anne hesitated and then awkwardly bent over to pick it up. When her face reappeared it was smiling with the hope that he had enjoyed the rear view, but he turned and went back into his office. Her smile widened with pain, and seeing her teeth I could also see the jawbone that held them, and her skull with its empty sockets and the whole of her clickety-clack skeleton. I could see right into her brain; it was shaking with fixation.

Just his name on a piece of paper could set her off. Even a word like Broyard—*barnyard, backyard*—sent her into an exhausted loop of fantasies. Everything else in her life, including her own therapy practice, was faked. The spell consumed 95 percent of her energy but she was surprised to see that no one noticed; the wafer-thin 5 percent version of her sufficed. She kept a list on her desk of all the things that used to make her happy:

Zydeco music
Dogs
My work
Rainy days
Thai food
Body surfing
My friends

But she couldn't generate enough sadness and regret to free herself. She lived for the three days a year he replaced her in her office and she worked beneath him. Through sheer force of will she became what he once said he wished his wife was: small, feminine, with a slightly conservative elegance. Being this woman, this receptionist, was her one joy. *Joy* is the wrong word: it fueled the spell and so the spell could continue, which is the only thing a spell wants to do.

Ruth-Anne filed the folder. Looking at her expansive back it was easier to remember my therapist who was so daring and so helpful, even at 5 percent. I owed her.

It took a while to get it going, but after a few seconds of rocking on my heels I began to sway to the twangy rhythm. Ruth-Anne raised her eyebrows, hoping I was just stretching my legs. I began hoarsely, unmelodically but with great force.

"Will you stay in our Lovers' Story
"If you stay you won't be sorry"

She looked up, or rather the spell looked up, slowly, with re-vulsion. The spell, in its tartan headband, was fuming. It looked from me to Dr. Broyard's door to its own monstrous hands and back to me as I raised my voice in volume:

"'Cause weeeee believe in youuuu"

Jack liked this; he bounced up and down in his sling.

"Soon you'll grow so take a chance
"With a couple of Kooks
"Hung up on romaaancing"

I only knew the chorus, so I immediately began again,

"Will you stay in our Lovers' Story"

Something strange was happening with Ruth-Anne. It didn't seem good. She was sweating; big damp rings were rapidly ex-panding from the sides of her blouse. She was dissolving. If this was the wrong thing to do, then it was very wrong. I shut my eyes, wrapped my arms around Jack, and chanted,

"If you stay you won't be sorry
"'Cause weeeee believe in youuuu"

The "in you" part sounded stronger than the rest, full-voiced and resonant. I cracked my eyes. Sweat was streaming down her

face and her mouth was pointed heavenward, as if she were singing to the gods, begging them to intercede on this matter, to
release her from her spell. We crooned together:

"Soon you'll grow so take a chance
"With a couple of Kooks
"Hung up on romaaancing"

But they do not exist, the gods. The only way to break the
spell is to break the spell. So now she hooked her thumbs under
her soggy armpits, trying to ride the twang, embody it. We came
around the bend and headed back into the start of the chorus:

"Will you stay in our Lovers' Story
"If you stay you won't be sorry"

Her shoulders were broadening, almost ripping her blouse.
Makeup melted into the wrinkles around her eyes and her jaw
galloped as she sang. Dr. Broyard opened his door, adjusting
his spectacles and watching us with a bemused smile—Kirsten
peeked out behind him. Too late, doctor! Too late! The spell
has been shattered into ten million pieces, too dispersed to flock
together.

But I was wrong. Seeing my triumphant face, Ruth-Anne
realized who was watching; her croon immediately withered to
nothing. For a split second she looked devastated, her eyes wild
with disappointment. Then the spell descended and she cozily
tucked herself back in, almost relieved, it seemed. She sat down
and rolled forward to her computer. I stood before her, my arms
hanging, chest heaving, but her eyes stayed locked on the screen.
As she repositioned her headband I turned to leave.

"Your card, miss."

"What?"

"Your appointment card."

Without a blink she handed me a card for an appointment I didn't have.

I put it in the glove compartment. Now that I had it I didn't want to look. Of course it was Darren. Why break a promise to learn something I already knew? This feeling carried me all the way home. I calmly gave Jack his bottle and put him down for his one o'clock nap. But the moment I shut the nursery door the equanimity ended and I could not get to the glove compartment quickly enough. I carried it inside in my fist and sat on the couch. I opened my fingers, smoothed the card and turned it over.

It wasn't Darren.

I ripped the card to shreds before remembering, too late, the old trick for getting someone to call by tearing their name up.

The phone rang almost immediately.

"You look the same," he said. "Kirsten looks much older but you look the same. And the little guy in front—what's his name?"

"Jack," I whispered. I sank to my knees, keeling over a throw pillow.

"Jack. He's a sweetheart—how old is he?"

"Ten months."

He coughed—he already knew that, he had done the math. My forehead had a fever, I was burning up. Oxygen. With the pillow under one arm I crawled to an open window and pointed my mouth at the screen.

"It's great to hear your voice, Cheryl. It's been a long time."

Phillip and Clee.

How had they met? How was it even possible? But why not? If one young woman, why not another?

"I think I owe you an apology," he continued. "I was in a difficult place when we last spoke."

"No need," I choked out. I couldn't remember what we were talking about.

"No," he said, "I *want* to apologize. I should have called when I heard she was . . . but of course I didn't know for sure. And then when I saw his picture—" His voice cracked. I inhaled wetly and he gasped a sob of relief, as if my tears allowed his tears. This wasn't the time for one of his long cries; I hoped he knew that. I blew my nose sharply on a sock. It was quiet for a minute. The curtain blew against my face.

"Here's an idea," he said finally. "I come over."

AT THE DOOR WE JUST stared at each other. He looked much older; there were heavy bags under his eyes. I felt like a wife who had waited in vain for her husband to return from war, and now, twenty years later, here he was. Ancient, but home. He stepped inside and looked around.

"Where is he?"

"Napping. He should be up soon, though."

I offered him something to drink. Lemonade? Water?

"Could I just have some hot water?" He pulled a packet of tea bags out of his back pocket. "I'd offer you one but this is a special formulation, made by my acupuncturist. For my lungs."

We sat on the couch holding our mugs, waiting. He kept glancing at me, trying to weigh my mood or show me how receptive he was. As if I would want to talk about it.

"Why did you step down from the board?" I said finally.

He leapt on this, launching into a lengthy description of his poor health and a recent trip to Thailand, how it really took him out of himself. Each word he said was boring, but collectively the melody of them lulled me. I tried to resist, but just the weight of him, in pounds and ounces, was a relief. Always being the heaviest person in the house had been exhausting. I sipped my tea and leaned back into the couch. When he left I would have to shift the weight back onto my own shoulders again, but that was a problem for later.

"I feel strangely at home here," Phillip said. He peered at my bookshelf and the coasters on the coffee table as if each thing contained a memory. Out of the corner of my eye I saw Jack beginning to wiggle on the baby monitor. I had a sudden wish to prolong this moment, or delay the next one, but a high and certain squawk echoed out.

"I'll go get him," I said.

"I'll come."

He followed me to the nursery, his breath on my neck. Would there be an unmistakable resemblance?

"Rise and shine, sweet potato," I said. They had no single feature in common but the likeness could be felt; it was waiting in the wings. I laid Jack on the changing table. He had a messy poop, many wipes were needed. Phillip watched from the corner.

"You have a special connection to him, don't you?"

"I do."

"It's beautiful to watch. Age just kind of slips away, doesn't it?"

His anus was red. I dabbed it with diaper cream.

"You're just a man and a woman," Phillip mused, "like any other couple."

I seemed to be putting the diaper on in slow motion; I couldn't get the tabs to stick, it kept opening.

"I'm more like his mother."

"Okay." He shrugged agreeably. "I wasn't sure how you were approaching it."

The pants weren't going on easily; two legs slipped into one hole. Phillip peered over my shoulder, watching the struggle.

"I heard there were some . . . complications. Right? A rough start?"

"It was nothing. He's fine."

"Oh good, that's good to hear. So he'll be able to run, play sports, all that?" He was nodding yes, so I nodded with him.

The moment I pulled up Jack's elastic band, Phillip swept him off the changing table, right out from under my hand and up toward the ceiling with an airplane noise. Jack squealed, not with glee. Phillip coughed and quickly brought him down again.

"Heavier than he looks." When he was safely on my hip Jack stared at the bearded old man.

"That's Phillip," I said.

Phillip reached out and shook Jack's soft hand, waggling his noodley arm.

"Hi, little man. I'm an old friend of your grandparents."

It took me a moment to understand who he meant.

"I'm not sure they think of themselves that way."

"Understandably. Last thing I heard she was giving it up for adoption. And no one knew who the father was."

There was a question hidden in his voice—he was 98 percent sure but he wasn't certain. She might have slept around.

"That was the plan initially," I said.

"Sounds like she had lots of partners."

I didn't answer that.

WE SAT IN THE BACKYARD while Jack ate a mashed-up banana. Phillip lay on his back in the grass and inhaled the warm air, saying, Ah, ah. Jack experimentally put a rock in his mouth; I pulled it out. We moved into the shade; I described my plans for a pergola to block the sun.

"I have a great person for that," said Phillip. "I'll have him come next week. Monday?"

I laughed and he said, "She laughs! I made her laugh!"

I tried to frown.

"If you don't like him, just tell him, 'I don't know why you're here, Phillip is crazy.'"

"Phillip is crazy."

"That's it."

I KEPT THINKING HE WAS about to leave, but he kept staying. He played with Jack in the living room while I made dinner. I moved quietly, trying to hear them, but they made no noise. When I poked my head out Jack was gnawing on a rubber hamburger with Phillip sitting on the floor a few feet away, his stiff knees awkwardly angled. He gave me a thumbs-up.

"Dinner's ready, but I have to put Jack down."

I gave Jack his puree, bath, bottle.

Phillip watched me as I sang the night-night song and settled Jack in his crib. We smiled down on the baby and then at each other until I looked away.

I apologized for the dinner. "It's just leftovers."

"That's what I love about it. How ordinary it is. This is how people eat! And why not?"

After dinner we watched *60 Minutes* on the new flat-screen TV.

"This is the only real show left," he said, putting his arm around the back of the couch, grazing my shoulders. I tried to relax and get into the program. It was about how counterinsurgency tactics could be used against gangs. When the commercials came Phillip muted it. We watched a woman wash her hair in silence.

"Look at us," he said. "We're like an old married couple." He patted my shoulder. "I was thinking about that on the drive over here, about all our lifetimes together." He glanced at me sideways. "You still think that?"

"I guess I do," I said. But I was thinking about Clee. I'd been her enemy, then her mother, then her girlfriend. That was three lifetimes right there. He unmuted the TV. We watched police officers going door-to-door to embed themselves in the community. At the next commercial break he went into detail about his lungs; they were hardening. It was called pulmonary fibrosis. "When your health goes, this kind of stuff really matters."

"What kind of stuff?"

"This." He waved his hand across me and the living room. "Security. Friends you can trust who are in it for the long haul." I didn't say anything and he looked at me nervously. "I'm getting ahead of myself, aren't I?"

I looked at my thighs; it was impossible to think with him right next to me, waiting.

"Of course I'm here for you," I said. It was a relief; being angry at him was hard work. He took my hand, clasping it quickly in three different ways, like a gang member. We had just watched two men on TV do this.

"I knew you would be. I don't want to point fingers or name names, but let's just say young people don't have the same values as people of our generation."

My mouth opened to remind him I was only forty-three but then I remembered I was forty-four now. Nearly forty-five. Too old to be making a point out of it.

After *60 Minutes* he went to his car and got his electric tooth-brush. "It's the one I keep in my car." He didn't have night blindness per se, but he was less and less comfortable driving at night.

"It's not an imposition?" he asked from the porch, taking off his shoes.

"No, no, not at all."

We brushed our teeth side by side. He spit, then I spit, then he spit. He plugged the charger into the socket above the counter; it had brownish gunk calcified in all its grooves and ridges.

"Don't worry," he said, "we'll get you one." I took a long time to dry my hands while he peed loudly, sitting down.

Was it okay if he slept in his boxer shorts? Of course. I put my nightgown on in the closet, wondering which one of us should sleep on the couch. When I came out he was in my bed. He patted the place next to him. For a moment I felt butterflies, then I remembered about our being an old married couple. We were past all that, and his lungs were hardening. I got us each a glass of water from the kitchen and set them on the bedside tables.

"Should we get sex out of the way?" he said.

"What?"

"A man and a woman . . . sleeping together. I don't want it to be an issue."

My heart hammered. This wasn't at all the way I had once pictured it, but maybe there was something very beautiful about it. Or honest. Or, in any case, we were going to have sex.

"Okay," I said.

"You don't sound very enthusiastic."

"I am!"

"Terrific. Hold on."

He jogged to the living room and came back with his cell phone and a tiny tube of pink lotion; he propped the phone up against my vitamin bottles. I was having trouble regulating my breath and my jaw was shaking with nervous energy. Phillip stared at my floral nightgown and scratched his beard a few times. Then he slapped his hands together.

"So. The deal is if you want to watch me, you can, but you don't have to—it doesn't do anything for me. I just need for you to be on your back and ready when I say *now*." He handed me one of my pillows. "If you could put that under your hips that'd be great." He filled his cheeks with air and released it. "Okay?"

"Okay!" I said brightly. I felt terrible for him except he didn't seem embarrassed. He tapped the phone. Shrieks and grunts jumped out before he quickly muted the sound and hunched over himself. The bed shook, all was quiet. This is what Kirsten meant when she said he had to look at his phone for a long time. How long was long? I quietly rolled up my nightgown over my hips. I got the pillow ready under me in case he said *now*. I thought about caressing his back. It had many tiny pits in it, a sprinkling of gray hair and freckles and red dots. I laid my palm between his shoulder blades; it shook with his body. I took it off. After a few minutes he picked up the phone, did some scrolling and tapping, and got set up again. I looked at the baby monitor; Jack was sweetly splayed with his arms over his head. Would it be easy or hard to sleep after this? Maybe I would have to secretly take some of my homeopathic sleeping pills. I shut my eyes to test how near sleep was.

"Now."

My eyes jumped open; I quickly spread my legs and adjusted the pillow as he swung around and on top of me, his penis red and shiny with rose-scented lotion. He jabbed it a couple times before he found the hole. He thrust very quickly, in and out, then slowed down. A little painful, but the burning warmed away. He inhaled and exhaled in long measured breaths.

"Good to go," he said, after a minute. He leaned down and pressed his thick lips into mine. It was a little difficult with the beard. He stopped and pushed the bristly hairs away from his mouth. Our teeth knocked.

"I'm thinking of that folk song about the old hen and old rooster," he whispered, thrusting. "How's that go?"

"I don't know." I wiped my mouth.

" 'Cluck, cluck, cock-a-doodle-doo and they tapped their beaks together . . .' Something like that. Do you want to be on top?"

His eyes were on my breasts. Maybe it was better if they hung rather than puddled. But I shook my head no. I wouldn't be able to think about my thing in that position.

I pulled my legs together and shut my eyes. It should have been easy but it took fierce concentration to imagine that he was on top of me. I had to erase him completely and reconstitute him, focusing on his imaginary weight as opposed to his actual heft. As always he was very encouraging; again and again he told me to think about my thing. I was nearing peak exhaustion when the real Phillip interrupted.

"Open your eyes."

To appease him I peeked for a split second and saw his mouth puckered in a tight ring; he was forcing air in and out of it. I quickly shut my eyes again.

Everything was scattered now so I gave up on my thing and tried to imagine the penis in me was my own version of Phillip's member and that I was doing the thrusting, into Clee. Once I got a hold on it, the scene felt very real. Like a memory.

"Where did you meet her?" I panted.

"Who?" He paused his exertions for a moment and then continued. "In a doctor's office. A waiting room."

"Dr. Broyard."

"Right. Jens."

She's reading a magazine and he sits down. He tells her a bit of trivia about the doctor's wife, how she's a famous painter. He doesn't recognize her until he asks for her name.

"Clee."

He smiles, putting it all together, looking her up and down. What are the odds of them running into each other like this? High. In this waiting room they are higher than average. That's why I sent her here. He says he thinks he knows her parents.

"You're staying with Cheryl Glickman? From their office?"

She winces at my name. I'm the woman who just told her her feet smell; I could still see her enormous smile and how it fell. She wanted *me* and I gave her a referral. Her leg begins to shake with anger; Phillip puts his big hand on it. She looks up at his gray beard, his tufty eyebrows. "What did you say your name was again?"

Even from her desk Ruth-Anne can see what will happen next. Spermatozoon enters the uterus, fertilizes egg, zygote, blastula, and so forth. Jack's consciousness begins on this day.

I didn't make him, but I did each thing right so he would be made.

That's how much I wanted you.

Looking at the baby monitor, I marveled at the web of people that had spun him into being and proud tears swelled behind my eyelids. My son.

"Everything fine?"

I nodded, tucking my joy under my face. Phillip rolled off of and out of me.

"It's okay," he wheezed. "I can't climax either anymore. And it's probably safer if I don't try—although what a way to go, right?" He rubbed my sweaty thigh a few times. "I want you to know I'm not afraid of it, but . . ." He swallowed. "No, that's not true. I'm very afraid of it. But I'm not afraid of being afraid."

I nodded. What were we talking about? Jack rolled over onto his side and then back again.

"I've kept my eyes on it this whole time, ever since I was young—so it can't sneak up on me. I want to know it's coming, I want to greet it."

Death is what we were talking about.

"*Oh hello,* I'll say. *Do come in. Let me get my things before we go.* But instead of getting anything I'll just let go of everything. Goodbye home, goodbye money, goodbye being a grand and wonderful man. Goodbye Cheryl."

"Goodbye."

"And then I'll go out the door, so to speak."

I could see the door, me locking it behind him. The bedroom felt strangely cold, almost cryptlike. Jack was on his stomach now.

"I have a will and funeral plan and so forth, but if you don't mind—"

Suddenly Jack screamed; it blasted from the monitor, ripping through the night.

"—if you don't mind," Phillip raised his voice to be heard over the cries, "I'll tell you some of the details. Have you heard of EcoPods? I'd like to be buried in one of those."

"I have to—" I pointed at the monitor. Phillip held up one finger.

"They aren't legal but if you—"

Jack sobbed; I rose to my knees. Phillip looked up at me, his eyebrows furrowed. "This is only the second time I've ever told anyone this."

The baby wailed in disbelief. I had never not come when he cried. I leapt out of bed and ran from the room.

HE WAS CUTTING A TOOTH. A bottle didn't calm him so I walked him around the house. That didn't work, so I put the carrier on over my nightgown and strapped him in. I slipped a jacket on and crept out to the porch. My shoes were right there, waiting.

The sky seemed to lighten as we walked. But dawn was hours away; it could only be the moon, or my eyes adjusting. Instead of walking in big circles as I usually did, we covered new ground, block by block. On Monday the man would come about the pergola. Phillip and I would have matching electric toothbrushes. The thing with the phone and his saying *now* would soon be normal. So would watching *60 Minutes*. Jack looked straight up, suddenly calm, his eyes on a pair of blinking lights.

"Airplane." I rubbed his back. "One day you'll go on an airplane." It disappeared, out of sight. The world felt warm and enclosed, as if we were safely inside a vast room. He craned his neck this way and that. I stroked his head.

"All the other babies in the world are asleep," I whispered.

My legs were hungry to move, almost bouncing with each step. I could go forever, my arms wrapped around the only thing that really mattered, a full bottle in one pocket and my wallet in the other. We had everything we needed. How far would I walk? Could I reach that mountain range in the distance? I'd never really noticed the enormous peaks; they seemed to have risen up just now, lit up by the city. I walked for an hour without thinking a single thought, Jack long asleep against my chest. Most homes were completely dark or lit only by a TV. A man put his sprinkler out. Otherwise just cats, everywhere. The mountains stayed the same size for hours, as if I was pushing them ahead of me with each step. Then suddenly they were right there; I was at the foot of one. Would I feel compelled to scale it? It was hard to see the top now; I leaned back, one hand on Jack's warm bottom. It couldn't be seen from this close. I turned around and walked home.

AT FIVE A.M. PHILLIP STIRRED. He started when he saw me dressed, brushing my hair.

"I don't know if you drink caffeine. I made some oolong," I said.

His head bobbled over to the steaming cup on the bedside table. His clothes were neatly folded beside it, the electric toothbrush on top. I'd wrapped the cord into a little bundle. It took him a moment to absorb each of these things. Then he slowly stood up and began to dress in the dark. I leaned against the opposite wall and sipped my tea, watching him.

"I imagine the climate in Thailand is great for the lungs. Maybe that's home?"

"Maybe, I don't know. I have a lot of options."

"Just an idea."

He buttoned and tucked in his shirt, pulled on his black socks.

"Your shoes are on the porch."

"That's right."

We walked to the living room, our mugs from yesterday sitting in the dark on the coffee table.

"He's sound asleep but if you want to have one last peek at him . . ." I held out the monitor. Phillip took it but hesitated before looking at the screen.

"Did he seem standoffish to you?" he asked.

"Standoffish? Jack?"

"Maybe I misread him. I felt a chilly reception." He squinted intently at the sleeping shape. Suddenly he straightened up and handed the monitor back.

"I doubt he's mine. You know how I know? I don't feel anything here." He jabbed his chest with stiff fingers; it made a hollow sound.

I stood in the doorway and watched him put his shoes on; he gave me a small salute from the porch then stumbled down the stairs. I shut the front door, very quietly, and lay down on the couch. Best to try to sleep a little before the day began.

EPILOGUE

The flight from China was full of families and it took a long time to deplane. Then there was an endless line at Customs and the teenager in front of them couldn't find his passport. Finally they were headed down the long corridor to Arrivals. Moms and dads and husbands and wives at the end of the hall were exclaiming and hugging. As they walked he wiped his face with his hand and smoothed his hair down. She looked at him nervously.

"Are we late?"

"We're a little late. It's okay."

"What if she hates me?"

"Not possible."

"What should I call her? Ms. Glickman?"

"Just call her Cheryl."

"Is that her? That woman waving?"

"Where?"

"Down at the very end. With the blond lady. See?"

"Oh. Yeah. She looks old. Clee came too, that's Clee."

"She's so happy to see you—oh, she's running."

"Yeah."

"It's pretty far."

"We could meet her halfway—should we run?"

"Really? I have my bag. How about you just run and I'll catch up?"

"No, no. We can walk."

"It's just—my bag. Oh wow. She's really gonna run the whole way."

"Yeah."

"Just go."

"Are you sure?"

"Yeah, give me your bag. I'll catch up with you. Go."

He ran toward her and she ran toward him and as they got closer they both started to laugh. They were laughing and laughing and running and running and running and music played, brass instruments, a soaring anthem, not a dry eye in the house, the credits rolled. Applause like rain.

ACKNOWLEDGMENTS

I would to thank Melissa Joan Walker, Rachel Khong, Sheila Heti, Jason Carder, Lucy Reynell, Lena Dunham, and Margaux Williamson for reading versions of this book and reacting so honestly. A particular thank you to Eli Horowitz, who read many drafts and was profoundly helpful. Thank you to Megan and Mark Ace for the family name Clee, to Khaela Maricich for sending Bowie's song "Kooks," and to my father, Richard Grossinger, for permission to excerpt his book, *Embryogenesis*. Thank you to Michele Rabkin for talking to me about adoption and Alok Bhutada for answering questions about meconium aspiration. Thank you to Jessica Graham, Erin Sheehan, and Sarah Kramer for taking such good care of my son while I wrote. Thank you to my agent, Sarah Chalfant, for saying "you will have a baby AND you will write a novel" and many other boldly inspiring truths. Thank you to Nan Graham for her staunch, unwavering support of my winding path and masterful feedback. Lastly, thank you Mike Mills, to whom this book is dedicated. Your love and bravery and willingness to tangle see me through every single day.

ABOUT THE AUTHOR

Miranda July is a filmmaker, artist, and writer. She wrote, directed, and starred in *The Future* (2011) and *Me and You and Everyone We Know* (2005), which won a special jury prize at the Sundance Film Festival and four prizes at the Cannes Film Festival, including the Camera d'Or. July's fiction has appeared in *The Paris Review, Harper's,* and *The New Yorker;* her collection of stories, *No One Belongs Here More Than You* (2007), won the Frank O'Connor International Short Story Award and has been published in twenty-three countries. The nonfictional *It Chooses You* was published in 2011. In 2000 July created the participatory website *Learning to Love You More* with artist Harrell Fletcher, and a companion book was published in 2007; the work is now in the collection of the San Francisco Museum of Modern Art. She designed *Eleven Heavy Things,* an interactive sculpture garden, for the 2009 Venice Biennale, and in 2013 more than a hundred thousand people subscribed to her e-mail-based artwork *We Think Alone* (commissioned by Magasin 3, Stockholm). In 2014 she debuted the audience-participatory performance *New Society* at the Walker Art Center and launched the app Somebody, a new SMS service. Raised in Berkeley, California, July lives in Los Angeles.

LIVINGSTON PUBLIC LIBRARY

3 1792 00498 4550

NGSTON PUBLIC LIBRARY
10 Robert H. Harp Drive
Livingston, NJ 07039

BAKER & TAYLOR